Michael Edward Miller

Alison Elizabeth Miller

www.faultlinehawaii.com

FAULT LINE

I dedicate this book to God, the ultimate creator, who I believe inspired me with ideas to write this wild adventure story. And to my darling wife, Alison Elizabeth, one of the sweetest and most creative people I know. Without her storytelling talent and patient endurance, this novel would not exist. And to the best mother-in-law a guy could ask for, Alanna. Her giving, positive, and encouraging spirit reflects the love of God.

Michael E. Miller

For my dynamic, imaginative, entrepreneurial husband Michael, who wrote the original and fascinating Fault Line in a screenplay format…and for my family – Mom, Dad, Eric, and Grandma. Thank you for your love, guidance, and humor.

Alison E. Miller

Copyright 2016 U.S. Library of Congress Copyright Office Registration #TXu2-025-821.
All rights reserved. No portion of this book, including the cover, may be duplicated, reproduced or stored in any retrievable system, transmitted in any form or means; either electronic, digital, mechanical, photocopied, scanned or by any other means, except for brief quotations in critical reviews or articles, without prior written permission from the publisher or authors. Those requesting use permission may contact the authors via email: andrews@faultlinehawaii.com

Chapter One

"River Mountain Cave"
Southeast Vietnam, June 2005

Hang Son Doong, or River Mountain Cave, is one of the largest and most extensive cave systems in the world. Running for nearly six, long, twisting miles within the Annamite Mountains of Vietnam, it houses some of the tallest stalagmites ever observed. In the main cavern, secured in a harness, floating in mid-air, Susan Andrews swings on the line. Excited and nervous, she glances up to the hilltop opening of the cave. Then she looks down, a thousand feet below...

"Incredible," she whispers to herself, as she rappels, enveloped by a passing shadow from a cloud overhead. She's an active geologist in the field and has explored many caves over the past decade, but nothing like this. The mouth of the sinkhole is expansive, lush with greenery, a universe unto itself. She watches her geologist-volcanologist husband, Tom, suspended twenty feet above her on his own line. No doubt he is experiencing the same sense of awe and yet he remains calm, maintaining his grip on a rock wall.

To protect their bodies from the damp cold and sharp rock edges, they wear neoprene suits, gloves, and spelunking shoes. With climbing ropes, they lower themselves down into the inky depths toward the bottom. Susan imagines that they must look like tiny, black spiders dangling on fine threads.

She slows her descent and looks up again. Tom is scanning a section of the wall. He stops and hacks away at the rock with a small pick-hammer, a real-life Batman minus the cape. *He's never one to slack on a mission. Especially this one, she thinks to herself.*

Yesterday, they camped on the flat, valley floor below the mountains, in an area checkered with rice fields and craters filled with water. The craters were remnants of the Vietnam War. Now the locals used them as aqua-culture fishponds. Death had transformed to life. The cave system was even a shelter for the Vietcong, a refuge from U.S. air bombardments. But today, the cave is a playground for twenty-first century spelunkers and scientists.

For two days, Tom and Susan explored the openings, stream crossings, permo-carboniferous limestone formations, and a doline where sunlight entered and trees flourished. They considered spending one more day in that section, surveying and mapping the terrain, but Tom insisted they hike out to explore another, more massive, second entrance. This was the mission that required a vertical descent.

"We've been here for over an hour and we're still only halfway down. This place is humongous…it's a subterranean freak of nature," Susan says into her headset mic, as a wind rushes by and goose pimples rise on her arms. Looking up and out, she sees the clouds darken, choking the sun's light to a few meager rays. She pulls the neoprene gloves tighter over her forearms, and calls out to Tom.

"It's starting to rain and the temperature's falling. Maybe we should head back up. It's almost five o'clock."

A light mist pin-pricks her face. She glances below, where the silvery sunlight fades, plunging into an indiscernible depth. Then she hears Tom gasp.

"Whoaaaa," he says. "I think I've found something. It couldn't be… no, it's impossible." He leans forward, chipping away at the wall with his pick-hammer while yellow particles eject into the space around him. "Got it!" he shouts, words echoing in the cave.

Susan's headlamp illuminates the yellow dust motes that fall from his hammer and surround her. *Cheep. Cheep.* The Geiger counter clipped to her waist signals an alert. She holds it up, viewing the LED display panel. A baritone voice echoes through her headset.

"Sounds mighty cozy down there, oh yeah…"

Jerry Russell. Programmer extraordinaire, fellow colleague, and contender for first place among adventure junkies (following Tom of course). Jerry's mapped out the entire cave, marking the potential hot spots for mineral deposits. Somehow, he's found ample time on this expedition to kick back, nurse an ice-cold Bia Hanoi beer, and hang out with his beautiful, Thai girlfriend, Soonlee, whom he insisted on bringing along for the trip.

"You sound relaxed up there," Susan says. "We're down here freezing our proverbial asses off."

"You know my style well, Dr. Sue. Free-spirited-wild-man, that's me," he says with a chuckle.

"That's the understatement of the year."

She thinks back to when she met Jerry at the University of Arizona. He could have studied computer science at Harvard, but he refused to "wear the geek badge" and he loved the party life at U of A. He made good money programming for the Andrews' geological database, while doing contract work for other companies on the side. Over the years, he settled down a little, but there's a part of him still stuck in his crazed undergraduate days.

As dust continues to fall from Tom's hammering, Susan's hazel-green eyes flash in the light of his headlamp. She studies the meters on her Geiger counter again.

"Hey, I'm picking up radioactive traces," Tom says.

Suddenly, Jerry is rapt with attention. "Come in. Hello? What did you say? Don't leave me hangin.' Please repeat."

"It could be…vitrellium," Tom says. "I'm about 95% certain that it is."

"Ahahaha!" Jerry cackles. "Oh my gosh, no friggin' way."

"Yes, friggin' way," Tom says.

"If we manage to discover vitrellium mineral deposits in Southeast Asia…Man, that would give us some notoriety and you guys would be the most awesome-ic geo-team I've ever worked with…."

"Awesome-ic?" Susan asks.

"Awe-seismic if you prefer? Who cares? Because if this find proves true, I swear I'll never work with another expedition team again."

"You call sipping a cold 'brewski' in the tropics work?" Susan says. "You'd never join another team because they might actually make you do stuff. But you're going to have to zip it for a spell. We're trying to focus here."

" 'Brewski?' 'Stuff?' 'Zip it?' Sounds like you're pickin' up on our American slang. I could be rubbing off on you, Dr. Sue."

"I sure hope not."

He laughs through the static. She can picture him back at the base camp, sitting by the tarp-covered communication table. Ropes, carabineers, and muddy clothes litter the ground. Or he could be taking a break from the database, reclining in a swing back chair, rumpling his aloha shirt.

Or maybe, he's lounging in a hammock, while he gazes out on the tropical landscape, immersing himself in the scenery where passion flowers burst with bloom and vines cling to dwarf palms. He watches the bamboo towers overhead, and in the valley below, mango trees ripen, their fruit hanging above grasses that sway in the wind. The philodendron leaves are the size of elephant ears and the roots of the Banyan tree are as thick as a rhino's leg. Everything pulses in the violet light of the tropics.

Then a loud, disgusting sound interrupts Susan's thoughts.

"Bwaaaahhh..." Jerry belches into the receiver. "How ya' gonna' top this? An all-expense paid working vacation. Plus, thanks to the U.S. non-proliferation treaties, and if we can confirm this *is* vitrellium, we'll increase our incomes substantially! I'm talking boku bucks, my friends."

"There'll be a few more hurdles to jump through before that happens," Tom says.

As Susan listens to the exchange, her rope gives a sudden jerk. "Jerry? What's going on?" she says. The rope slackens as it drops her down a foot, then stops. Worry etches across her face. "This isn't funny. Stop the nonsense."

"I'm not sure what you're referring to," Jerry says.

"My rope is slipping..."

"Huh? I'll check it out..."

Deep within the cavern, the rope's tension releases.

"Susan!" Tom cries, reaching out for the rope as it slides past him. He manages to grab a hold of it for a split second, but the speeding line burns through his hand.

"Oh no!" he cries.

Susan lets out a high-pitched scream. Her feet fly up and she plummets downward. She tumbles, flips into a back handspring, hands flailing. Frantically, she reaches to her chest harness to release the Apex BASE parachute.

"No!" Tom shouts. Words ricochet between cavern walls. "Jerry, I'm going down for her, okay?"

Tom unsnaps his harness and drops down a couple feet. He tugs the ripcord to release his own BASE parachute. All at once he's falling, while the parachute unfolds. He keeps an eye out for any obstacles or snags. Counting down in his head, he twists right and left, his headlamp shining toward the cave's floor. He tries to gauge the distance and hopes not to land on a sharp stalagmite.

Ten, nine, eight, seven, six, five...

Falling, he lands in a murky pool of water with a splashy kerplop. His mid-section absorbs the force. He surfaces, covered in mud. Heaving and spluttering, he catches his breath.

Perched on a rock above the pool, Susan calmly adjusts her gear. Tom waddles toward her and stops in a shallow section, wiping mud clots away from his eyes and chin.

"Bravo Thomas! That has got to one of the most exquisite, mud dive belly flops I've ever seen," she says, chuckling.

Tom growls. "You knew this was here!"

"Like I had time to say anything! But hey, gravity sucks. At least we're alive. Heaven knows how we're going to climb out of here." Getting to her feet, she balances on another rock. "Check your receiver, Tommy. Mine's out cold."

"I'm not picking up any signals either."

"Great. These U.S. government issue receivers are rubbish," she says, flicking the mud off her receiver. "They could have set us up with the new Hey Phones. You know, the ones developed with the British Cave Rescue Council and the Cave Radio Electronics Group?"

"You Brits have a better way of doing things, huh? I find that hard to believe."

"At least we're not injured." Lowering herself into the mud, she trudges toward him. "Yikes, gets a bit deeper here." She stops at chest level, feeling the cool sludge infiltrate her vest.

"Hey, Hey, I bet those phones are impervious to mud," Tom says with a sly grin.

"Very funny. We're not supposed to be down here, but it's better than being stuck in some stuffy office, I suppose." She looks up to the light from the cave entrance over a thousand feet above them and knows in an hour the tropical glow will fade to a faint lavender.

"Things don't always go as planned." Tom starts to free himself from the parachute.

"I'm not sure you'll find that deposit again. At least we're together down here, wherever that is."

"Appreciate the cheery attitude," he says with a sarcastic tone. "I'm not feeling so confident with Jerry being incommunicado." He wipes the last clumps of mud off his neck. "As far as the vitrellium goes, we'll just have to take another look tomorrow." He sits down on the rock and removes a shoe to shake out the excess water. "Shall we take stock?"

"Broken rope," Susan says.

"Receivers down."

"Jerry should be lowering the retrieving ropes…"

"Harder to climb back up."

"Let's try to stay positive, love." She looks around at the cave walls, then back at him. "You know, my love, you still look quite attractive." She walks closer to him.

Tom wipes his face, a lock of hair falling over his eye. "Glad you think I'm worth a gander." He pauses and tilts his head. "Did you hear something?"

"Only the echo of our own voices."

"I think you should get out of the water," he warns her.

"Come on," she says with a seductive slur. "I love a man in mud."

"No, wait, I'm not joking. Get back on that rock, now!"

Within seconds, the muddy waters rise around them, whirling slowly at first, but gaining momentum. Tom lunges and tries to grab her hand. He's only inches away from grasping her when a current sweeps her off her feet and carries her down to the back of the cave.

"Susan!"

As the swirling water rushes in and fills the pool, Tom strokes after her, but the powerful flow is pulling her further into the darkness.

"I'm coming, Suzeeee…."

"Help me…."

She gurgles on the dirty water. She watches the whirlpool slosh around her, her body tumbling, as she covers her head to protect it.

Tom yells back, but he's still attached to the parachute and it drags him down beneath the surface. He attempts to clasp its lines, but the raging water pushes his hands away. The level rises higher and higher. He has just enough time to snatch a breath before the powerful current grips him, pulling him off his own feet. Remembering the high school water polo days, he kicks his legs egg-beater style and tightens his abdomen to rise up above the water.

His headlamp shines. Light rays dance on the walls and ceiling. To the left, there is a series of stalactites, like monster's teeth, hanging down from a cave's mouth. On the right side, sharp black rocks jut out from under the water. He could be impaled from above, beside, or below. Up ahead, he sees Susan's headlamp bobbing, the light flashing in the distance. Then the light disappears. He grits his teeth as he watches her being sucked into an overhead tunnel. The current pulls him along and he accidentally gulps cave water.

He can't imagine the thought of losing his beautiful wife. Two hours ago, they were standing at the top of the River Mountain Cave, ready for an adrenalin-pumped adventure, but safe. In the dappled forest light, Susan's hair had a lustrous copper tint, touched with gold, like a rare mineral that he had just discovered. As lovely as that recent thought is, he'd never forgive himself if it was last happy memory of her.

"Hold on, babe," he calls out. He resumes his stroke and makes contact with her while his right hand clutches at a rock outcropping above the waterline. With his left hand, he grabs her sleeve, twisting the material.

"Gotcha."

"Tom-meee..."

"Don't worry," he reassures her, but the hold is tenuous. A surge of water barrels in and dashes against them. Struggling to hold her, she slips away again.

"Damn," he gasps. Using his legs to propel him, he claws at the tunnel ceiling with both hands and angles his head up to take a few breaths, before he releases from the wall, dropping back into the turbulent flow.

They speed down the twisting tunnel, bodies zipping from side to side. The flow increases with force and velocity, bludgeoning them against rocks and low ceiling sections, ripping their wetsuits as the tunnel turns into a speeding water-slide ride.

Susan catches glimpses of Tom while he swims toward her, closing the gap between them. Closer and closer. He dives and gains hold of her outstretched hand. Their fingers interlock, nails digging into each other's palms – *I've got you*, he seems to say. A charge of gratitude and relief courses through her.

The flow begins to subside. The tunnel widens, with more space to breathe and calm oneself...the air circulates...and then, the outside light seems to increase...

"No way!" Tom shouts.

Susan spins around in a panic. "No, no, no, no," she says, spitting out water. In desperation, Tom snatches her other hand and then, *PWAAAAHH!*

The tunnel spits them out as though shot from a water cannon and they soar, ejected into the air. They trundle downward, with the thunderous, muddy waterfall pounding upon them.

Chapter Two

"Stolen Data"

Back at the base camp, an onslaught of rain drenches the equipment. Soonlee hurries to cover it. Jerry runs over to the mango tree where Susan's rope was tied. He bends down and picks up the cut rope to examine it. He saw the rope fly past him, but he couldn't predict that it would be tampered with.

"What the hell? Who would do this?"

He looks around and scopes the perimeter of the camp for any intruders. No one is here besides Soonlee. He tosses the rope aside and reactivates his headset receiver, shouting into it.

"Tom? Susan? Can you hear me? Come in!"

He stands up and walks over to the cavern sinkhole opening. He wishes he could stop the downpour. The Andrews could be trapped or hurt, if they're even alive. Dropping down to his haunches, he peers into the sinkhole.

Soonlee stands under a tent canopy. "You see them?" she calls out as her eyebrows twitch nervously.

"No," Jerry answers. "They must be way the hell down at the bottom. There's too much foliage and it's way too dark to see 'em."

Rain thrashes the camp, accumulating in puddles and torrents. Water funnels down the tarp and batters Jerry's amassed collection of empty beer cans. *Rat-atat-tat-tat*. It's not letting up.

He yells into his mouthpiece. "Guys, if you can hear me, I want ya' to know, I'm comin' in, you hear me? I'm comin' for ya'!"

He dashes back and forth, rushing to secure and set up his rope system, along with two rescue ropes. He pulls on his wetsuit, momentarily slipping in the muddy ground before he grabs his repelling gear.

"You need help?" Soonlee asks.

"Yeah, babe. Help me secure this."

She adjusts his harness as he puts on a BASE parachute and wraps a bandana around his head.

"You don't have to do this," she says, reaching to kiss his cheek.

"I'd much rather stay up here with you. But I gotta' find these guys."

They kiss each other on the lips, a lingering kiss moistened by the tropical downpour.

"It's gonna' be okay," he says. "All right," he shouts into the receiver again. "Gear on, I'm good to go!"

He turns toward Soonlee. She clips the helmet strap and he fastens himself to his rope. He drops over the other ropes, turns on his headlamp, and lowers himself backwards over the slippery edge into the sinkhole abyss. The rain gushes.

"You scared, Jer Bear?"

"Nah, Jer Bear doesn't get scared," he sings out with false bravado as he makes the-sign-of-the-cross in deference to his religious mother. He clings to a side rock wall. "I just don't like plunging into waterfalls. I can't even see the frickin' bottom. Keep the flashlight on, little to the right, okay. It's going to be mighty slick down there."

Soonlee nods, holding out a powerful flashlight with one hand, watching him descend into the cave. Her other hand controls the rope. Her eyes are intent and fixed. Even the pounding rain can't distract her. But while she watches Jerry descend, neither of them see what's happening in the base camp behind them.

Under the jungle foliage, three commandos, camouflaged with face paint, watch Jerry and Soonlee. The soldiers blend into the undergrowth. One of the soldiers has his eyes and an AK-47 trained on Soonlee's back. The other two soldiers break away and head straight for the center of camp. With combat knives strapped to their waist belts, they lift tent tarps to reveal computers and high-tech geological equipment – calibration weights, compasses, sensors, sieves, and pick-hammers.

They ignore the geological tools, but work quickly to gather up the files, laptops, and computer storage units. Within seconds they are gone, disappearing into the jungle, footprints erased by the rain.

This is the end. The grand finale!

Susan's stomach lurches while she clutches onto Tom's hand. She feels the tension in his neck and the beating of his pulse through the fingertips. They were flying for a second. Now they are hurtling down to the canyon floor, nearly two thousand feet below them.

It was a good life. I love you Mum, Dad, Sissy, Tom. If it's gonna' end, at least I'm with Tom.

Suddenly, she feels a powerful jerk and Tom's hand grips her wrist.

They come to a swinging stop. He groans with the pain of her weight as his parachute harness tightens.

"It caught on something," he says.

"Don't let go of me!"

He twists his neck and glances up, then back down at her. "I won't. Don't worry. Wow, that rock just saved our lives." He smiles at the success, but the pendulum swing of their bodies reminds him of the current danger. Pain racks throughout his body. "Hold on, it'll be alright."

"What else can I do?" she says as she sags under him. The rain lightens up. Sunshine peeps through the clouds, accompanied by a rainbow. The waterfall flow has slowed down and the air is still and almost peaceful.

It was like being on a carnival ride, Susan thinks. *Minus the safety contraptions. Bloody hell, don't look down.*

Tom's arms quiver. His face reddens.

Then Susan catches herself looking down again. "Please don't let go." Hot tears trickle down her cheeks. "Please, don't..." She starts to hyperventilate and her legs shake.

"I won't, I promise you," Tom says, "But stay calm. You'll have to pull yourself up to redistribute our weight. With your right hand, grab my left foot."

"I can't do that. I can't even move."

Both her mind and body freeze up. Charged with desperation, she lunges and reaches for his foot. Then he swoops down, using his free hand to raise her up to his waist. She finds herself hugging the barrel of his body, her thighs wrapped around his middle section. Shaking, she rests her head. "I do like this position much better."

"Yeah, me too." He sighs. "Keep talking. It'll help us think this through. The parachute might still be functional. If we can free it from this ledge..." Tom lifts one arm and tugs at the chute lines.

"What? Wait a second. Hold on there, Geronimo. What if the chute rips? Or it won't open? Or it won't hold the both of us? These are only meant for 150 some kilos."

"You mean three-hundred and thirty pounds."

"I don't care what system you use."

"One-twenty-eight and one-eighty, makes three-hundred and eight pounds, Suze. We're under the weight limit."

"You think I'm honest about my weight?" she says. "We actually are under the limit and it's still a bad idea. This can't hold us."

"I'm a little…ah, hung up here. Excuse the terrible pun. You got a better suggestion?"

She looks up. "The ledge we're hanging from is big enough for both of us to rest on. We'll climb up the chute. I'll go first and secure the line."

Tom tightens his grip around her waist. "That would be a feat. But even if we can climb up, what then? We sit up there all night, soaking wet, freezing to death. What happens if the chute gives way when you're half way up? We'll both die. And we've got *those* guys to consider…they're off season, but they're here…"

Susan follows his gaze across the sky to a flock of large buzzards surfing the warm air currents and circling above them. She bites her lip, but she's resolved to be strong.

"Okay, I got it," she says. "We separate. I'll climb up the ledge, kick the parachute free, and you glide down and find us some help."

"What kind of help? You'd still be stuck up there."

"Helicopter or something."

"If I land safely, I'll have to hike back to our camp. I'll barely make it there before dark. Then I have to drive a few hours to the airport." He pauses and sighs. "In the morning, I have to find someone to help me rent a helicopter, with a pilot, and then we all have to fly back here and rescue you? Do I look like Indiana Jones?"

"No. You're missing the fedora."

"Suze, this is no time for jokes! And I'm out of breath too. Stop talking."

"You started it. You don't think I'm totally freaked out?"

Tom glances back to the ledge. "No, we're gonna' have to stick to my plan. If it doesn't work, at least we'll end our lives together…and I couldn't think of a better position to do that in."

Tom looks lovingly at his wife – her flushed skin, her eyes bright with tears. "You are so beautiful." He leans forward to kiss her. She accepts with trembling lips.

"Suze," he whispers. "We're going to do this. Now just lean backwards and arch away from me. We need to get some momentum going."

Tom hoists her up, tightening his grip around her waist. Attached at the hips, Susan arches back as Tom holds her and they rock back and forth in a seesaw motion.

"Kind of ah…kinky, eh? In these ripped wetsuits," he says with a wink.

"Only you would think of that at this time. We could die!"

"*You* started it…"

As the rocking motion picks up speed, the parachute's top slides to the ledge. Small pebbles and dirt fall down on them. Then suddenly, the parachute breaks and they free-fall, speeding toward the ground. In a fit of panic, Tom tugs on the chute straps above him, trying to open it.

"Oh God, please help us!" Susan shouts into the rushing air.

They speed down to the valley floor, a flat expanse of foliage dotted with sharp, black rocks. Susan can hear the sound of impending death – the crunch and crackle of entire bone structural systems, the thrash of dismemberment, a whoosh of fresh blood.

"Tom!"

"Susan!"

Pwooooohh…

The chute opens with a gentle stretch, as though nothing ever happened. Aloft with the wind, Tom and Susan float down, a hundred feet above the ground, until they land in a soft tumble, falling over each other onto a pile of leaves. *Terra firma.*

"You okay, Suze? No broken bones?"

"None whatsoever."

They sit up, dazed and exhausted.

"We did it. I can't believe it," Tom says.

"That was insane," Susan says while she catches her breath. She swings her arms around Tom's neck.

"Don't get too excited yet. We have to walk back to our camp."

"More like slip and slide with the rain."

Mud has already encased their feet, crusted over the zippers of their wetsuits, and streaked across their faces. But outside the cave system, the temperature is warm and humid. They unzip and peel back their suits.

Susan follows Tom, keeping her eyes trained on the ground, occasionally glancing up at his bare shoulder and tattoo. *$KAlSi_3O_8$*. It's the chemical formula for orthoclase feldspar, or K-feldspar, one of the silicate minerals in igneous rock. K-feldspar forms in rectangular prisms, with two perpendicular vectors and a third vector that doesn't meet at 90 degrees. A monoclinic crystal system. Tom's had the tattoo since before they met, and in twelve years it hasn't faded. If anything, it appears darker against the smooth, hairless spot on his shoulder.

While walking, they discuss certain surprises of the River Mountain Cave – the depth of the second doline, the green foliage in the first one, the rivers of mud, the flash floods in the passageway, and the hell ride that led to the waterfall plunge.

"That was unexpected," Susan says. "Catching my breath still."

"Certainly. Do you realize that we may have been the first research explorers of this cave?"

"There may have been others. Local explorers and such."

"Yes, but we may be the first geologist team," Tom says with excitement as they trek up a hill. "We could come back and map this place. Make it famous. Leave our mark." He watches a lock of reddish gold hair fall over her eye. She knits her brows and at once he sees that contrast of innocence and her particular thirty-something worry.

"What's wrong, babe?" he asks.

"Oh, nothing."

"Which means *something* important."

She sweeps her hair back. "I just miss home."

"We'll be back there in forty-eight hours."

"Yes, yes," she says.

How does one explain the concept of home to the perpetual wanderlust man? There's not even a pet at home to miss. With all the demands of work and travel, they don't have time to take care of one. She misses the comfort and familiarity, the feeling of being settled. It's a recent but dramatic change in her mindset.

"Hey," Tom says peering at his receiver. "I'm getting a signal. No audio from Jerry, but he's not far from here. We're close to camp." He looks to Susan. "Just try to enjoy our adventure on the last day. Think – thirty years ago or so, this place was a potential bomb zone. You could die in a war. But now, it's so peaceful and beautiful, plus it's a pretty cool country. Not temperature wise, but you know, Fonz cool."

She chuckles. *I have liked it here.* She thinks back to the delicious street side pho in Hanoi and touring the museums and temples for a half day. She learned about Caodaism, a mix of Catholicism (introduced by the

French colonists), Buddhism, and indigenous folk traditions.

She enjoyed the city, but presently, they are a world away from the hustle and bustle and it's gorgeous. The birds chatter. The sultry rain opens her pores and the scent of the jungle's flowers intoxicates.

"Jerry!" Tom calls out.

Jerry and Soonlee are walking toward them, a hundred yards outside the base camp.

"What happened to you guys?" Jerry says. "I went almost all the way down to the bottom and it was flooded. You look like all hell, but I'm glad you're okay."

"We are. It's a miracle," Tom says.

Jerry's temporary smile of relief fades to consternation, as he hands them bottles of water. "I hope y'all don't get too upset."

"Why, what's going on?" Susan asks.

"Do you want the good news or the bad news first?" Jerry offers.

"Crud," Tom says. "I don't know. Normally, I'd say bad news, but I'm not sure how 'bad' bad is. So, shoot me the good news."

"Well, you'll probably still win that geoscientist award thingy. Between this find and the Hawaii research, you're the top dog."

"Tell me something I don't know. So that's the good news. Now, what's the bad news?"

Susan watches Tom scratch at dollop of dried mud on his face. He's so casual about everything and yet logical. He's weighing the known good news and figuring the bad news is in equal measure and Jerry will tell him something minor, since Tom has been indifferent about the award.

Maybe there was a miscalculation in the doline depth recording. Perhaps there were more hidden caverns than they estimated or they didn't consider the effect of the monsoon rains. These are all forgivable errors. But something is amiss with Jerry. Some circumstance has obliterated his goofy smile and he's never looked this serious in his life.

"Our data. Actually, *your* data and equipment…"

"Yeah, what about it?" Tom asks.

"It's been stolen."

"What? How? Who could have?"

"I don't know, but it's all gone," Jerry says, whimpering. "I'm so, so sorry."

"Whoa...but...how could you have known, Jer? Damn. We weren't prepared for this."

"Must have happened while I was distracted trying to rescue you guys. Those rip-offs probably cut off Susan's rope, too. It wasn't any accident, man."

Stunned, Susan and Tom look at each other. They're speechless.

Chapter Three

"Geoscientist of the Year"

Six Months Later
Hyatt Regency Hotel
Los Angeles, CA

Wild and crazy...stupid and negligent...

Susan is never sure where to place the blame for their stolen laptops and files. They shouldn't have explored the second doline. Jerry never should have left camp. Fortunately, Tom had the older information saved on his home desktop.

But what third party would want the data and how would they interpret it? Who would want the files?

It confounds her. Leaning in front of the hotel bathroom's vanity, she applies her makeup. She spreads glittering, light brown shadow on her eyelids and opens her eyes, standing, half-way dressed in a slip and a flesh-toned lace bra. She dusts her cheeks with bronzer, but the harsh fluorescent light makes her skin look pale.

"Ginger kid for life," she says with a sigh. A diamond solitaire necklace sparkles below her delicate collarbone. She puts on a sage green chiffon dress, pressing her hands down to smooth out any wrinkles that the dry cleaner didn't catch.

"Have you seen my purse, love?" she calls out.

"Right here next to my jacket," Tom shouts back.

"Thanks."

Without glancing at him, she knows how he's sitting in the living room. His feet are up on the Ottoman, tie askew, uncomfortable in his tuxedo pants. He's not one for formality. He'd wear swim trunks and a worn out T-shirt every day if he could. He had spent too many years in Southern California.

They met there, at Caltech. She was a recent Oxford grad, finishing her post-doc. Years before, she had read Dr. Thomas Andrews' articles in

Geoscience Journal. One of the articles was on the Cenozoic rock strata of the Tucson basin; the other discussed the volcanic basalt sea caves of Hawaii. To her, the research was expansive and fascinating, covering faraway iconic American subjects. Applying to, and then attending Caltech, were the most outrageous decisions of her life at that point.

"It's a bit rash," Susan's mother said a few months prior to the departure.

"I agree. But it's an incredible opportunity. I'm beyond lucky to be in this program."

"Why can't you just stay here? What's wrong with studying in England?"

"Mum, please try to understand."

"I never would want to impose upon you lovey," her mother countered. "But California? There's a reason they call it 'the land of fruits and nuts.'"

"And some very incredible geological features. El Capitan, La Brea Tar Pits, San Andreas Fault. I'm not going to spend my life studying rock cairns in Lockerbie, okay?"

"What's wrong with that?"

She mentioned Lockerbie as a joke, but clearly her mother didn't get it and there was no way that she could. She had worked in marketing at a flagship British department store. The Lowell descendants had never lived outside the U.K. They wasted away, gossiping on Sundays and perpetually drinking tea and being British in all the prescribed BBC show ways. Indeed, it was hideous.

So why not venture out and be a maverick?

Susan planned to return to England, but the moment she walked onto the Caltech campus, with its sprawling green lawns and endless sunshine, she knew she wouldn't leave.

During the summer before her teaching schedule started, she accepted an invitation to the Geology Department's annual "Seismo Social" event, where she would meet up with advisors and colleagues.

"I'm sure it will be a proverbial geek fest," she joked to her housemate. "There better be some wine."

Dressed in a light eyelet dress, she arrived at six p.m. The event was way beyond her expectations. The organizers had set up large canvas tents on the quad, festooned with twinkling lights. They were prepared for a late evening. It was fully catered with a Mexican food theme, where caterers served shrimp enchiladas, massive mounds of nachos, "shaken" margaritas, and a frosted cranberry jello "Earthquake Cake," stenciled with the words: **SAN ANDREAS**

After dinner, Susan waited in line for a piece of cake, slightly blinkered from a lime margarita. She watched the Geology faculty interact. Some laughed uproariously while others huddled in small groups discussing their special interests. They were all informal at the school, donning faded cargo shorts, t-shirts, and surfer "flip-flops."

Where was stodgy old Dr. Mortimer Ross in his tie and tweed jacket? Where were the lab coats and spectacles? How could anyone really take these young California party scientists seriously? But, they were the best of the best.

Spun out in thought, Susan didn't see the looming figure behind her. He slid by, walking to the dessert table, essentially cutting her in line.

"Hey," she called out.

The waiter cut a medium slice of cake and scooped it onto a plate designed with seismograph patterns. The waiter then reached over the rude cutter man. "Here you go, Miss, lots of frosting for you."

And then the cutter and Susan stepped toward each other. *Whoosh – plop!* A collision of cake. The gelatinous, dyed frosting covered her dress from chest to hips.

"Oh my gosh, I'm so sorry," he sputtered.

She gazed up to him. *Oh my gosh* was right. She couldn't help staring. As he tried to suppress a chuckle, his dark, wavy hair bobbed up and down in a spastic motion. Stubble dotted his face. There was a quivering dimple in his left cheek and a movie star cleft in his chin. He was handsome. Very handsome. A clumsy slob, yes, but sexy.

"Here, I'll help you clean up." He leaned forward with a napkin to swipe her front side.

"No, it might smear. I'm fine. I'll just go to the ladies' room."

"Ok, Susan. McCarthy." He winked as the wafts of sweet frosting proliferated the air between them.

"How do you know my…oh, yeah, the name tag," she said as she fumbled to regain composure. "Amazing, it was spared from the recent seismic activity."

"Ha, nice one." The stranger extended his hand. "I'm not one for name tags. I'm Tom Andrews."

"*You're* Tom Andrews? *Dr.* Thomas Andrews? Of the Hawaiian cave and lava tube research? The Southeast Asia explorations?"

"Among other things."

"I am a huge fan! I've read your articles for years." She reached out to shake Tom's hand.

"Glad to hear that, since you know, we'll be working together."

She blushed. It almost wasn't fair that such an attractive man was also a brilliant researcher and writer. His smile spread, to accentuate full lips and perfect, white teeth, as his eyes glimmered in the late afternoon sun. Indigo blue eyes, a color she had ever witnessed before, and in those eyes, there was sheer joy and playfulness, but a sense of depth, too. Right away she knew he was a bit wild. She couldn't help but think, *You, Dr. Andrews, are the one I've been waiting for…*

Now, after twelve years together (five dating, seven married), she feels as though she is still waiting…waiting for him to grow the heck up. At times his charm allows her to forgive him for the terrible domestic habits and yet it's too much. He eats in bed and loses things. He never unloads the dishwasher, nor does he pick up after himself. In his kooky mind, it's okay to let the bills pile up in a tower.

This evening, when she walks into the hotel living room, she sees heaps of towels on the floor and the foot drying mat strewn across the couch. The TV hums along, but Tom's not watching it. He faces away, sitting on a bar stool, with Thor Heyerdahl"s Kontiki in his lap. Lately, he's been on a kick of re-reading his favorite books from childhood.

"You ready?" she asks, grabbing her purse.

"Just a sec." His eyes skim the book's text, while his cell phone sits in the crook of his neck. Of course multi-taking is most fervent when they're getting ready to go somewhere. He says a quick good-bye into the phone and turns to Susan.

She stares at him. "You've been waiting for me all this time and your shoes are still not on. Who was that on the phone?" she says.

"My Mom."

"What does she want?"

"Nothing really. She just wants to hear about this trip, I guess. I'll be ready in a jiff."

"Can't we do anything without her knowledge?"

"She's excited for me and the award." He strolls over to the couch where his shoes lay and he puts them on as he gazes at the TV.

"The man of honor shouldn't be late, Mr. Geoscientist of the Year."

"*Doctor* Geoscientist of the Year. But that's beside the point. Tonight, he's escorting the most beautiful woman in the known universe," he says, grinning like the Cheshire-cat.

"Classic Dr. Charmer."

He stands up and leaps toward her for a hug.

"Me shoes are tied, milady!"

"It might be funnier if you tripped over the laces."

"You want the Stooges foreplay routine, huh?"

"Oh, good lord, no…" she says, sighing. "What are we going to do with that bow-tie? It's all askew."

She leans back to adjust the tie and straighten his cummerbund. It's definitely a step-up from the flip-flop days. She straightens her dress. "So, do you still think I'm the most beautiful woman in the universe?"

He nods. "Absolutely."

"But Doctor Andrews, there are over ten billion galaxies in the known universe and our galaxy alone has at least a hundred billion stars in it. So far, we've only examined a few star systems in comparison. So, based on those irrefutable facts, how can you be one-hundred percent certain that I am the most beautiful woman in the universe?"

"Well, I've done some intense, first-hand research. With up-close, personal attention and knowledge of the field." His smile widens as he runs his hands over her bottom.

She fidgets. "That tickles!"

He stops and smiles again.

"Thank you darling," she says. "But if you don't hurry, you'll be late for your own award ceremony."

On the TV screen behind them, the news report airs a video of young Koreans rioting in the streets of Seoul. Firing tear gas, the police chase them. Other images show the police beating students with clubs. Plumes of fire consume cars and buildings.

A newscaster drones on about the mayhem. "The government is in disarray as the riots in South Korea continue and begin to turn deadly. Soldiers, students, and various workers have united in their demands, rumored to be instigated by a new political party known as the Korean Unification Front, possibly backed with funding from the North Korean government and perhaps other unknown support."

Tom watches and pauses, listening to the TV reporter.

The newscaster continues – "Outside U.S. military bases, the protests have become violent, but the U.S. government still refuses to..."

Susan grabs the remote and turns the TV off.

"Hey, I was watching that," Tom blurts out.

She registers his miffed look. "We need to go."

"I'm just trying to stay a little informed about the world. You're the one who wants me to move beyond geology obsessions."

"Did I say that? All right, there are strange happenings in Korea, but we can't make it less crazy. I'm tired of hearing about government this and that."

"I did agree I wouldn't take on any more government contracts, unless they're Hawaii related."

"Hawaii is the compromise, yes. Remember we could have died on that last Vietnam expedition."

"And an earthquake could hit this hotel."

"Thomas, we could worry about an infinite number of things," she says, shaking her head. "But I know where you could start."

"What? Where?"

"Down at your feet."

He follows her eyes to the towels on the floor.

"Oh yeah," he says. "Sorry about that."

Chagrined, Tom picks them up and carries the pile outside to the balcony, where he hangs the towels on the chairs. He places a hand on the railing of the fifth-story balcony. The air is dry, but nothing like their home in Arizona.

"For such a fancy hotel, it's a lousy view of a parking lot...and a dirty, overrated city," he grumbles.

The city is a sea of incandescent lights, traffic, and miniature-looking people. Ficus and jacaranda roots battle for breathing room within the cracked cement sidewalks. Venus, the morning star, twinkles in spite of the omnipresent smog.

He steps back inside. "L.A. isn't really my style," he says, "but you already knew that." He walks toward her. "Fantastic foxy lady, are you ready for dinner now?"

"Aye, aye captain. Lead the way," she says, taking his arm.

He whisks her through the room and out to the foyer. Her dress lightly grazes the marble hallway floor while she catches a glimpse of their reflections in the elevator's mirrored doors. *We do clean up well*, she thinks. When they step into the elevator, she senses his nervousness.

"Worried about the ceremony?" she says, pressing down on the Lobby button.

"No, I'm thinking about the Homeland Security and NSA nonsense. They advised me not to publish my findings on the susceptibility of trigger points in Kilauea's fault zones and sub-surfaces. It doesn't make any sense."

"The government doesn't make sense, but I suspect they have their reasons."

"A credible threat shouldn't be about politics. They're frickin' fools. My Big Island data provides more than enough evidence to warrant the preventative measures that I suggested."

She nods in agreement. The elevator dings and the door slides open to reveal a hall crowded with formally dressed employees directing academics and guests into the banquet room.

The host spies them walking out of the elevator and his eyes light up. "Dr. Andrews!"

"We've been spotted," Tom says.

"Isn't that the idea?" Susan counters.

The host guides them into the ballroom while guests stop to greet Tom. He shakes their hands and looks back to Susan with raised eyebrows, as if to say, "Nice people and I have no idea who they are."

He's too uncomfortable to ask for their names. The host directs Tom and Susan into the lavish banquet room. Tom scans the international crowd of academics, specialists, and dignitaries. Susan marvels at the intricate, glittering chandeliers suspended from the ceiling. Women parade in designer dresses. The men wear tuxedos. It's a far cry from the field uniforms of Carhart pants and work boots.

"More people here than I expected," Tom says. "I was figuring this would be more of a 'secret society' type meeting."

"It's quite the hobnobbing scene. And all for you."

"So they tell me. Maybe we should get a drink first. I think I see Dr. Haverford, but…"

Before Tom says another word, a swarm of reporters shove their way through the crowd. "Dr. Andrews, I have a question for you," one says.

Another reporter unceremoniously pushes his way in. "Dr. Andrews, a word please?"

Looking over his shoulder, Tom says to his wife, "Hold that thought honey, I'll find you at our table. Wherever that is."

The reporters sweep Tom away.

Susan lingers a moment, observing the elaborate flower arrangements on each table. Young women servers, of various ethnicities, but all thin and pretty, sashay through the crowd maze, offering appetizers. Geo-scientists hold conversations throughout the room, some arguing furiously in corners, others grinning in efforts to gain favor with a superior. A few people look as awkward and alone as she does.

Perhaps it's the nature of the field. She recalls introverted James Hutton, "the father of modern geology." Born in 1726, alive at the height of the Enlightenment, he dedicated his life to understanding erosion and sedimentation. He originated the theory of uniformitarianism, in that the Earth formed by natural processes over geological time.

In the Scottish Highlands, Hutton discovered that granite was formed from the cooling of molten rock, not from precipitation as was hypothesized. At the Sicar Point sea cliffs, he observed ripple marks, confirming his proposal that the rock beds had been laid horizontally in water. He theorized that there were cycles of deposition, uplift, and erosion, with the thickness of the rock indicating that it was a slow process over thousands of years. Since then, further observations, plus qualitative and quantitative data confirmed Hutton's theories.

The Godfather of Geology spent years alone. He never married.

Today, even with 21stcentury technology and networking within the field, some geologists spend every waking hour in study. Few people outside of the academic sphere can understand that level of commitment. Susan was like that herself at one time. As for Tom, he was a focused intellectual, and yet he had an extroverted personality. He could talk to anyone. He could speak in public, in a manner that was both eloquent and relatable. And it didn't hurt that he looked like a model or celebrity.

Tom Andrews, GQ Geologist. Now there's a headline for you, reporters.

She chuckles to herself, ready for a glass of wine. A lithe, honey-haired server walks by carrying a tray of champagne glasses, but she ignores Susan.

She taps the girl's shoulder. "Excuse me?"

23

The girl spins around and stares blankly like a googly-eyed Pomeranian.

"Yes, I'll have one of those, thank-you-very-*kindly*," Susan says in a mock-Audrey Hepburn accent. *Sometimes you have to kill them with graciousness. Young, pretty idiots.*

She scoops up two glasses and immediately downs one. The rose champagne bubbles dance on her tongue and fizzle down her throat. She sets one champagne flute on the server's tray and wanders over to the assigned table, happy to see the familiar face of Dr. John Haverford, Tom's mentor at Caltech. They shake hands. He asks her what courses she taught when she was there ("Mostly, Stratigraphy and Sedimentation") and she asks him about his recent studies.

"You think Tom will ever show up?" Dr. Haverford asks, laughing. "I have to say, he's quite the schmoozer."

She squints at the table placards: Dr. Thomas Andrews and then Susan Andrews. Just Susan Andrews, no professional title of McCarthy, no hyphenated name. *I earned a doctorate, too. The nerve!* Nearly seven years of graduate study – analyzing, writing, researching, processing micro-paleontological samples…and she's just a tag-along to Tom. *I gave up a job in California, potentially a career, to follow that nutty man to the Sonoran Desert. But it doesn't mean I didn't work my bum off!*

Inspecting her glass, Susan signals a passing server for a top-off and takes a seat. She turns her attention to the stage. After ten minutes of introductions, followed by "thank yous" and "wish you wells," Tom takes the stage as the audience claps.

He stands at the podium and accepts the much-coveted plaque and grant for $10,000. It's something to be proud of for sure. He deserves it. He turns to face the audience, beaming and reveling in the excitement, like the crazy kid asked to "be on your best behavior." Above him, a banner reads:

U.S. Geological Society
Geoscientist of the Year

Stepping up to the microphone, he leans forward to address the crowd. "Good evening, friends and fellow colleagues, I'm going to keep this brief and meaningful. I'd like to thank some very special people who have made this incredible journey possible. To Dr. John Haverford, who is here tonight – thank you, dear friend. Dr. Hans Mueller of the Hawaii Volcano

Observatory and to Dr. Tan Yamasaki at Mount Fuji, you two will always have my undying gratitude. Such incredible mentors since day one. And for the one person I owe my entire career to..."

Susan sets her glass down and starts to rise, expectant. *This is it. A moment of recognition. Finally, a taste of acknowledgment.*

"My dear mother, Mrs. Genevieve Andrews."

Susan's shoulders collapse as Tom continues talking.

"She can't be here today, I wish she was, but without a doubt she's the one woman who made me who I am. Since early childhood, she always encouraged me in all my scientific endeavors. Thank you, Mom. And thank you ladies and gentlemen."

With a frozen stare on her face, Susan looks down, disappointed. As the applause washes over her in a nauseous swell, she notices her glass is almost empty. She downs the rest of the champagne. *This calls for a third glass.*

Chapter Four

"The Abduction"

Hawaii Volcanoes National Park

Every U.S. National Park is beautiful in its own unique way. Yosemite has its granite cliffs, tall waterfalls, and old growth forests, while the Grand Canyon has its multicolored layers of sedimentary rock. Yellowstone has erupting geysers and mammal species. The Grand Tetons are known for the contrast of rugged mountains and piedmont lakes.

There are the high hinterlands of Wrangell-St. Elias, south central Alaska, known for majestic mountains, volcanoes, and glaciers. There is the humid Florida Everglades, the largest tropical wilderness of the U.S., home to many protected species, and then, in Maine, Acadia National Park, with its scenic coastline and epic sunrises. Each park is a treasure to the nature photographer, the hiker, the climber, and adventurer.

Hawaii Volcanoes National Park is no exception. It includes 500 square miles of land encompassing the earth's highest active volcano, Mauna Loa. The flanks of Mauna Loa sit on a sea floor, 16,400 feet deep. From the sea floor to its summit, it would be considered the tallest mountain in the world.

Located close to Mauna Loa is the Kilauea Volcano, which includes the main caldera of Kilauea and a smaller active vent Puʻu ʻOʻo in the east rift zone. At the center of the Kilauea shield volcano is the Halemaʻumaʻu crater, where continual eruptions have been recorded since 1790, when pyroclastic flows killed the native Hawaiian warriors of Keoua Kuʻahuʻulaʻs army.

Some two hundred years later, this National Park has been the site of over fifty major volcanic eruptions.

"Making it one of the most active volcanoes on earth," driver James Elhorn tells the visitors on his Aloha Tours bus.

Heading south from Hilo town up Highway 11, the bus accelerates up the road's gentle incline. James straightens his baseball cap and squints in the glare of the morning light. He's thirty-eight, but laugh lines have already etched into his cheeks, his face worn from the sun. He's apple-shaped, thirty pounds overweight, shoulders set in a permanent hunch. His hair is thinning and yet there are qualities about him that are attractive – friendliness, reliability, genuine contentment.

He has followed this same route for fifteen years. He gets older. The forests grow taller and wilder. Yet the sleepy east Hawaii towns of Keaʻau and Kurtistown never seem to change that much. He sees gas stations, general stores, and a scattering of plantation-style houses. Maybe a new restaurant or art gallery will open up here or there, only to close a year later.

It's rural living and James likes it that way. He enjoys the relaxed style and quiet unpretentiousness of the Big Island, but a higher salary would be ideal. He has his wife to think about, pregnant with their second child, and then there's his seven-year old daughter Micaela, whose talents for music and dance should be honed with lessons. *More activities to pay for, rising gas and food prices, astronomical rent. It never ends.*

He peers into the interior rearview mirror to check in on his elderly tourist passengers. They are American Korean War veterans from the mainland, some accompanied by their wives. The Greatest Generation. They made it through the tail end of the Great Depression, only to find themselves at war with psychotic tyrants.

James doesn't take a political stance on Korea, but he respects the veterans. They paid their dues and were willing to make sacrifices, something he feels his own selfish generation could never understand.

"Hope you're enjoying this scenic drive," he relays over the intercom. Slowing the bus down, he gestures toward the road just outside their windows. "So here's a little side note for you. These Big Island roads are the best in the State. With the abundance of lava rocks here to crush, you add some tar to it, and boom! You have Hawaiian-island-ready-made asphalt."

The tourists nod with understanding. Flanked by chaotic matrices of tropical ginger, koa trees and fire engine red ʻoʻhia trees poke their way through prehistoric looking hapuʻu ferns with their furry, curling tendrils. Sunlight filters through the morning mist and reflects off plant leaves and the neon yellow moss.

A recent rain amplifies the sweet fragrance of the blossoming yellow and white wild ginger that blooms on the roadside. The passengers smile, seeing the varied and abundant flora, as James slows and takes a right, then a quick left, onto a side road that parallels the highway.

"We're coming into the small town of Volcano Village, where you'll see shops and restaurants on our right. Usually, it's clouded over by now," James says. He leans over the steering wheel to peek up at the blue sky. "But not today. This is a rare treat. Looks like it will be sunny all day for our Park tour."

The bus slowly rumbles through the town. Shops and restaurants border the side of the road.

"Depending on where you travel on this *big*, Big Island, you'll encounter a number of different climate zones, ranging from the Kau desert on the south side to the humid tropical forests on the east side near Hilo. The Big Island hosts a vast range of climates. The island encompasses just over 4,000 square miles. And it's still growing.

"If you venture up to Mauna Kea, which in Hawaiian means White Mountain, you'll find a dozen international observatories with state-of-the-art telescopes. You'll have to take a separate tour up there in a four-wheel drive van to experience the unique tundra climate, where snow falls in the winter months.

"The summit is 13,800 feet high, so the low temperatures up there can average just above freezing. Frosts are common year round. Right here, we're below 4,000 feet. This area is known as a wet, temperate zone. If it clouds over, the temperature can drop rapidly. So hold onto your jackets and sweaters."

The bus pulls back onto the highway, accelerating up the hill as he continues to inform the passengers. "We're almost to Volcanoes Park," James says, "where we'll go to the visitors' center, and then after that, take a lunch break."

They pass the "Hawaii Volcanoes National Park" sign, its painted, wooden block letters projecting from a chest-high rock wall. A tourist family stands by their rental car, smiling and taking photos next to the sign. James steers into the park.

"In case any of you have asthma or lung conditions, I want to warn you about the vog. It's a visible haze of sulfur dioxide mixed with oxygen, moisture, dust, and sunlight. The volcano produces about 100 tons of sulfur dioxide daily, some days even more. A lot of it settles in the Kona district, blocking and filtering out the sun. It's a hassle for local residents and tourists, but everyone has a different sensitivity. Please let me know if you need any assistance."

The bus rattles down past the guard shack and James waves to the uniformed park ranger standing in the booth. Continuing along the double lane, the bus passes a ranger station before reaching the Visitors' Center.

The Center houses a long one-story building with a covered deck. On the deck are topographical maps, modern exhibits, and screen displays. New rent-a-cars and buses from various local tour companies fill up the parking lot. Like schools of hapless fish, the tourists stream in and out of the museum's doors, viewing the indoor attractions and outdoor exhibits.

Under an awning, hyperactive children spastically press buttons on the exhibits to light up the maps of the volcanoes. The U.S. and Hawaii state flags billow in the wind. Trees sprinkle their small, brown leaves on the lawn and across the road. Puffy clouds congregate. It's just another average Hawaii summer day.

"So inside the Visitors' Center we have a theater," James says. "It features films about local eruptions and Hawaiian history. We'll come back to the Center, but first we're going to stop by the Volcano House for a stunning view and lunch."

He drives on, turning left past a line of cars, before the bus navigates through a lava rock portcullis to a separate lot for the rustic two-story Kilauea Volcano House lodge and restaurant.

"Here we are ladies and gentlemen, at the famous Volcano House. You'll be able to get some great food, souvenirs, and most importantly, you'll have a fantastic view of the caldera," he announces with pride through the intercom as he brings the bus to a halt. "We'll reconvene back here at one o'clock."

The passengers chatter away, getting to their feet, while James climbs out. One by one, he escorts the tourists off the bus. They are a nearly homogenous flock of bald men in bright aloha attire and happy wives clutching outdated cameras.

"There you go, Ma'am...right this way," James helps a woman step down from the bus. *Gotta' hand it to these folks. Eighty years old, married for decades, and here they are, still together and going on a romantic adventure.*

Another tour bus pulls up behind them in the loading zone. Asian tourists – couples, families, and single people – disembark from their bus. With cameras, they smile for one another and snap photos in front of the hotel.

The rest of James' passengers disembark from the bus and he follows them for a few steps as they meander into the lobby. Tourists crowd the Volcano House. Some browse in the gift shop, while others head straight to the viewing deck. Once he's sure the passengers are situated in the new environment, James makes a beeline through the door and climbs back onto the bus. He parks it in a designated bus parking spot and reaches for a pack of cigarettes in his backpack.

With all this vog, it's the worst damn habit to have, he thinks. *I'm just killing myself and spending money I could save for traveling with the fam.*

He scurries out of the bus and heads down a palm tree-lined pathway along one side of the Volcano Lodge. He lights up and takes a few deep drags, enjoying the rush of nicotine in his system. He can't help but feel foolish. He's probably wasted countless hours with these stupid smoke breaks, time he could have spent teaching Micaela guitar. When was the last time he picked up the instrument? He can't remember.

The cigarettes distract him. He never smokes in front of his family, but they are already familiar with the acrid odor that permeates his clothes and skin. His wife grumbles at the stinky laundry and Micaela makes "yucky faces" at him. He's tried the patch and gum, and even taken that medication with the stupid TV advertisements. In spite of his daughter's digs, he can't seem to give the smokes up.

He extinguishes the cigarette and tosses the butt in the trash. He makes his way past the Lodge. It's an older building with history dating back to 1846 (the first and only hotel in the park), red-shingled with newly repainted white shutters.

Slowing down to a casual walk, James watches people shuffle for vantage points along the overlook railing, trying to get the best shots of the gigantic caldera before the clouds roll in and block the view. One couple in particular catches his attention – Howard and Irene O'Malley. They stand arm in arm by an exhibit sign. James recalls them from the bus, chatting away like best buddies. They're loud talkers and he's close enough now to them to eavesdrop on their conversation.

" 'Here and there were gleaming holes a hundred feet in diameter, broken in the dark crust and in them the melted lava,' " Irene reads from the exhibit sign. "Mark Twain wrote that. When he visited here in the 1860s."

"I bet that was a sight back then. Must've been pretty active and wild," Howard says.

"More like spectacular," Irene says, staring out at the shield volcano. Water vapor mixed with sulfur dioxide escapes from the interior vents. The rim of the Kilauea shield volcano is almost oval in shape, a vast expanse measuring two miles across, surrounded by cliffs four hundred feet high. "So inside the volcano are the smaller calderas. This one called Hale-mumu... Gee, I can't even pronounce it!"

Howard laughs. "Says here, 'the cliffs and surrounding areas are riddled with miles of lava tubes, formed as the lava flows southeast through these rift zones, some eventually exiting all the way into the ocean.'"

"Wild fire and deep seas. It's as if we're witnessing earth in its infancy. Imagine that," Irene says. She takes her husband's gnarled, liver-spotted hand, so much like her own hands, and she gives it a loving pat.

"I wish we were young again, Howie. We're both getting so old, but hopefully better," she says with a slight grin.

"Yeah, soft and bruised like overripe bananas."

They take a seat on a wooden bench and observe a local tour helicopter flying above the caldera. "Maybe we should pick up some Dramamine for you," Irene says. "For our helicopter flight tomorrow."

"Nah, I don't need any of that crap."

"But honey, you could get sick, like you did after the lu'au."

"That's only because I drank one too many of those damn mai tais! Besides Dramamine doesn't work on me. I'm really looking forward to the helicopter tour. During the war, we used to call the choppers 'guppies,' because they were so shaky. They were nothing like these new-fangled, smooth 'copters they fly today. Hey, wait a sec."

He jumps up for a moment, a surge of energy charging through him, his arms spread open. "I'm still young on the inside, maybe not as handsome anymore. But heck, I bet I can pilot one of those hi-tech birds they're flyin' right now!"

"What a sight that would be. Oh, Howie, you're a hoot."

"I could fly 'em, gosh darn it!" he says while he slaps his hand on the railing.

"All right dear. Just so long as your young insides don't wind up on your old outsides."

"Oh, ha-ha, very funny. Sometimes you drive me crazy with your worry. You sure know how to wreck the mood, 'Reeny." He smirks and presses his upper teeth down to his lip. Deflated, he sits back down. "I reckon I'm not the same as I was back then, but I do love *you* more than ever."

He wraps an arm around her bony, bird-wing shoulder blade and she nuzzles her nose into his soft, thin pullover sweater. They cozy up together on the bench. "This is the best anniversary we've ever had," Irene says, contently, closing her eyes.

Still standing off to the side, overhearing their dialogue, James smiles. A light mist descends on him, tickling his cheek. A shiver runs through his body. He zips up his jacket and heads to the restaurant for lunch.

Forty minutes later, James hovers beside the open bus door while the elderly tourists re-board the vehicle. James helps Irene up the steps and turns to Howard, the final passenger, who shoos him off.

"No thanks, but I don't need any help. I'm healthy as a horse."

"Alright sir, whatever you say," James replies as he watches Howard climb the steps with a quiet grunt and a pop of his joints.

What a stubborn old dude he is, James thinks.

Once everyone sits down, James ascends the steps and takes a seat behind the wheel. He flicks on the intercom.

"Welcome back, ladies and gentlemen," he says as he's about to pull the door shut. "We'll be leaving now…" his voice trails off when he sees two young Asian men standing at the door. Both wear baseball caps pulled down low. One of them holds a cumbersome duffel bag.

"Hello? Can I help you?" James asks.

The taller of the two moves toward the bus steps, about to enter when James says, "I'm afraid you got the wrong bus, sir. This is a private charter. If you can't find your bus, you can return to the Lodge or maybe check with the next bus down the line."

He turns and points behind them. Both men look up with expressionless faces. The shorter man holds the bag. He has dark skin and wide cheekbones.

The taller man is angular and pale, lean-muscled, and sleek as a puma. His eyes pulse with a cold intensity. He dismisses James' suggestions and springs up the bus steps, with the shorter man following him. Inside, they look around the bus interior, taking an inventory of the sights and sounds.

"Do you speak English?" James asks.

Without a word, the two men walk toward him.

"Sir, if you're looking for the Japanese bus, it's right back there."

"We're not Ja-pa-nese!" the tall man growls.

The shorter man leans in close, his breath heady with a peppermint scent. "Now...shut the hell up."

"Whoa, easy there, guys. I really apologize about the Japanese comment. Didn't mean to be insensitive. But as you can see, we only have senior citizens on this bus."

James starts to rise out of his seat. *What to do? Should I demand they get out? Call security?* They have effectively barricaded the door.

"Listen, guys, I don't want any trouble. If you'll please exit the..."

The shorter man unzips his bag. He flashes an Uzi machine gun to James and without taking it completely out of the bag, rams it into James' side.

"Holy crap." His heart beats so loudly he can't register if the passengers have seen what has just happened. Folding in half, he falls back into his seat, sucking in breaths between groans.

The short man leans in again, spitting into his face. "Do like I say, fatso. Shut up and drive or die. Now go!"

Clutching his torso in pain, James nods his head, bobbing it up and down like a frightened child. In all his years of driving buses, he's never encountered anything like this. The company never briefed him on how to handle a terrorist or a bus hijack. They didn't even give him a protocol to follow! Eyeing the curve of the roundabout, he struggles to think straight. It's not only the pain of the machine gun pressed against him, but also the greater psychological pain of knowing the lives of his passengers are at risk.

Should I yell at the top of my lungs?

He whimpers, paralyzed in his seat, hands clawing the steering wheel. He has to stay calm. He does not want the passengers to know, even if they are suspicious. His radio receiver, which allows him to contact the dispatcher, dangles just out of his reach. How he musters an untapped energetic angst, he's not sure, but he catches his breath and spits through locked teeth.

"Get the hell off my bus."

"Ha. You're not so smart, bus driver," the tall man says. "Now listen to me."

Click. A steely-cold Glock pistol hidden from the passengers' view now pushes up against James. His back aches from the pressure. The man takes off his baseball cap, throws it down, and then lifts off James' company Aloha Tours visor and puts it on his own head. He whispers in James' right ear with a clear, assured tone.

"I tell you this. When I was a boy, back in Korea, I wanted to drive a bus, but I never had a chance. Until now." His smile spreads wide, revealing perfect white teeth. "So drive now…or I'll splatter your brains all over the dashboard. Then I'll finally get my chance to drive a bus. Lucky me."

He pushes the pistol harder into James. There's no point in fighting. James reaches for the ignition switch and turns it over. The shorter man plays "bouncer" in the aisle, blocking the passengers from any view of the cab.

Passengers crane their heads to see what's happening, muttering in hushed voices. Veterans send cool stares at the men, trying to understand what's taking place and sizing them up.

James navigates the bus down a hill and through the guard gate without incident. The taller man stands over him, pointing directions as he keeps his pistol shoved in James' side. "Faster. Faster. Now, slow down. Turn left there."

"There's nothing there," James protests.

The man points a small remote control device at the roadside. A metal gate, camouflaged by the foliage, automatically swings open, revealing a narrow, unpaved road. James brakes and turns onto the road as tree branches and bushes scratch the side of the bus. The gate closes and the bus trundles through a thick jungle area of trees and undergrowth, clearly off the regular path. The passengers look at each other with questioning eyes.

"This is not the bus route," Irene says, trembling with anxiety in her voice.

"I was thinking the exact same thing," Howard says. "Something's definitely not right."

Chapter Five

"Where's my GPS?"

Sonoran Desert Highway,
30 miles southwest of Tucson

With a Cat Stevens tune blasting on the car's CD player, Bernard "Bernie" Wilkes taps his fingers while he drives, watching the sky's color shift from blue into an intense sunset palette.

"Oh wow, this place is so unreal..."

He drives a '95 Chevy Metro, on loan from his mother. With his flip-down aviator sunglasses on, the polarized lenses heighten the evening colors in an array of bright orange and purple. He rolls the window down and extends a pudgy, sunburnt arm, feeling the wind whip across his fingers.

He leans his head out for a moment, but his greasy hair doesn't move – the result of yet another shampoo free week. Mom isn't around to line up fruity hair products in his shower caddy and with collegiate freedom, there comes a certain dismissal of basic hygiene. Students are busy with work and regress to a "I-just-don't-give-a-shit-anyway" attitude.

In the case of Bernie Wilkes (who doesn't give a *darn*, "cussing is inappropriate"), these particular habits were never really learned. He's always relied on his Mom's cues for functional routines and life skills. So when he's alone and fending for himself, his hair smells like a fast food restaurant and his armpits exude a damp, acidic reek.

"But, darn it, who cares?" he'll say. "I've got five more important things to do." And he'll list them out loud. "My class coursework, acapella group, Tae Kwon Do practice, video games, and reading comic books. Do you know how rare the 1938 Adventures' Comics issue is?"

He picked up the habit of reading comic books when he was six and that hasn't changed in over a decade.

The car chugs along the uphill grade at forty miles an hour as Bernie sings in a loud but perfectly pitched voice, "My lay-dee d'Arbanvee, why do you sleep so still, I'll wake you tomorrow aa...ah, ah, ah!"

He hears a *put, put, put, put*. The Metro splutters.

"No, no-no-no-no. Not now, please not now," Bernie pleads to the car. He rocks forward, grasping the steering wheel with tense knuckles. "Just a little further, pleeeeaazze..."

Smoke billows out from under the hood and a steady *clunk-clunk* sound follows as the engine convulses. He looks down at the radiator gauge, which is well above the hot level, and at the engine warning light which is on.

"C'mon, Mettie ol' girl. We're almost there." As he pulls over to the side of the road, the car grinds to a halt. He puts the car in park and turns the ignition over. The car rumbles.

"No way!"

He slams his palm on the steering wheel. He pushes the door open and exits the car. Trudging up to the front, he lifts the hood and a puff of hot steam hits him in the face causing him to rear back. The engine smolders and the radiator smokes as though there's a dragon's mouth inside the car. The curtain has closed. Death blow to the Metro.

"Darn it!" Bernie cries out. He shuts the hood and turns away, kicking up a patch of gravelly sand. "Sorry, Mom. I killed your car." He flips his sunglasses up and scans the desert highway.

"This is not good, no, not good at all."

Twenty minutes ago he saw a modern-day cowboy driving a pick-up truck with a Texas license plate. Other than that, he hasn't shared the road with anyone else in a long time. The sun begins to dip below the horizon. It's all desert flora and fauna, sand and rocks and violet sky. Sagebrush lizards bask in the twilight glow and hunt for insects. A warm breeze floats through the creosote bush and whisks away the last of the spring cacti bloom. He hears a coyote howl. He thinks he sees a rattlesnake shimmy behind a rock.

"Was that a snake?" he whispers. "Sure hope not."

If he stays here for much longer, it will be dark soon. The temperature has dropped since the afternoon, but it's still substantially hot, probably in the 90s.

It's only about a mile away, he tries to reassure himself. It's not going to be a regular walking mile though, but rather a *sweaty-thirsty-bone-tired-after-twelve-hours-of-traveling-uphill-hike*. Yet some force is prodding him to go. Is it instinct? Something primal? Or a sense of adventure? *Forget those coyotes and snakes, I'm going for it!*

Bernie reaches into the car and grabs his laptop, a half-full water bottle, and a worn-out nylon backpack. He hurls the backpack over his shoulder and begins hiking up the road toward the high desert hills.

"Amazing," Susan says as she peers out from the deck. She's lived here for three years and has never seen a sunset quite as beautiful as this one. It's a veritable canvas of cantaloupe, indigo, soft hazy yellow, and flaming red. Tall Saguaro cacti cast long shadows across the plains and foothills. Spindly ocotillo dance in the refracted light. High-altitude cirrus clouds sweep across the sky under a blanket of cirrocumulus cloud formations that remind her of a mermaid's tail.

The exterior solar charged pathway leading to the house illuminates her Zen rock-desert garden. A few months ago, before the intense mid-summer heat set in, she was out here raking circular lines and tending to the sage and lavender. Since then, the herbs have wilted a little. The hearty cacti and agave thrive. Xeriscaping *is* Arizona gardening and Susan's eyes become accustomed to the sandy neutral tones of desert plants. The bright shades of valerian and aster flowers stand out that much more.

Situated on the alluvial plain, Tucson and its environs are surrounded by the Santa Catalina and Tortolita Mountains, the Santa Rita Mountains, the Rincon Mountains to the east and closest to the Andrews' home, the Tucson Mountains. Eruptions formed the ranges, with the volcano collapsing to create a caldera that filled up with subsequent lava flows and the cooling of plutonic rocks.

The desert is incredible, and yet, Susan had never wanted to leave California. It meant bowing out of her job as an assistant professor and saying goodbye to friends and students. But Tom had found the ideal position at the University of Arizona, where he would only have to teach part-time, giving him breaks to venture off to different places for research. There was also the golden promise of tenure.

Tenure. It's something Susan can't even think about for herself. She could go back and teach college, but most days she tutors high school math and cares for the interminable needs of the house and garden. During the hot days, she tries to stay cool and protected from the glaring sun. At times the sadness of change is hard to bear, but the glorious Southwest environment has its special magic. Not even the most colorful Pacific sunset in California, with its famed "green flash," could compare to the *Arizona Outback*.

With a final look at the dwindling light, she heads inside, ready to resume evening duties. In the house, the air conditioner blasts away and she walks over to the kitchen to finish cooking dinner.

"Susaaaann! Susaaann!" Tom calls out from another room. Then she hears the sound of shuffling papers. He might be lifting something too. "It was right here!" he yells to her.

"What are you looking for?" she hollers back.

"My GPS."

"Which one?"

"You know, the one Mom gave me," he says, wandering into the kitchen.

"Oh, *that* one. Of course, why did I even ask?" Susan mutters, partly to herself, partly to Tom, but mostly into the steaming vat of angel hair pasta. She stirs the tomato sauce and grimaces. "It's on the bottom rung of the night table, by your camera."

"I can't find my camera either and no GPS here. Are you sure you didn't move it?"

"No, Tom," she says, trying to hide the crossness in her voice.

He pokes his head back into the kitchen. "Hey, that spaghetti sauce smells great."

"Come in and try it while it's simmering. Here, have a bite." She greets him with a heaping spoonful of tomato sauce. In his eagerness, he slurps it down.

"Just like your Mom's?" she bobs her head to one side, waiting for a smile of approval.

"Mom's was a bit more... flavorful. More oregano maybe." He stares at the wall in a brief reverie.

"Really? I actually copied her recipe. She sent it to me last spring. Maybe she's worried you're not eating well enough," Susan grumbles.

"Yeah, okay," he says. "I have to get back to the detective work." He strolls out into the foyer.

Susan turns the burners off and follows him out through the living room. "Oh, yes, I almost forgot how you really love *her* tomato sauce and everything else that she makes and does!"

He turns his head, eyebrows knit in confusion.

She continues. "Your mother can't do anything wrong in your book. And, you don't even hesitate to call her for advice on our personal lives."

"Not now, Suze. I need to find my GPS."

"Evasion tactic! No, you don't need anything. But *we* need something. It's called freedom. It's called privacy. Cut the umbilical cord, Thomas. It's time for independence from the Motherland. You can't do anything without her approval. I bet you get her okay to trim your nose hairs."

"Okaaay..." Tom says. Half-distracted, he reaches up, feeling his nose hairs. "You know, they've never been tidier, my love." He crinkles his chin, shrugs his shoulders, and resumes his search. "I don't get it. I know I saw it here." He sifts through the bills stacked on the foyer table.

She follows him, arms crossed. "Don't walk away from me. You're avoiding me."

"Look, I'm not avoiding you," he says, turning to face her. "I just don't understand your train of thought. It's illogical. Mom's sauce?

Nose hairs? Our personal lives? Where's the connection?"

"Last week," she announces.

"Last week? Well, there's another connect-the-dots. What about it?"

"The awards ceremony?" she offers.

"Oh, ok. How'd I miss that? What did I do wrong? Clue me in. I had some wine."

"And then some more wine," she says.

"I talked to the other Johns. Not John H, I think it was John Currier and John Metzger –"

"Leaving me alone for half the night."

"We were discussing X-ray fluorescence in sedimentary samples. It might have interested you. Seriously, darling wife of mine, what gives? Is this about the award?"

"Bingo."

She looks at the chunky silverware set atop colorful Guatemalan napkins and the hand painted ceramic dishes. She brushes her fingers against a vase full of fresh desert lilies. Unlike this conversation, they are simple. They don't make excuses. They don't have domineering mothers.

Hesitant, Tom reaches out to stroke Susan's hand, but she scooches away.

"Please don't touch me," she says. "First, you left me at the party. Then you got up there, in front of everybody, and thanked your mother."

"Ah no, so you're mad about Mom for the zillionth time. What else is new?" he throws his arms up into the air. He starts to walk back to the living room and turns again to face her. "And what does any of this have to do with my GPS?"

"Volumes! Everything! Tom, you don't go anywhere without it. You're attached to it in the same way that you're attached to your mother's opinions. Can't you see what she's done to you? The dependency and need for approval?" Susan pauses to catch her breath. She paces around him, her mind spiraling, trying to equilibrate like a neurotic nautilus. "What did she say to you when you won the N.G.S award?"

"She said it would have made her happier if it had been the international one."

"See, that's exactly my point! 'Made her happier.' You can never make her happy. Because *she* is a miserable person and a bloody perfectionist to the extreme. So why even try? You're the National Geoscientist of the Year and she still can't accept you."

Tom stares blankly at the door. "Susan, she's my mother."

"And, you're playing some bizarre mind game with her. You're like this fawning little puppy that puts up with all her abuse, hit after hit, and then just go right back to her for more, like everything's fine and dandy. If this isn't some crazy Oedipal complex, I don't know what it is."

"Come on, that's a bit melodramatic. Look, I love my Mom, but I'm not *in love* with her."

"You sure have bamboozled me."

Tom struggles to rein in his impatience. "I'm sorry for asking her advice about those minor things, like you know, having kids and all."

She catches the sarcasm. "Fine time to bring this up, Tom." She can't hold back the tears and they begin to stream down her flushed cheeks. "You're not the only one here. I gave up my career and California to be with you."

A loose strand of wavy hair falls over her left eyebrow. Defeated and discouraged, she trudges back to the kitchen.

"All right," Tom says to the empty room. "She's gonna' keep bringing that up. I can't win."

A sudden buzz of the doorbell cuts through the silence. Tom is both relieved and annoyed. He runs his hand through his hair as he approaches the door. "I'm coming!"

For a moment he entertains the thought of his recently ordered Volcano Tilt Meter, gleefully delivered by a cute, ponytailed Fed Ex lady. But no, that wouldn't happen. He picks his mail up at the University and it's too late for a Fed Ex delivery.

Even when they do deliver to this area, most postal workers have hard luck finding the Andrews' out-of-the-way house. The rock-hewn home blends easily into the larger stone formations like a rust-colored chameleon. Its exterior is constructed from layers of gray and brown slate. A Geode Abode.

Tom swings the door open, promptly assaulted by the odiferous smell of grease and body odor. Before him stands a sweaty teenager. He's pale as a turnip and can't be more than sixteen years old. Fine layers of dust have settled on the boy's crooked wire rim glasses and his clothes are caked in dirt and desert sand.

Of average height, with a torpedo-shaped body, he looks like he was plucked straight out of a comic book convention and thrust into the Arizona sun for more than a few uncomfortable hours. His shoulders hunch over and he has an overbite that no Svengali orthodontist could ever correct. Wide-set fish eyes blink twice when he asks in a nasal voice, "Dr. Andrews?"

"Yes? What can I do for you?"

"Hello. My name's Bernard Wilkes. I'm here, with the Caltech Internship program. And I just want to say..."

"Great, glad you could find our place. It sounds like you've been practicing that canvassing speech for a while, kiddo. Good timing. I've got some cash on me." He pulls a five-dollar bill out of his pant pocket and hands it to Bernie. "Here ya' go. And have a great day!"

"No wait, wait, you don't understand."

Tom slams the door.

Outside, a band of crickets thrum, in a sad, stringed vibrato. Bernie turns away from the house, peering around the garden and landscape entryway. *Someone put some real thought and work into this place. Wonder if I'll get to see the inside?*

He plops down onto the porch steps, burying his face into his hands, and sobs.

He didn't even give me a chance. I mean, don't they know that I'm coming? It's too much to think about and he's too tired and thirsty to even move. He contemplates heading back to the Metro, but that would be another hour of walking back down the road and the heat has immobilized him. He lays his head on his backpack and closes his eyes. Maybe the nice Dr. Andrews (the one he imagined) will appear at the door.

Inside, Susan spoons tomato sauce over the pasta, pausing to glance at Tom. "Who was that?" she asks.

"Just some college kid on a fund-raising gig. You remember that character Piggy from Lord of the Flies?"

"No."

"You didn't read it in middle school?"

"No. I think that was one of your quote-unquote 'uniquely American experiences.' British ruffians on a Polynesian island? I think those kind of books were banned at my school."

She glances at Tom's messy hair and the marching line of sweat droplets on his brow. He's not smiling. The GPS is still missing.

"Anyway, this kid reminded me of that character," Tom says. "Or maybe I'm mixing it up with the movie."

"So you're going to invite him in?"

"Piggy? I don't think so. If I was him, I'd shift my butt into high-gear and zoom outta' here."

"So…he drove all the way here, from the city or maybe farther, only to have you slam a door in his face?" she says while she shakes her head. "What college does he go to?"

"Caltech."

"What? Tom! He's the intern we're having for the summer! Did you really forget?"

She sets the spoon down with force, watching sauce splatter onto the countertop. "You only spent a decade there, and who knows… *you* might be asking for a job from this kid someday." She clenches her teeth in exasperation. "Do I have to keep track of everything?"

She walks over to the door and turns the porch light on. Opening the door, she sees Bernie propped on his side in a fetal position.

"Hi there," she says.

"H-ello," his voice strains, a reedy falsetto. He peeks out from his huddle for a moment, like a forest squirrel hiding in a tree knot. Scared, but still curious.

"Bernard, right?" Susan crouches down to place a hand on his shoulder, ignoring his grassy body stench, though it's hard to do so. "You're the summer intern, right? I'm Susan."

He rises to his feet. "Hi, Dr. Andrews. Or do you go by Dr. McCarthy?"

"Susan, please. And come on in. I'll get you an ice cold glass of cherry lemonade. You'll feel better. You can take a hot shower soon."

Bernie raises an eyebrow and his lips part into a whispered thank you as he follows her into the house.

"I'm really sorry about my husband's behavior," Susan continues. "He must have forgotten. He's, well, how can I explain?"

"It's okay. But, my car died a couple miles down the road. I think it's the engine. The radiator over-heated. I'm not mechanically minded, with cars that is. As my mom would say, all's well that ends well. I am supposed to be here, you know," he says, reassuring himself as much as to her.

From his backpack, he picks out a crinkled, ketchup-stained paper and hands it to her. She skims the page:

California Institute of Technology
Department of Geological Sciences Internship Program

Wilkes, Bernard A.J.
6551 Pine Meadow Avenue
Portland, ME 04109

Below that is a signature, chicken-scrawled and slanting at 45-degrees. The B, A, and W are the only recognizable letters.

"Did you drive all the way from Maine?" Susan inquires.

"Yes, ma'am. I was visiting home for my summer break."

"I'm amazed you made it here in one piece. You must be famished and dehydrated from your hike. Walking in this heat can be truly unbearable. Glad you have some luggage with you. We'll take care of your car issue as soon as possible."

A shout startles them from the other room. "I found it!" Tom rushes in, eyes widening in childish delight. "It was next to the camera. But *not* in the library. It was in our *bedroom*, on the bottom of the night table."

Susan sighs. "Like I said, right next to your camera."

Grinning from ear to ear, Tom nods his head. "Amazing." He sees Bernie and sends him a quick wave. "Oh, hey kid."

"Bernie, have a seat here in the dining room and I'll be right back with your drink," Susan says as she pulls Tom aside. "Can I speak with you in private for a minute?"

"Okay," he says, confused. She takes his arm and they head into the kitchen.

Bernie notes the serenity of the house and its surroundings. Soundless, except for the low hum of an air conditioning unit. The coolness feels marvelous. He lets out a deep breath and sighs. Taking a seat, he raises his arms behind his head to cool off his armpits. He looks out the window and observes a waxing crescent moon rise over the jagged mountains peaks.

What he can't see is that the desert is already abuzz with nocturnal activity. Snakes lurk in the creosote. Kangaroo rats burrow holes in the sand, while lizards lick crusted insects off pebbly rocks. He's glad he's not out there. For him, this is a much more delightful vantage point, comfy and protected in a custom home, with its peaceful enclosure of sandstone and shale. All quiet on the set.

Glancing over to the tapestries on the dining room wall, he sees one that looks like an Asian tapestry of a bird flying above an ocean of waves. Another tapestry is an abstract tessellation pattern composed of alternating black and yellow zigzags, possibly of South American origin. The patterns mesmerize, colors against a colorless wall. Bernie's mom would say Susan's decor is "very feng shui," whatever that means. As he sits there, he overhears tidbits of the couple's conversation.

"I'm not joking here," Susan says. "Remember? The Caltech apprenticeship program?"

"I forgot."

"He's going to be here all summer."

"Who? Piggy?"

Bernie fidgets. He hears Tom's comment, but even Susan doesn't seem that excited to have him here. He drops his head. *Tom is a jerk. First he slams the door in my face and now he's name-calling?* Bernie stands up. He's dealt with bullies, though it's a little disappointing to see meanness in a professional man. The best thing to do is ignore their conversation and remind himself: *They requested me to be here and give them whatever help I can. So we'll all have to make the best of it.*

He continues to scope out the house. It's a single level home with thick, white adobe walls, tile floors, and Spanish alcoves. It's the kind of house with fantastic acoustics, where you could hear a pin drop three rooms away. He's tempted to walk over to the library-study. Most likely it's Tom's special room. But before he has time for a proper browse, Susan and Tom are standing behind him.

"Uh-um," Tom clears his throat.

"Bernard," Susan interjects, twisting a strand of hair into a curl as Bernie turns to face them. "We're both completely happy to have you stay with us." She hands Bernie a glass of lemonade.

"Thank you so much," he says between gulps. After drinking for a couple seconds, he can barely swallow his burp. "You can call me Bernie. All my friends do."

"All right," Susan says.

"We're fine with you staying," Tom mumbles. "And sorry, about closing the door on you."

"It's okay. I promise I'll be neat. I can see you run a tight ship here, Dr. McCarthy, just like my mother."

"Thank you Bernie," Susan says. "Good to make mums happy, right? Ha. But, please, just call us Tom and Susan."

Tom rolls his eyes.

"So, why don't you two get acquainted while I finish fixing dinner?" Susan says. "After we eat, I can show you to your room." With her last stroke of patience, Susan leaves the library.

Bernie turns to Tom. "Dr. Andrews, I'm a big fan of your work, particularly your scholarly essays that I read this semester in a geology course. I come from a long-line of scientifically minded folks. You might even say it's part of our DNA."

"That's interesting. You can join me in the study. Check out our 'lab' as I sometimes call it."

Bernie follows Tom into the room. There are large glass cabinets displaying various quartz rocks. Dozens of textbooks, manuals, and reports line the shelves.

"Dr. Andrews, have you ever heard the joke about a geologist's favorite game?"

"Oh, brother..."

"Igneous erodes to sedimentary, metamorphic alters sedimentary and –"

"Igneous melts metamorphic?" Tom interjects. "This is a joke, huh?"

"Then you have heard of the understandably, less popular geologist version of the rock-paper-scissors game, known as rock-rock-rock?"

"Funny! We play that every day and it still doesn't get boring," Tom says.

Bernie laughs. His eyes wander and settle on a large topographical map of the Hawaiian Islands on the main desk. A number of red round headed pins mark locations around the Kilauea volcano on the Big Island. Like army peons, the pins are clustered together with a large battalion on the volcano's southeastern flank.

"Checking out the map?" Tom asks.

"Yes, although I imagined you had all your maps on a computer versus a paper map model."

"I have a consultant for that. Sorry to disappoint you. I'm not the Geology Tech Wiz you may have imagined, with holograms and spinning plates and all that jazz. I'm old school. More of a hammer and hand-lens kind of guy."

Absorbed, Bernie studies the map. "So the pins represent current seismic activity?"

"They represent some recent activity at Kilauea in the past thirty days. Magma is churning underneath, but there is also possible structural weakness at the base of the volcano, far below the earth. Most of the earthquakes are so tiny they can only be detected by the seismograph. The largest recorded quake in Hawaii was in 1868, with an estimated magnitude of 7.9 along the Mauna Loa south flank," Tom says pointing near the southern tip of the Big Island.

He continues. "The north flank of Kilauea is immobilized by the adjacent mass of Mauna Loa, which in turn causes Kilauea's south flank to move outward to make more room for the additional magma."

"And so the south flank then shifts seaward in response to the pressure causing earthquakes?" Bernie says.

"You know your macro-geology, Mr. B."

"Thanks. So, is there any explanation for having a higher rate of activity like it is in this particular month?"

"I've been compiling a detailed analysis to evaluate any significance, but I still have to run more data with my tech consultant."

"You don't run the data yourself?"

"That's mostly Jerry's job." Tom leans over the map and examines the southeast ridge.

"Any indication of a big eruption or earthquake in the near future?" Bernie asks. He watches, fascinated.

"Honestly, we really don't know yet."

Tom inspects the map further, his nostrils flaring with intent. "Measurements have indicated a significant amount of volcanic slippage and we can only deduce that there may be some large magma re-distribution happening. At least that's the natural course of events."

He pauses, tracing his finger along the ridge. "If a major earthquake were to happen, it would most likely occur along this rift zone on the Southeast coastal region. Hopefully, it would only instigate minor seismic activity…although you never know with Kilauea. It's unpredictable and there could be a lot of pressure built up. It's a big, bad-ass volcano."

Chapter Six

"The Hostages"

Hawaii Volcanoes National Park

At 1:30 in the afternoon, the Aloha Tours Bus comes to a stop in a tree-lined area, a few yards from the caldera's cliff. Within seconds, six armed Korean soldiers in dark camouflage uniforms break cover and surround the bus. They throw a camouflage tarp over the roof and then cover the sides of the bus with tree foliage, effectively hiding the vehicle from aerial views. Armed with AK-47s, two additional soldiers appear and head straight to the bus and march inside it.

The passengers protest and yell to no avail. They were unprepared for anything like this. The tall man and his partner survey the hostages' nervous faces, knowing these elderly people, however tough they were fifty years ago, are subdued and not in control.

"Thanks for the ride Mr. Bus-Man," the tall man says, snarling at James. "Now out of your seat and move back. Keep moving."

James obliges and tries to catch his breath. "There," the man orders, shoving him down into an open seat.

James looks behind and notes Irene's frightened state as she clings to her husband's arm. *I'm scared too*, James wants to say out loud, but his attention diverts to the other passengers. Their eyes are open wide with fear and apprehension.

"Turn around," a deep voice calls out.

It's not one of the original hijackers nor any of the young soldiers. This Korean appears middle-aged, his hair graying at the sides. He is shorter and more slight than most of the soldiers, but he is definitely the commander in charge. He speaks in a tone that is forceful yet smooth.

"I am the officer in charge. Ho Dam. You are being held by the Korean Unification Front. Until your government removes its troops from our homeland, you will not return to yours."

One of the U.S. vets, Mark Gerlach, mutters to himself, "You sick, yellow commie bastard."

Amidst the cries, Ho Dam can still hear the comment. He hones in on the words and stomps down the aisle toward Mark. Ho Dam rolls up his sleeve and holds out an exposed arm. "Look closely. Do you actually see any yellow? Aren't we all shades of brown? I would say that *you* are the sick bastard."

Before Mark can answer, Ho Dam slaps him hard in the face. Mark lets out a pained moan and crumples down.

Ho Dam whips around, brandishing his weapon at the other passengers. He stomps back up the aisle. When he reaches the front of the bus, he spins around and points his UZI up, firing three rounds. *Pop-pop-pop.* The bullets burst through the ceiling in a deafening rattle. The passengers shake and cower down into their seats. Two more armed soldiers rush through the door. They are all clutching AK-47s in their arms, training their weapons on the crowd.

"Listen carefully," Ho Dam says. "If anyone tries to escape, you and your loved one will be shot and thrown into the caldera. If your government attempts any rescue, we will kill all of you! Do you understand?"

Several passengers nod in agreement. Ho Dam turns and storms out, leaving his men to threaten the passengers.

Hours later, night has fallen. Within the stuffy bus, many passengers have resigned themselves to sleep. Disoriented, dehydrated, and tired, James tries to think. He takes note of the two armed guards at the door.

Irene is wilting in the heat.

"We gotta' do something," Howard whispers to her. "This is insane. At least they could give us some damn oxygen," he says while he reaches over to slide the small window open.

A rifle barrel from outside rises to meet his hands.

"Whoa, whoa! Don't shoot! Just trying to get a little air." Even in the night shadows, Howard can see the white of the guard's teeth and his mouth fixed in a bull-dog snarl.

"Don't even think about it, Mr. O'Malley," Ho Dam calls out from a few feet behind the guard. His voice reverberates off the lava rocks, low and cool and confident.

"How'd you know my name?" Howard asks.

"I know everyone's name on the bus."

"And how the heck did you manage to do that? You don't strike me as the friendly schoolmaster."

"Good joke, Mr. O'Malley. I just grabbed Mr. Elhorn's clipboard. Easy peasy, as they say. You don't strike me as the 'top student,' but I'm watching you."

"I'm not afraid of you!"

Howard looks further out, but he still can't see Ho Dam in the dark of the night. The outside guard has a rifle pointing at him. The two guards from inside the bus are now at his side, threatening him with their weapons as well. He's scared of course, but he won't show an indication of it. He knows these men feed off of fear like ants on sugar.

"Well, well, Mr. Macho Man," Ho Dam says. "How 'bout I have one of my men blow a hole in your head? Or how about a dozen shots all at once that'll kill your wife, too? That doesn't scare you?"

The outside guard shoves the rifle closer to Howard's face. Reluctantly, Howard pulls his head back in the bus and slides the window closed. He controls his shaking and plops back into his seat with a "Humph." The two guards next to him return to their posts in the front of the bus.

Irene pats his shoulder.

"Damn, at this point, it doesn't look like we'd have much luck with a takeover," Howard says to both Irene and James. "There are at least a dozen of us vets in good, healthy condition, but still we're all unarmed."

James shakes his head in non-verbal agreement.

"We have to keep waiting," Howard continues. "These guys will get tired and they'll need to do a switch-out. But who knows how many henchmen he's got waiting in the dark?"

He pauses, thinking. "Maybe we could create some late night commotion. I don't know, someone having a panic attack? The guards would rush to see what was happening, then we jump them, take their weapons, and bolt through the exit door. We'd have to wait until early morning – when they're really tired and we can see where we're going."

"Don't be crazy, Howard," Irene whispers back.

"Well, we've got to do something. We can't let them use us like human pawns."

"Whatever it is, please think it through. You'd not only be risking our lives, but everyone on the bus," James says.

Suddenly, the bus shudders, cutting their conversation short.

"Whoa... what the heck?" Howard exclaims.

There's a violent shake that tosses some passengers to the floor. Others grasp for their seat belts, hastily securing them, clutching their armrests and holding onto the seat backs in front of them.

"What's happening?" a woman screams out.

"Help!" another man wails as he's jolted from his seat.

"Earthquake!" James shouts.

The passengers shift and brace themselves. The bus heaves and rolls forward. A guard rushes to the driver's seat and stomps on the brake, yet the bus continues to gain momentum. Another guard yells frantically in Korean and pulls on the emergency brake, but it's useless. He searches outside for his comrades, but they're busy scrambling as best they can to get away from the shaking vehicle.

While the bus lurches forward to the caldera's edge, tossing the passengers like confetti, Irene cries out.

"I've got you," Howard reassures her. He wraps an arm around her, but his own body is sweaty and his hands move in spastic gestures.

The bus bumper slips over the edge. Pebbles dislodge from the cliff face in a tumbling hail of debris. Tremors rock the ground beneath the vehicle. Unable to look anymore, Irene buries her face into Howard's shoulder. The intense shaking continues as they move closer and closer to imminent death.

Chapter Seven

"The Situation Room"

The Pentagon, Joint Chiefs of Staff Room

"Know this, American leaders...." the heavily accented voice resounds over a live-fed broadcast. "We demand a full U.S. Military withdrawal from your American bases in South Korea and five hundred million U.S. dollars wired to the Central Bank account, number 39-0754762231. This is just compensation for the families of those who your military massacred during the Korean War..."

Accompanying the voice is the rugged, scarred face of Commander Chu Lee, an older, seasoned North Korean military commando. He wears olive green battle fatigues and a gray cap. The camera pans over the backdrop of a private garden, while a white flag with a blue design of the Korean peninsula billows in the wind. Then the camera zooms in, focusing back on Chu Lee's face.

"You have seventy-two hours from 6:00 a.m. Pacific Time to complete this task. Failure to do so will result in the deaths of forty-five Americans whom we have seized.

"For those of you who doubt our resolve, know that we have already detonated our first explosive device near the Kilauea Volcano in Hawaii, triggering a minor earthquake. This is only a prelude to the devastation that will follow if our demands are *not* met.

"Many other high explosives are set to detonate in more sensitive areas of the volcanic plain, which, if activated, will send powerful tsunami waves across the entire Western Pacific coast. Collateral damage is likely. The choice is yours. Meet our demands, or be responsible for the destruction of your cities and the deaths of many of your citizens."

The eyes of U.S. Joint Chiefs of Staff General Robert McGregor, CIA Director Douglas Berkowitz, and Secretary of Defense Alex Hanson scan the room clockwise, then counterclockwise as National Security Adviser Michael Durante joins in the group. They wait for each other to answer, but for a moment it is silent and foreboding, like the collective stare of a military Argus.

Finally, General McGregor speaks up. "For years there have been talks of Korean unification, but the R.O.K. and D.P.R.K. hate each other. Is this just more rhetoric or some kind of bluff from Kim Jong-Il? And what's this Unification Party all about? We're not about to leave such a strategic location. We're not going to withdraw 30,000 troops. Furthermore, we don't negotiate or give in to terrorist demands."

General McGregor's experience harkens back to the days of Carlos the Jackal and the Air France hijack. He's dealt with the "major bullshit" as he calls it. Takeovers are a predictable terrorist phenomenon, although he never envisioned Hawaii Volcanoes National Park as a target site. It's all starting to make sense – unpredictable locale but relatively close to Korea, easy access from the airport, no armed guards at the Park, poor phone reception, a major visitor destination point, and a targeted elderly hostage group.

Certain questions arise. *Who is the leader? Who is the second-in-command? How many soldiers are involved?*

The General pounds his fist into the table, rolling his knuckles in a sine wave. He stands up. His fingers span and put pressure on the table as he lowers his voice to a growling whisper. "What the hell is this *really* about?"

Douglas Berkowitz clears his throat. "It goes back more than fifty years to the Korean War and an incident that happened at No Gun Ri in the summer of 1950. Their Commander is Kim Sung Cho, who heads KUF, the Korean Unification Front. Our Intel informs us that he is one of the leaders of this fringe, paramilitary North Korean group.

"Recently, they've infiltrated and enticed riots within South Korea. It started with some radical students, idealistic kids that envisioned a unified county, but now the military is joining their ranks. Until recently, the protests were peaceful, but the situation has escalated. KUF is well-financed and backed by the North and probably China. They have no issue with military spending. They supply equipment and weapons to the riots in the South."

Alex Hanson taps his fingers. "General, as you know, during the Korean War our troops swept the countryside several times. The North would beat us back to the South and we'd have to regroup. With the help of reinforcements, we'd fight our way back up. We napalmed and bombed the hell out of their country in several drives to keep the North at bay." He looks down at the table with a solemn expression.

"Many innocent civilians lost their lives," Hanson continues. "In one incident, our investigation stats show that perhaps five hundred Korean civilians were accidentally massacred at No Gun Ri Bridge. There are debates about the actual number of civilians killed and wounded.

"The Koreans have petitioned every U.S. administration, including this one, since 1960, asking for recognition and monetary compensation. Condolences have been made, even by our own administration, but we've traditionally refused to acknowledge any U.S. involvement.

"It would seem that this is their last ditch effort to get recognition. The fact is, two million Koreans died in the three year 'conflict,' as it's called. No Gun Ri was a blatant trigger point."

"That's an affirmative," Michael Durante chimes in. "Even though it's been fifty-some years, the Administration's official position is still: No recognition, no admission, and absolutely no compensation."

"Well, congratulations, Durante," General McGregor replies, irritated. "We've just created our newest hot bed of hostility. Now, don't bullshit me. Five hundred, accidentally massacred? Did we or did we not kill those civilians?" he says as he sits back down in his chair.

"Unfortunately, it may appear, yes," Michael Durante answers.

"We're going to need our best Special-Op's Incursion Team Leader on this… and we'll need him now," Alex Hanson adds.

General McGregor motions to an attaché stationed behind him to come forward. He whispers in the man's ear and they confer in hushed tones, before McGregor announces.

"We got him. Served in Grenada, Desert Storm, Somalia, Kosovo. He's a Delta Force SOG Commander with an impressive and successful career. Got about as much tact as a battleship in a pond, but he doesn't play politics and he's a helluva' leader that his men respect. I'd bet my life on him to get the job done."

"All right," Alex Hanson replies. "Assign him and ready a task strike team. Immediately."

Fort Bragg, North Carolina
Joint Special Operations Command (JSOC),
Home to the Special OP's Delta Force
Counter Terrorist (CT) Group Training Center

Thirty Special Forces trainees, known as Fresh New Grunts (FNGs), tread water in the training center pool. Blindfolded, they can't see the approaching boots, but they hear the sound of the heavy footfalls. With tied hands and feet, the troops breach the surface, their throats burning from the chlorine. They gasp for air before sinking back down in a continuous, tortuous cycle. Heaving and spluttering, they summon all their strength to stay afloat.

They hear him and they know. He's coming. He's almost here. Maybe it'll be over soon, or maybe it could get a whole lot worse.

"Ten minutes. Thirty seconds. You grunts tired, yet?"

The voice of Colonel Sal Rosetti booms off the walls of the natatorium. His nostrils flare as he funnels in the surrounding smells – ammonia and bromine, lycra and nylon, the rubbery plastic scent of lane lines and buoy markers. His deep set eyes nestle below an overhang of thick, fuzzy eyebrows. Like dark monstrous beetles, the class-A, black military jump boots *click-clack* across the indoor pool tiles, stepping in a steady two-by-two beat.

Compact, in his late 50s, Colonel Sal is fit, with the strength and endurance of a man half his age. His biceps approximate the size of a man's thigh and his neck is reminiscent of a bulldog. Under the mask of seriousness, he hides a smirk of contentment. His temple veins pulsate below a short military crew-cut. Carrying his crisp officer's hat under his arm and a file under the other, he stops at the pool's edge.

Two lifeguards run up to him, their red swim trunks flash like semaphore flags. "Sir! Sir! We got a sinker."

Sal twists his head in the direction they are pointing to and grimaces. "Looks like it."

A muscular twenty-three-year-old, no weaker than the rest of them, has mentally retired. He's nine feet under the surface and seconds away from a shallow water blackout.

"The kid's name is John Foster, as in Foster Freeze," Sal says. "And he might just freeze up if we leave 'im in there any longer. Better go retrieve him."

The lifeguards immediately dive into the pool.

"Six minutes, thirty seconds, keep it up!" Sal yells to the rest of the grunts, as they continue to bob. He keeps time in his head without glancing up at the pool clock. He doesn't consider himself unique in this regard. After so many years of military training, his brain works like an automatic stopwatch. Once upon a time, he was more of a dreamer, a young man distracted by a cloud or the pattern of a woman's beautiful dress. But that era has long since passed.

He watches the lifeguards drag the waterlogged Foster out of the pool. They flop him down onto the tile floor. One of the guards cuts the ties off his hands while the other checks vital signs, ready to perform CPR if necessary.

"He's not coming around!"

"Keep at it!" Sal orders back to the lifeguards.

"Sir, he's still not breathing."

"Ahhhh, shit, do I have to do everything? Get the hell outta' my way," he growls, pushing the lifeguards aside. He hands off his hat and file to one of the lifeguards and kneels next to John. He lifts him, pulls him up over his leg, and pounds on the limp grunt's back.

Whack! He slugs the trainee as the other FNGs continue to struggle, treading water and bobbing up and down.

Sal pounds again. "Now you listen up, amigo. You hear that, Foster? That's your team breathing for you. Now dammit, you need to start breathing for *them*!" He hits him extra hard on the back again. "One for good measure..."

"Hffftwwwaaaahh..." John heaves and coughs out a fountain of water with dregs of bile. His eyes flutter in shock.

Sal hoists him up and flings him over to the lifeguards before he looks back down the pool. He nods in mute approval at the FNGs who continue to splash, heave, and flail like wild marlin.

Stamina is a mind game, Sal thinks. *Without a mind sharp as steel, I wouldn't have lasted a day out in the field and neither will these men. They're not aqua-men, they're not super heroes. But their brains and bodies are being honed and whetted, grinding beyond the point of pain. When the pain climaxes - that's where it all begins. Move past it and you win.*

"All right, fish chum, one more minute left," he calls out. Before he can yell at them more, his cell phone rings. "Blocked call," he complains, but he answers with the same clear, stentorian voice. "Hello, this is Colonel Rosetti."

The Pentagon Situation Room

It's 12:25 p.m., six hours ahead of Hawaii, and the clock is ticking. General McGregor beats his fingers on his legs and stares at the elderly geologist standing before him. Wire-rimmed glasses drift down the nose of Dr. Hemsley, while he strokes his long, gray, Merlin-like beard and briefs the staff on the volcano.

"Gentlemen, of course, you are familiar with the Pacific Ring of Fire, yes?" Dr. Hemsley says. He draws a stylus across the computer monitor screen, highlighting the Ring of Fire in orange.

"In the middle of this ring is the mostly submerged Hawaiian-Emperor volcanic mountain chain. Thousands of years ago, these islands formed across the Pacific Tectonic Plate. They have been moving slowly northwest, across a stationary mantle plume known as the *Hawaiian hotspot*. The movement is very gradual, only about three to four inches a year. But as this happens, the hotspot continues to rise through the mantle, the layer between the Earth's core and its crust."

With the stylus, Dr. Hemsley focuses on the Hawaiian Islands. "Eventually, the main Hawaiian Islands will become atolls, like those of the Midway Islands. Perhaps, in a couple million years, they will disappear and submerge completely, when the edge of the Pacific tectonic plate that supports them slides under the Eurasian plate." He pauses to gesture to the left edge of the map.

"But not to worry, new islands will most likely continue to form above the Hot Spot area here." He points to the hot spot located off the Big Island's southern coast

"We're not worried about something that may happen in millions of years," Alex Hanson states. "We only need the pertinent information about the immediate terrorist threat, doctor."

"Well, yes of course, sir," Dr. Hemsley says with a nervous chuckle. "I get carried away."

A focused image of the Big Island's volcano and southern coast appears on the screen. Flashing red dots cluster in various areas of the map.

"Now, earthquakes are not uncommon in this region. These red dots indicate the larger ones over the past few years. In fact, there are over

100 earthquakes happening almost every day at the Kilauea Volcano. The majority are too small to detect, but our sensors measure them anyway." Alex Hanson rolls his eyes, turning up his palms.

Dr. Hemsley ignores the eye roll and clears his throat. "In this region, earthquakes can result from three distinct causes. One: injection of magma through the crust into a growing mountain. Two: deformation of a subsiding volcanic mass. Three: landslides of unstable mountain and cliff side slopes.

"And that's the scenario we're looking at…the last possibility. If any type of high-explosion, by a terrorist or some other trigger, occurs on this sensitive area, the entire coastal slab could possibly fracture and slump off into the ocean."

Michael Durante guffaws, shaking his head. "A slump, so what? We have Navy scientists that monitor the area. We're very aware of the frequency of earthquakes and volcanic activity there. Isn't that part of Hawaii's coastline uninhabited anyway?"

"Yes, it is. For the most part. However, even if just a few miles of the coastal cliffs were displaced into the deep water canyons offshore, it could potentially create tsunami waves of gigantic proportions. Do you know how many bombs were planted? And what magnitude they are?"

"We're not sure yet," Douglas Berkowitz says.

Dr. Hemsley stares back at him. "Okay. Let's look at the worst-case scenario. If the entire twelve-mile section of this coastline were to give way, and drop into the deep coastal waters that border them, the event could generate a sizable tsunami. And by the time the waves hit landfall, they could enlarge to hundreds of feet tall, traveling several miles inland."

He clicks the monitor remote to show an image of tsunami wave lines extending out from the volcanic coast.

"Within minutes, the waves would wrap around the Big Island, with devastating impact on all sides. In a half-hour, the waves would hit Maui, within an hour Oahu, then Kauai. It could impact the whole Pacific Rim region. The loss of property and life would be…well, catastrophic. This is a real threat."

The Joint Chiefs of Staff break into a batter of alarmed conversations until a high-pitched twang sounds from a cell phone.

"Just a minute, quiet please. I have to take this call," Alex Hanson says. He listens intently and then speaks in hushed tones with an air of reluctance.

"All right, we have our orders," he announces to the room. "Evacuate

Pearl Harbor, Honolulu, and all coastal regions across the State of Hawaii. We'll need our best Hawaii volcano expert on this, a geologist with expertise on the Big Island Volcano, who can advise on-site with the Special Forces.

Make sure he's got on the ground, accurate knowledge of the area. And I'll add, make certain that he's crazy enough to put his life in danger. This is a rush order!"

Chapter Eight

"Beware of the Doonies"

Night settles in. Susan escorts Bernie to the guest room. She flicks the light switch on to illuminate a nautical-themed space. A Calder-style fish mobile hangs from the ceiling, jangling in the gust of the air conditioner. There's an old, rusted porthole refashioned as a wall mirror and wooden blocks that spell out *CAPTAIN AHAB'S CABIN*. Rows of tiny blue anchor stencils punctuate the crisp white wallpaper. Conch shells, narwhal figurines, and wooden model ships line the bookshelves.

"Wow," Bernie says, while he examines one of the ships. "The HMS Victory, Lord Nelson's flagship. Nice. I used to build ship models. Can you believe that the fore topsail of the HMS Victory covered an area of 3,618 square feet? Seems almost impossible. But it hasn't been hoisted since the Battle of Trafalgar."

He's not looking at Susan, but trailing off, staring at the ships and then down to the floor. He looks back to the shelves and eyes the titles on the worn, vintage book spines; Master and Commander, Moby Dick, The Bounty Trilogy.

"You could say my father had sea legs," Susan laughs. "He was a civil engineer, but he came from a long line of naval officers. Loved books and liked American literature too, as you can see. Unfortunately, he was a real Scotsman, in *too* many ways." Her voice strains. "Loved the bottle."

She hesitates before meeting Bernie's eyes with a reluctant smile. "After he passed away a few years ago, we inherited all his treasures and knick-knacks. My Mum certainly didn't want this stuff. She considered it rubbish, but I have a strange affinity for it. So I decided to dedicate this guest room to him."

She picks up a scrimshaw basket. It was the last gift her father gave to her mother before he died of liver cirrhosis at age 54. It was Susan's last year of college. He would not live to see her graduate, to pursue her passions, to marry...

Her lashes flicker for a moment and she wipes away a tear. "I'll let you get settled, Bernie. You can take a shower. The bathroom is down the hall. There's a dresser for your clothes. Please let me know if you need anything else."

"Thanks, Doctor Andrews. Oh sheesh, I mean Susan."

"No formalities needed," she says. "Enjoy our hard Arizona water. I'm going to head to bed myself. Sleep well, and again, just call me if you need anything."

Bernie sets his backpack down and empties out its contents: a laptop computer, khaki shorts, socks, shirts, underwear, a toiletry bag, compasses, plastic baggies for sampling, pencils, notebooks, the American Geological Institute (AGI) glossary, and a stack of Marvel comic books. He folds the clothes and places them in the dresser. He sets the comic books atop the nightstand.

"A place for everything and everything in its place," he says to himself with a grin.

Susan walks down the hall to the master bedroom. Tom is lying in bed clipping his toenails. She wonders why he has to that, ruining romantic moments with nasty habits, but it's too late to make a fuss. "I'm going to take a shower, dear," she calls out to him.

She strips off her clothes, throws them in the hamper, and enters the shower. She turns on the faucet. Hot, mineral-heavy water pelts her body. As she soaps up, she thinks about Tom, the good things, fixating on the picture of his indigo eyes. Her imagination scans down to his wide shoulders and the perfect patch of dark hair on his chest. For a split second, she can almost smell the intoxicating, pheromone scent of his body after a workout.

He is oblivious to his own attractiveness, which makes him that much more handsome and desirable. There's the smoothness on the sides of his body and the genetic blessing of toned obliques or what the women magazines refer to as "sex lines."

A shiver runs down her spine in spite of the hot water. She spins around. The water coalesces on her hard nipples. *This is what you do to me, Thomas. That and blooming ovulation. Mercy.* After several minutes, she steps out and slips into a light, cotton nightgown.

She enters the bedroom and he looks up.

"Tonight?" he asks with hope flickering in his eyes. "A truce?"

"If you're lucky…"

"I'll make you a pillow fort and you can just lay back, lovey. I'll make you feel sooo fine."

It all sounds amazing, but she resists despite her own longings. She can't let him win every battle.

"You're still mad at me, Suze."

"Sort of."

"Oh come on, please let it go."

She slips under the covers next to him. The light blue duvet undulates over and around her like a twisting sea serpent. Turned-on, yet angry. She distracts herself with particulars of the room. The blinds need to be washed, the floor swept. By her calculation, the outside air temperature has dropped at least ten degrees since dinner (such is the desert) and the hall air conditioner still hums, making her teeth clack.

"You want the air conditioner off, babe?" he asks.

"No." She rolls on her side to face him. "You can warm me."

"Now that's more like it…you wanting something… and that something could be me?"

She reaches her hand out and places it on his chest, stroking his soft hair. The scent of a fresh light cologne pulsates in the cool air. He can lay there and tempt her with his physical presence alone. She feels him harden. He's perfect there too, of course.

"I'm sorry for the things I said," she coos. "You know that I pretty much always want you."

He wraps his arm around her and pulls her closer. "It's alright. I guess I had it coming. I apologize, especially about my speech in LA."

"Apology accepted. Yes, I think we can make up," she purrs.

He kisses her neck, moving down to her clavicle. He alternates between kisses and light, feathery strokes. The tingling sensation travels from her forehead down to her toe.

"That might just work," she says, laughing, as she closes her eyes and relaxes into the caress.

"You *are* in the mood," he says, "I'll turn the A.C. down a notch, okay, then I'll be right back."

"You read my mind. Thank you, love."

Tom slides out from the covers. She watches his calves flex as he shuffles out, clad in gray silk boxers. He tiptoes out and into the hall.

Turning the corner, Tom notices that the light in the guestroom is on. Softly, he calls out Bernie's name. No answer. He peeks inside the room. It looks like Bernie is asleep. Tom reaches up and clicks off the bedroom wall switch.

"Ahhaa…Ahhaa…Ahhaa!!!" the high pitched scream echoes down the hallway. Shocked by the outburst, Tom flips the light back on.

Susan rushes to the guest room and sees Bernie sitting up in bed, trembling, his eyes wide as saucers.

"What's going on?" she asks.

"I don't know. I only turned the bedroom light off," Tom answers, dumbfounded.

Susan brushes past her husband and takes a seat beside Bernie.

"Bernie? Can you talk?" she says. She takes a Kleenex and wipes the sweat off his face.

"I'm okay," he says, calming down, hair matted in spiky tangles. "I'm okay. I'm so sorry."

"Has this happened before? Do you get seizures?" she asks.

"Yes," he says, embarrassed. "It's happened before, but it's not a seizure. It's because of the dark. I apologize for the commotion. I get real nervous when the lights go out, so I sleep with a nightlight on."

"We had no idea." She rests her hands, palms up, on the duvet.

"It's okay, it's not your fault. It's the Doonies' fault."

"Rest assured, Bernie, there are no Doonies here. They're not in the room, and they're definitely *not* under the bed." She leans down and glances under the bed. "Just checking."

"I don't believe in monsters under the bed. I'm not that crazy or childish," Bernie says matter-of-factly. "No, the Doonies were these kids in my neighborhood. Three bully brothers that lived next door to us. One of their favorite pranks was to tie me up to the basement radiator and leave me there for hours. In the pitch dark. With the menacing, horrible sound of the radiator.

"The Doonies would duct tape my mouth so my screams were useless. I was in fourth grade. I thought it would get better. But in middle school, they would stuff me into a dark locker and leave me there too, after calling me all kinds of names."

Bernie pauses to catch his breath and control his tears. "I was smaller back then. In fact, I think that's the reason why I started to overeat junk food and gain weight. Anyway, the Doonie brothers used to absolutely terrorize me. To this day I still can't sleep without a nightlight. I know it's silly, but I just freak out. And even though I'm a Tae Kwon Do student and I should be more brave, I have this irrational phobia of the dark."

"You can say that again," Tom says. "Well, damn those stinking Doobie brothers. Aren't they a rock band, too?"

Through drying tears, Bernie avoids looking back at Tom. Tom scratches his head and trudges back to the master bedroom.

"I'm really sorry for the disturbance," Bernie offers.

"It's all right now," Susan says. "Just try to relax. We'll keep the light on every night here for you."

"Thank you. You're so kind."

Like a little kid, she thinks. *But ever so polite.* "You're very welcome."

She watches Bernie slide down under the covers and close his eyes in a meditative manner. She exits the room and leaves the light on.

Chapter Nine

"Kilauea Caldera"

*Jaggar Observatory Conference Room
Hawaii Volcanoes National Park*

Outfitted in gray battle dress fatigues, Colonel Sal Rosetti stands, looking out through the tinted glass windows of the second story observatory loft. There's a panoramic view of the steaming Kilauea Caldera where sulfurous fumes rise from lava rock vents. Vog mutes the sunlight's rays. Off in the distance, the cobalt blue ocean shimmers, coral reefs undisturbed by any rain or soil erosion.

Hawaii is a peaceful place. In terms of war, nothing serious has happened in the islands since the Japanese bombed Pearl Harbor. Now, with the support of a dozen military bases, it's unlikely that anything serious will happen again.

Sal arrived with the troops in Hilo just an hour ago. Accustomed to long international jaunts, the ten-hour flight on the C-5 Galaxy was no problem. The troops were happy and spent the time cracking jokes and playing cards.

I suppose any excuse to go to the islands, Sal muses.

He's survived the hundred and fifteen-degree heat of the Arabian Peninsula and watched the slaughter of innocent Bosnians. They can handle this. No problem.

Sal looks out to the Kilauea Caldera and Hale'uma'u Crater. It's a wide, hazy expanse of bleak grayness. Barrenness. Nothingness. *Why in the hell would anyone choose to spend a lifetime studying this godforsaken volcanic wasteland? Seen it once, you've seen it for the rest of your life, as far as I'm concerned.* He doesn't have much interest in geology or the earth's formation, or anything that happened millions of years ago. At the end of the day, he's a "people person," invested in their success and focused on the near future.

With his feet securely planted hip-width apart, hands clasped behind his back, he glances over at the meeting table, with the twelve members of his Delta Force Team seated around it. Then he peeks down at his watch which reads: 17 hours, 14 minutes. Dr. Elizabeth Redland is fourteen minutes and thirty-eight seconds late and counting. In Sal's book, that's extremely late.

Forty-one seconds, forty-two seconds…

Suddenly, the door flies open and a lean feminine figure barges into the room. There's a flash of a red flannel, Levi jeans, and high top hiking boots. A fine haired, static ponytail whips around as the woman bee-lines to the Colonel.

She extends her hand to shake Sal's hand, while apologizing, "I'm so sorry I'm late. You're Lieutenant Rosetti?" she says while her pale green eyes search for affirmation.

"Colonel," he replies. "Apology accepted." He lets go of her hand and exhales a deep, resonant sigh.

"Oh, okay. Thank you, sir. I'm Dr. Redland." She points to the laminated tag with a photo of herself. In the photo, she's younger and earnest looking with glasses and flushed cheeks. "I've worked at Jaggar for almost twenty years. I was practically a teenager when I started here." She pauses for a beat, mumbles something to herself and then turns away. "This'll just take a moment or two…"

In kinetic motion and quick rabbit dashes, she moves about the room with even greater alacrity, failing to notice the meandering muddy dirt trail she's tracked inside while she makes last minute adjustments to the technical equipment. Her fingers dance over the computer keys with a flurry of strokes, pulling up a digital, aerial image on the overhead monitor.

"Voila! This is it."

"This is what?" Sal counters.

"The Caldera, of course." She grins. Her ponytail swishes forward, lassoing her thin, sun-tanned neck.

Sal scowls with impatience. "Yes. We can also see the famous Caldera right outside the window."

"No, *this* is the spot," she says, drawing her cursor over the photo labeled Kilauea Crater. "Where the terrorists could be hiding. Their command central so to speak."

"I see a pile of rocks," Sal says with a flat tone.

Dr. Redland zooms in on a dark spot located halfway up the wall of the crater. "Around here," she says. "Mind you this is just a hypothesis. We haven't actually located the cave yet. Kilauea measures two by two miles. It's a vast area. We're theorizing that the KUF troops may have repelled over the crater at night and found a hidden lava tube that connects to the much larger lava tube system."

"So this is what we're going with...a hypothesis? And you have no actual visual on the enemy?" Sal clears his throat. "We don't know if they've infiltrated a cave. We still have to find the bus." His lips are pressed so tightly together that his chin wrinkles up like a walnut.

"Well, they can't feasibly operate out in the open."

"I know that, Doctor Redland, and I appreciate your thoughts on the Korean Unification Front, but you need to know that our primary goal is to locate and rescue the hostages, whatever the cost. And secondly..."

"Colonel," Dr. Redland interrupts him. "These terrorists could detonate more explosive devices in highly sensitive fault areas. They've already made threats to do so and have detonated one. If any more happen, well, it could potentially initiate volcanic activity or an eruption of devastating proportions."

"I've already heard the report from Dr. Hemsley and I have my orders. But quite honestly, I don't give a rip about hypotheses or potentials. Furthermore, I don't like to be interrupted. Do I make myself clear to you, Dr. Redland?"

The SO Team members break out in a hushed collective chuckle, oblivious to the intensity in Dr. Redland's expression. Embarrassed and angry, she turns away and fixes her attention on another photo image on the display monitor.

Sal continues. "We are going to rescue those hostages. Period. That's going to take some strategic planning." He leans close to her and lowers his voice. "Please, just show us where you think the bus location is. We'll have to keep your scientific possibilities on hold for now."

"Fine," she says, failing to hide her glare. She steps back to the computer and clicks open another folder. A file label appears on the screen, then a satellite image of the volcano area. She traces across a photo and stops.

"This is the area where the bus is located, camouflaged and hidden from aerial surveillance, in a narrow vegetation line next to the caldera rim. The coordinates are nineteen north, twenty-five minutes, sixteen seconds, by west one five-five, seventeen minutes and thirteen seconds. Colonel, you should be aware that the area of your approach will be across a barren lava field. That doesn't afford much protection or cover."

"Is there any way to see enemy movement on this program?" Sal asks, concerned.

"Negative. These satellite images are only picking up permanent structures and the KUF members most likely covered the bus roof with foliage. Also, the soldiers would have to be out in the open to pick up images."

"So we're not sure how many soldiers we're dealing with? We can assume their weapons and equipment are inferior to ours, but they have the home court advantage."

"I don't give military advice, Sir. But in this setting I would suggest a night attack. It's the only way to get near the bus without detection."

"That would be our plan. Thank you, Doctor, for your advice and words of caution." With a perfunctory salute to her, he turns and signals his team. The swiftly exit the room as Dr. Redland drops into a chair, exhausted.

Chapter Ten

"The Hostage Cavern"

It's almost midnight. James sits blindfolded, trying to remember how they got here. One moment, they were on the bus at the crater's rim, scared for their lives. Now they're sitting in a dank cave lit by dim propane lanterns. As his senses return, so do the memories.

The earthquake happened. Yet everyone was safe. After sunset, a Korean soldier gave the "all clear" signal and ordered the hostages to walk up the field to a small lava tube entrance. In single file, each hostage crawled into the tunnel. James struggled to squeeze himself into the tube's entrance. The guards shoved and mocked him.

"Go fatso!"

"Get in there, chubby man," another soldier taunted.

Perhaps the insults were the most humiliating part of the experience. James couldn't talk back. Not when a loaded Kalashnikov rifle was pointed directly at his skull.

Then the hostages began an arduous trek down long, dark tunnels, shoved and forced through an underground maze with only the guards' flashlights to navigate the way. Some of the hostages lost their balance and fell to their knees, cutting and bruising themselves on the tunnel's rugged terrain. The guards kept prodding them along, herding them like frightened sheep into the maws of a heated furnace.

Another horrific aspect of the trek was the complete darkness of the lava tube, save for an occasional weak flashlight beam from one of the guards. It was all made worse by the fact that the hostages' hands were bound in front with zip-ties.

The soldiers cursed at them and lashed out, beating on them, constantly hurrying them along. At one point, a soldier shouted something to James and though he couldn't decipher the words, James understood the cruel intonation. He already felt the weight of responsibility for his passengers. This helplessness. He couldn't even make a distress call or offer any chance of rescue or comfort for the group. *Didn't they at least deserve that?*

When they finally arrived in the large cavern, the Korean soldiers ordered them to sit against the walls. The soldiers turned their flashlights off and set up an array of lanterns. James could see the ceiling peak at twelve feet above them where whitish mineral deposits dripped and very fine roots spread like spider webs. The lava rock walls protruded in all directions. Below, the ground was a mixture of loose rubble and sizable boulders, with a flattened area for Ho Dam to be center stage. *Calling this place a villain's evil lair would be a gross understatement*, James thought to himself.

Many of these American War veterans had come close to death before, years ago in battle. They were not strangers to suffering and yet they must have felt bewildered. Some prayed and called out to God.

James himself wasn't a religious man, but as the adage goes, "there are no atheists in fox holes." He wondered if Hell existed and if this place was a preview of that type of horrible afterlife existence. Hot, scary, and confusing. Reeking of sulfur, with hard-hearted, demonic captors who would not back down.

He shuddered at the thought, and then, he surprised himself. He bowed his head and prayed. "God, if you're listening, I know I don't deserve it because I've ignored you most my life and I ask you to forgive me for that. But, we're in a desperate situation here. If you don't help us, I don't see how any of us are going to survive.

"So please God, I don't want my daughter to grow up without her Dad. I want to see the new baby and be a good husband. And these veterans, you know they've been through enough already, so please save them."

James ended his prayer while the veterans' wives moaned, coughed, and cried out. The prayer would not be answered right away. No miracle yet.Instead, two guards shoved rough wool blankets at the hostages and yelled at them – "Sit! Stay there! Shut up!" A third soldier tied bandanas over their eyes. They squirmed to try to get comfortable. No one knew what would happen next.

Hours later, the anxiety intensifies. James' stomach growls with hunger. Parched throats rasp in a ceaseless round of coughs and hacks. James finds that his lungs are irritated as though he's smoked a whole carton of cigarettes in a few hours. He splutters and tugs at the ties around his wrists.

"Quiet!" A harsh, loud voice cuts through the moaning din. "Shut up or I'll beat you!"

"You're an animal," Howard returns, spitting out his words.

"With no regard to decency or humanity," James adds. "These are old folks. They have medical conditions."

"At least give us food and water," Howard says.

"We're suffering here," James says under his breath.

"You'll get no mercy from us." The voice draws closer, feet crunching on the gritty rocks. James cringes as Ho Dam lifts back the bandana blindfold, allowing him to see.

"Watch," Ho Dam says. He strolls back to Howard and shines a flashlight on his face. "Remember, old man. I can stuff a rag in your mouth at any time to keep you quiet. Or I'll make you choke to death."

Ho Dam's hand reaches down, slight and sinewy. Fingers pause for a moment and then brush Howard's cheek. James expects to see a blow, but strangely, the slap or punch doesn't follow. Ho Dam retracts his hand from the old man's face. "Do you hear that O'Malley? The quiet? The nothingness?"

"I'll stop my reasonable requests. What do you want?" Howard says.

"That is a good question," Ho Dam says with a widening smile. "Right now, O'Malley, I want to think in the dark and enjoy the silence. I am *not* an animal, but as your own history has shown, you Americans condone violence against the helpless and innocent. I hope to change that story."

"If you got some burr up your butt about what happened during the Korean War years ago, look I'm sorry. Okay? That was a long time ago. I was a young kid then, most of us were. Stupid and green. I didn't care for war any more than the average citizen. I just did my job, served my country. We all have some degree of remorse, but we've had to move on. I suggest you do the same."

Ho Dam's body throbs with rage. He lunges at Howard, kicking him with one swift and forceful blow to the stomach. Howard crumples over and moans.

"It may have been easy for *you* to move on," Ho Dam shouts, "but you cannot speak for all! This is our story, too." He spits at the old man, then turns and rushes out of the hostage cavern.

Walking through a tunnel, Ho Dam's anger cools. He thinks of Kim Sung telling the story, the story he's heard so many times before, that it's almost become his own memory, images branded into his psyche:

Summer in the mountains of South Korea
A beautiful young woman walking the countryside
with her three young children
Herded along with other villagers by the American soldiers
Planes battering the sky
Napalm and bombings
Villagers trying to hide... failing and dying
Death, destruction, and terror everywhere

He pushes the thoughts away. He walks and turns left through a narrow lava tube that connects to a smaller cave which serves as KUF command center/operation base. Equipment crates, ammo boxes, hand-held weapons, rifles, and stockpiled RPGs clutter the cavern. Ho Dam's senior officer, Kim Sung, is hunched over, pecking away at the keys of his laptop, and glancing at a paper map.

Kim Sung is a stout man with a double chin and swollen hands. He's as cool headed as Ho Dam is unpredictable. Raised in a small village outside of Seoul, Kim Sung trained in the South Korean army after secondary school. He studied engineering, but discovered a passion for politics in his dream to one day see a reunited Korea. He swore allegiance to the Korean Unification Front and its leader Chu Lee. They demanded the removal of U.S. hegemonic forces in South Korea. And Kim Sung agreed.

The KUF manifesto reads: "It is time for the sun to set on the United States. We can never be free with the presence of the U.S. military stationed on our soil and at our borders."

Kim Sung agrees whole-heartedly and he will fight for the cause, whatever it may take. So while he sits in a dank cave, four-thousand miles away from the Korean peninsula, he stays focused on the mission.

He can listen to orders via an underground radio transmission, developed for the mining industry. It uses ultra-low frequency (300–3000 Hz) signals, which can travel through several hundred feet of rock strata. An antenna cable is hidden on the surface, providing adequate signal coverage. Using the Earth's magnetic fields to carry its signals, the connection is weak, but enough for him to talk with Commander Lee as needed. Kim Sung's hand slides over to a low, fold-out table, where an instrument panel sits, connecting him to Commander Lee's Hawaiian dispatch. The reception is temporary and spotty, but Kim Sung knows the orders. He adjusts a knob on the panel when Ho Dam enters the command center. He salutes the younger man and senses his impatience.

"Yes, Ho Dam?"

Ho Dam salutes him back and announces, "Sir, the hostages are bound and accounted for in the main cavern."

"Good work. You and your men are to be commended. Now we wait."

"Wait? For what? For the Americans to attack us?"

"No, we wait for Commander Lee's next order. This is not the time to act impulsively. For every action there is a consequence. Any hasty moves without proper orders will not bode well."

Ho Dam shakes his head and looks away. "What's that? Another one of your Buddhist sayings? Or did you read it from a fortune cookie? Look, this is our moment. We are in control. It's our time to strike or they will find us and kill us."

Kim Sung looks back up at him. "I assure you, we will act. And it will be soon. For now, follow my orders and take your position. Do not do anything until you have been told to do so."

Ho Dam's face pinches with irritation. He walks out in a huff.

Kim Sung folds up the map, musing over the younger man's rashness. Patience was a skill Kim Sung had to learn early on. The unification effort has taken years. The talks began in the 1970s. In 1990, prime ministers of each country met for the Inter-Korean summits ("reconciliation, nonaggression, cooperation, and exchange").

More recently there was the North-South Joint Declaration, which called for reunification by the Korean people. *By* the Korean people – not the U.S. That is one of the reasons it is imperative to remove the U.S. military in South Korea.

We don't want to create another war, Kim Sung thinks. There have already been too many wars, too many innocent people dying. At the same time, he cannot forget the past. He saw the suffering. He reflects back to the Korean War. The Southerners called it "The 625 Upheaval." The Northerners called it "The Fatherland Liberation War."

He was only a boy when the War started, but he remembers the tragedy as if it was yesterday. Strange how the thoughts creep back in, inflicting him with a deep sadness and anger. He sees himself:

He is eight years old. He is with his mother, younger sister, and his infant brother. His mother wears a traditional white cloth shirt and long skirt. Her long, dark hair is tied in a loose bun.

She holds his brother, and together they walk with a crowd of villagers. They have left their village of Chu Gok Ri, walking in shoes made of recycled rubber and strips of old canvas. The North Koreans seized the nearby town of Yongdong and now the Chu Gok Ri villagers are essentially refugees. The American soldiers find them. The Americans don't ask questions or if they do, no one can understand.

All the waiting…all the silence…and what came in between…

Kim Sung sighs. There are no answers for tragedy. But he does have a fault zone map from the scientist. He prefers to think of it as "re-purposed" rather than "stolen." He also has information about the rare, radioactive vitrellium, which may be important for a later time. A united Korea would need to create new, destructive weapons. They need that resource. But the memories seer into his brain yet again. Korea, decades ago:

The villagers run into a squad of American forces. The soldiers make the villagers spend the night by a riverbank. Light winds cool them to sleep. It could be any summer night where they fall asleep to the strum of insects and the twilight shrill of evening swallows. Then, in the middle of the night, gunshots awaken them as soldiers cut down a half dozen refugees trying to escape from the group.

In the morning, the young Kim Sung can taste his mother's fear. Even this early, her sweat is metallic, fueled by anxiety. She has already felt defeated by the death of Kim Sung's father just a few months ago. He was a good husband and a loving father, but his immune system wasn't strong enough to fight the smallpox epidemic. Everyone else in the family survived. His mother still mourns, while Kim Sung barely understands death. His father leaves, becomes invisible. Kim Sung feels a certain weightiness. The weight of lost dreams, suspended hopes.

But he is also just a boy. He follows his mother and then runs ahead to tag his sister. Distracted, he picks up a stick and pokes her. Fun and games.

"Stop," his mother scolds him, but she doesn't speak in a disciplinary

tone. No, it is her apprehensive voice. Normally, she would slap Kim Sung's hand since he has a wild side and deserves reprimanding, but she doesn't care to draw attention to herself or the family.

The villagers march forward, wet grass clinging to their shoes. Around noon, near the railroad tracks, the U.S. soldiers stop them. They search his mother and the rest of the villagers, confiscating kitchen knives and anything that could be a potential weapon.

The soldiers point at the villagers. They speak in a strange language that sounds friendly one moment and menacing the next. Kim Sung's mother pulls her baby boy close to her, feeling the soft beat of his heart against her own. Kim Sung is more afraid of his mother's condition than his own, though she stays calm.

The soldiers push them to wait under the No Gun Ri Bridge railroad underpass, where they are held captive by armed guards from both sides. The structure consists of two, double concrete tunnel arches, with a road under the left arch and a stream bed under the right arch. A railroad track runs across the top of the bridge.

Underneath, there is some shade, though not enough to quell the oppressive summer sun. Villagers wilt in the heat. Old men and weary women crouch down. Families with young children watch one another with tense glances. Of course the young Korean men of fighting age are not here. No hope of rescue. Who will protect them? They wait. Some fall asleep. Silence lingers.

Fifty years later, Kim Sung would like to forget the tragedy – the captive waiting, the dread, the fear on the adult faces, that fretful silence. He cannot. The silence has become anchor-heavy, dropping him down to a lower depth of grief, where he can't equalize the pressure. Dropping him down to the murky, cold seafloor, chained to the bottom.

Denied retribution and retaliation for so many years. And now, he must swim to the surface and call for the voices that are unable to speak for themselves. He will give them back their breath.

"Yes," he says to himself, "the time has finally come."

Chapter Eleven

"The Big Mix-Up"

The copper kettle whines, first softly, before it crescendos to a high pitch, as beads of hot water splutter onto the stove. Susan lifts the kettle up and pours the water into a ceramic mug. The Earl Grey sachet bobs on the surface, and sweet herb scents waft through the kitchen, discordant with the bitter aroma of Tom's coffee. But Susan knows it's what he needs. After the restless and disappointing night, they both crave their respective stimulants.

She spreads butter on wheat toast. Tom sits at the kitchen table, shirtless, in khaki pants. He munches cereal flakes while he marks up a graduate student's paper with a bright purple pen.

"You know, your Word program should have a colored correcting pen," Susan says, gently teasing him. "It would make correcting papers easier."

"Hand corrected is more personal," he says, continuing to scribble away. "Agh. This student's data is totally off. He might as well be an undergrad. Speaking of which, where is our pudgy, little house guest?"

"Be nice, please. You promised to give Bernard a chance."

"Bernard. Ha. What a name. And who says I'm not being nice?"

She walks by, with his coffee in hand, her housecoat brushing up against him. She sets the mug down and then embraces him, wrapping her arms around his mid-section.

He's mostly lean muscle, sinewy and strong, and yet she finds comfort in his torso region and the little spot of tender flesh on his belly. She is reminded of that sweet moment last night, his body radiating a lovely liquid heat, a warmth she wants to linger in forever, even on a summer morning.

He could cancel class last minute and I could change into something else, but no, we have a house guest. With reluctance, Susan has accepted the interruption.

Tom looks up and brushes her thigh. "I could definitely use a couple more hours of sleep, but this helps, thanks," he says. The steam rises over his nose while he chugs the coffee down. "Screaming maniacs and midnight adrenaline rushes aren't exactly ideal conditions for a professor's teaching schedule."

"Well, professor, maybe it would help to just imagine young Bernie as a nephew, or the son that you never had."

"He wouldn't be any son of mine. Nerds like him…we used to tease those kinds of guys in school. His type, you know? The acne prone, narrow shoulder, non-athletic geeks. They gave us cool nerds a bad name."

"Wow. I didn't realize there was a pecking order in nerd-dom. And speaking of…"

Bernie shuffles into the kitchen. In a white Tae Kwon Do uniform, he grins and breaks out into a falsetto singing voice.

"Good morning, good morning all! I just lo-o-ove the sciences, I've finally found my call! Geoscience, Geoscience! Tis' the best subject of all!"

He sings the last line with an Irish brogue and his mouth expands to reveal a bottom row of crooked teeth that look like jagged piano keys. His arms unfold, palms up, as though welcoming a crowd. "Oh, what a glorious field it be! Turn some rocks over and see, what you can see-e-e." He finishes on a drawn out note.

"It looks like you're a morning person," Susan says. "Fantastic. You probably don't need any coffee. I didn't know you were a singer, as well. And the, um, martial arts uniform?"

"Yes, I am a singer. As a matter of fact, I'm minoring, no pun intended, in music studies. I'm a proud member of the A Majors. That's the premier acapella group at Caltech. I'm also taking Tae Kwon Do classes. As you can see, I'm only a beginner, hence the white belt, but I take my classes seriously and practice every day."

Bernie lashes out with a sloppy kick. "This is the ahp-chagi, the front kick." He pauses. "And the dui-chagi is the back kick." He throws a leg from behind, almost knocking over a stool.

"Careful with the furniture," Susan says.

"Heaven help us," Tom mutters.

Bernie sits down at the table, oblivious to Tom's crossed arms and raised brows.

"You know what Bernie? I was just telling Susan that we might need to think about…"

She cuts him off. "He was telling me that it's a pleasure to have an understudy like you and how happy we are to host you this summer."

"Really? Thanks. It's so exciting for me to be with you both," Bernie says.

Susan glares back at Tom until he looks away. He stuffs his paper stack into a leather satchel and signals his departure with a nod. He hops up and embraces Susan, kissing her pillow-creased cheek. "Love ya' hon." He throws on a polo shirt.

"Heading to class now?" Bernie asks. "I can be ready in a jiffy."

"No-no-no. Not today, kiddo. But if Susan's up for it, she could familiarize you with some of our studies and samples. See ya' later." Tom turns and dashes out.

"I'd absolutely love to see samples," Bernie says to Susan. He reaches for Tom's bowl of soggy cereal like it was his own. Adding more flakes to the bowl, he grabs the spoon and begins to shovel the food in his mouth while he slurps the milk down. A drenched flake sticks to the side of his lower lip as milk drips off his chin.

Oh, dear, Susan thinks. *He's actually eating Tom's leftover cereal mush.*

"Nothing like a desert climate and a goodnight's rest to get the appetite stimulated," he burbles.

A few minutes later, after Susan washes the twice-used dishes, they enter the study room together. In the morning light, it seems dark and sterile, climate-controlled by the rumbling air conditioner. White wall shelves run along one side, illuminated with LED lights. Inside the shelves are large quartz geodes, fossils, and petrified wood.

Susan rolls out a rickety metal cart. It's defunct, with a wobbly wheel, but each drawer is alphabetized and labeled. She scans down to the U-V section and pulls the drawer open to reveal a crowd of sample trays.

"Old stuff here. Volcanic samples. If these samples were any older we'd need to use mass spectrometry, but there's no need for K-AR dating. We know they're from the 1983 Pu'o'o eruption."

She hands a sample to Bernie. He examines it, taking a moment to register the form – grayish black, like some ancient lithified froth.

"Reticulite," Bernie says. "Most likely formed during a vigorous fire fountain. Porosity is about 98% percent."

"Fantastic job," she confirms, exchanging another sample. "And this?" She hands him a dish that holds a series of irregular shaped objects.

They're polished, smooth, and black. Some fragments are elliptical, some are spherical, while others resemble mini gall bladders inflated with bile.

"Colloquially referred to as Pele's Tears," he says.

"You know how they form?"

"Well, technically they *de*-form, based on eruption, surface tension, viscosity of magma, and wind resistance."

"Yes. Which is the main factor though?" she inquires.

Bernie tilts his head. "There is a direct correlation with velocity. A lower velocity of erupting magma corresponds to the formation of Pele's tears. A higher velocity corresponds to the formation of Pele's hair, which in reality is fragile volcanic fiberglass. The threads can reach as long as six feet. The gold color of the 'hair' can be attributed to weathering effects."

"I'm quite impressed. Guess, you wouldn't need to check the references. Anyway, this is the Volcanic Debris file, should you want to look at it. We don't have any plans to return to Hawaii for a while."

She slides the drawers in and pushes the cart to the corner of the room. "You know there are a lot of superstitions about taking Hawaiian volcanic rocks," she continues. "About how it can anger Madam Pele, the Volcano Goddess, and how it can bring about bad luck if you take rocks off the islands. But that's rubbish, nonsense you know? All respect to the culture, but fear is not healthy. Science can free society from fantasies. But then sometimes it takes…"

Whop-whop-whop.

"What's that noise?" Bernie says.

The popping sound increases, becoming intensely loud. The cart rattles. The shelves and displays vibrate as Bernie's eyes widen. They both turn around and bolt down the hallway.

"Is it an earthquake?" he screeches. "The last major one in Arizona was in 1976 near Prescott."

"Only you would know that! But, no, look out there."

She points at the window. Outside on the driveway, kicking up a huge cloud of dust, they can make out the form of a UH-60 U.S. Blackhawk Army helicopter touching down on the pavement. The rotor blades slice through the air in a steady thunder of noise.

"Holy crud!" Bernie exclaims, shaking with a mix of anxiety and excitement. Dirt clouds billow under a helicopter. Three G.I.s leap out and dash toward the front door.

"Wait here," Susan says as she tightens her housecoat. Bernie hesitates, then scurries after her. She opens the door to the sight of an officer and two enlisted men. The officer has a military cap on and the enlisted men wear matching aviator glasses. They have crew-cuts and obscenely large biceps. They look like twin bodybuilder bookends with the officer in the middle.

She shouts to be heard above the rotor blade noise, while Bernie squeezes in next to her. "What's going on here? Why did you land in our driveway?"

"This is an emergency situation, Ma'am."

"I can see that."

"We have executive orders. We will explain as soon as possible, but we need your cooperation." The officer turns to face Bernie. "Dr. Andrews, I'm Officer Meyers. We're here to escort you to Vanderburg Air Base."

Officer Meyers puts his hand on Bernie's shoulder and turns him over to his men. They snatch him up and start walking him to the helicopter.

"Wait!" Bernie and Susan cry in unison.

The helicopter's noise deafens her protests. "He's not my husband! He's not Dr. Andrews! He's an intern here for the summer."

Bernie struggles, but his soft body is no match for the muscular GI Joes. He asks what is happening, but the men don't respond.

Susan follows the entourage, her heart thumping in her chest. She waves her arms in the last futile attempt to get their attention, but her slick-soled, house slippers betray her, sending her tripping down the pathway.

"Bernie," she whimpers.

It's too late. The crew and Bernie are onboard. A burst of filth and dust blow into her face and temporarily blind her. She cries out again, clutching her housecoat and waving with her left arm. The Black Hawk cargo door slams shut. It lifts off the ground and veers upward, like a deranged gigantic bird of prey hurtling into the sky.

Inside the helicopter Bernie tries to remain calm. He taps his fingers on his lap and peers around the aircraft, recalling some facts about the Black Hawk model. In comparison to the average civilian helicopter, the Black Hawk is a beast. It has a crashworthy external fuel system and can hold up to 10,000 pounds, along with armaments such as rockets, missiles, and gun pods.

Bernie sits in one of the armored troop seats and clears the dust off his glasses with his uniform top. A military official, Lieutenant Kowalski sits next to him.

"I'm afraid you're making a grave error. I'm not Dr. Andrews!" Bernie yells above the engine's roar.

"What-what did you say?" the Lieutenant asks.

"I'm not Dr. Andrews. I don't even look like him and he's twice my age."

The Lieutenant takes off his headset, his eyes searching in confusion. Anyone could wear a martial arts uniform, maybe for morning exercise, but as he looks closer, he sees this is a young man with zits and greasy hair.

"Sir, I'm Bernard Wilkes, Dr. Andrews' assistant."

"You're kidding?"

"No. But I'm happy to help with the situation."

"Dammit! I thought you looked young. We don't have Dr. Andrews' photo on file at the moment, but still, how the hell did we miss that?"

He stares at the other officers. Frustrated, Lieutenant Kowalski rises and makes his way to the cockpit. "What is this? Military intelligence?" he barks to the pilot.

From Bernie's vantage point, he can't hear them, but he sees a flurry of angry gestures and their looks of surprise and embarrassment. He turns his head to look out the window as the Lieutenant makes his way back from the cockpit.

"I see him. He's in a red jeep!" Bernie hollers. "It's Tom. It's Dr. Andrews."

"Okay, thanks for the visual," the Lieutenant booms back. "We've identified the vehicle." The Lieutenant heads back to his seat, with just enough time to clip himself in before the helicopter swerves, banking at 90 degrees. Bernie's stomach drops.

Within seconds, the Blackhawk catches up to Tom's Jeep, which is barreling down the highway, a flash of bright fire-engine red contrasting to the monotone desert. The helicopter zooms above and swoops parallel until it passes 500 feet above the Jeep. It then swiftly turns and lowers, hovering in front of Tom at rooftop level. The Lieutenant leans out the cargo bay doors and barks through a megaphone:

"DR. ANDREWS. DR. THOMAS ANDREWS. BRING YOUR VEHICLE TO A COMPLETE STOP, IMMEDIATELY. THIS IS A COMMAND OF THE U.S. MILITARY. BRING YOUR VEHICLE TO A COMPLETE STOP."

Brakes slam, the Jeep skids to the right, and Tom pulls to the side of the road. He slides down his driver's side window. "What the hell is going on here?"

The helicopter settles down onto the asphalt in the middle of the road, in front of his Jeep. Tom folds his hands on the steering wheel. He waits and watches as Officer Meyers and a GI run to him. The car door swings open.

"Dr. Andrews?"

"Yes?"

"You *are* Dr. Andrews, correct?"

Tom nods in affirmation and raises his hands into the air.

"No need to raise your arms, sir. You're not under arrest. We have a national emergency situation that requires your immediate presence and expertise," Officer Meyers announces, staring intensely at Tom.

"I'm in the middle of my summer session and truthfully, you guys could have killed me and yourselves landing that thing."

"Sir, we just notified the University not to expect you. This is a national emergency. I have orders from the White House. We're going to have to escort you out of here."

"What? Who's giving this order?" Tom turns off the ignition and jumps out, flailing his arms. The GI advances on him, grabbing his shoulder and holding out a hand.

"Your car keys, sir."

Exasperated, Tom drops the keys in the man's hand. The GI hops into the driver's seat and turns over the ignition. He drives further off to the right side of the road for parking.

"You can't do this. It's totally illegal!" Tom says.

"Sir, this is a matter of the utmost importance. The president and our military require your complete cooperation," Officer Meyers says, while leading him inside the helicopter. With some rough assistance, Tom climbs aboard, but immediately he turns to face them.

"I demand to know," he says. "What exactly is going on here?" The military officers don't respond even when Tom glares at them.

"Hey, Dr. Andrews. Isn't this so cool?" a familiar, high-pitched voice asks. Tom spins around, shocked to see Bernie with a military flight helmet strapped to his bobbing head. "Can you believe it? They thought I was you! Oh my gosh, how funny is that?"

"What the hell are you doing here?"

"There's no need to cuss."

"What the fuck is going on?" Tom looks over to Lieutenant Kowalski. "I want to know why I wasn't notified in advance."

"We'll brief you soon," the Lieutenant says. "For now, this is a secret operation."

Tom turns to Bernie, who shrugs his shoulders.

"I have no idea either, but it's pretty incredible, huh?"

"Does Susan know?" Tom asks.

"Yeah, she freaked out. I'm sorry she's not here."

Tom slaps the padded seat. "You're a big help."

The helicopter engines pulsate and the aircraft accelerates. A tumbleweed rolls down the side highway, a tangled mass of thorns and sand. Tom leans back and curls his index and middle finger around his tie, loosening the knot, and noticing that a wide sweat ring has formed around his neck. He stares off into space. His mind spins like the spastic blades above him. *What could this possibly be about?*

Chapter Twelve

"The General"

Hilo International Airport
Lyman's Field
Hilo, Hawaii

"It's a real nightmare," Lieutenant Kowalski says. "Apparently, during your River Mountain Cave expedition, some of these KUF terrorists, or at least someone connected to them, stole your data. So they saw all the maps of Kilauea's active fault zones and the research on cliff side slippage. They've studied your tsunami theory from explosives planted in the volcano's fault zones."

"And no doubt, my maps of the hidden lava tube systems in the area," Tom says.

"Looks like it," the Lieutenant says.

"So you want me to find where the Koreans are hiding out?"

The Lieutenant listens and nods, affirming Tom's role. "Yes," the Lieutenant says. "The military also wants to know where you think they've hidden their bombs."

"Geez, in the volcano area alone, there are literally hundreds of possibilities for underground hideouts and sensitive fault zones. With your time frame, it'll be a shot in the dark finding them."

"I'm afraid so, Dr. Andrews."

Tom and Bernie travel by helicopter to Vanderberg Air Force base in Santa Barbara. From there they transfer into a C-130 military transport plane. Six hours later, the plane glides down to the tarmac at Lyman's Field, Hilo International Airport. Among the passenger jets, private planes, and tour helicopters, the plane looks like an intruder.

Rain falls in large, languid drops. The military officers escort Tom and Bernie off the plane and lead them across the tarmac to a row of older aircraft hangars.

After the desert's dryness, Hilo's climate is an assault of humidity. Tom's work pants stick to his legs while sweat dampens his shirt. Bernie has changed into a strange mixture of civilian clothes – an oversized vintage aloha shirt with baggy, olive green cargo shorts and canvas shoes – courtesy of the officers. He stumbles into a puddle, splashing himself, soaking the shoes and staining his new white socks with dirty water. Despite this, he rejoices in the comfort of solid asphalt under his feet. The rain intensifies. With the officer's release, Bernie and Tom dash into a shaded, empty hangar.

An officer stands in the shadows behind them, a tall, looming figure off to the right side. When he approaches, he looks like the mythic Cyclops, his left eye covered by a black cloth patch. His jaw is as massive as an anglerfish. He wouldn't be out of place in the benthic ocean zone among the cookie-cutter sharks and bristle mouths. The four-star studded epaulettes of his uniform shine in fragmented light. He ends a call on his cell phone and speaks to them, his huge square jaw moving slowly.

"Dr. Andrews. I'm General McGregor. My apologies for landing you out here in the rain, but the main terminal is full of evacuees."

McGregor shakes Tom's hand with an iron grip. "I understand that Lieutenant Kowalski has informed you about our current situation. Is this your assistant?"

"Yes...and no... well," Tom stammers as McGregor watches him. "What I mean is, I have been given some of the details, but this is..."

"Bernard Augustus Jaggar Wilkes," Bernie says as he steps forward to shake McGregor's hand. "Sir, as I duly informed the commanding officer back at the base, my great-grandfather was Thomas Augustus Jaggar, the Kilauea Volcano Observatory founder, who, I might add, penned the phrase, 'Ne plus haustae aut obrutae urbes.' 'Let no more cities be destroyed or buried.' He knew how destructive a volcano could be."

General McGregor tilts his head and softens his grasp. "Excellent Latin. Studied it myself back in high school. And I'm sure you're a fine man like your great-grandfather. We're lucky to have you on board, Dr. Wilkes."

"Just Mr. for now, but thank you."

"Wait a second, you never mentioned your great-grandfather... impressive," Tom says to Bernie as McGregor cuts him off.

"Well, then. Time is of the essence and since you've already been briefed on the situation, there have been some more recent developments."

McGregor's voice competes with the rain that plummets down on the steel hangar's roof. Bernie looks up at it and shudders for a moment. Then he draws his attention back to the General's military jacket. He's fascinated by the gold Washington profiles in a series of purple hearts and he whispers a nearly audible "whoa."

"It's been confirmed that the terrorists have abducted a tour bus of American Korean war veterans and their wives," McGregor says. "They have threatened that if we initiate military intervention, they will detonate other explosives planted along sensitive faults in the volcano and kill the hostages."

"The Lieutenant told me that they've planted bombs in and around the Kilauea Crater and its rift zones," Tom says.

"That's what we believe. Actually, they could be anywhere along the Kilauea plate. We really don't know where for sure, or how many they've planted."

Tom and Bernie exchange alarmed glances.

"This sounds like an extremely dangerous situation, General," Bernie says.

"Affirmative," McGregor says as his cell phone beeps. "Pardon me. I have to take this call." He turns around and walks a few feet back into the hangar.

Bernie leans close to Tom. "Do you think he'd mind if I ask him for his autograph?"

"I don't think that's a good idea and yes, I think he would mind. The man is handling a national emergency with possible global ramifications."

McGregor ends his call and approaches them. "We need your advice on where you think the additional bombs may be planted."

Tom pauses and paces, glancing out across the tarmac into the foggy drizzle to the long queues of planes lined up on the runway. Hurrying about with much confusion, task forces evacuate hundreds of civilians onto the planes. Without turning back around, Tom asks, "But, that first explosion…it wasn't near a fault zone?"

"Right. The explosion was closer to the southwest end of the national park. Perhaps it was a show of force," McGregor says. "A threat. No casualties that we know of, thankfully." His phone buzzes again. "Hold on. This'll just take a second."

Bernie and Tom gaze out from the hangar. The rain lightens up. The pavement has absorbed the excess moisture, obscuring it to a shade of dark gray. Sunbeams break through the cloud cover while vapor rises off the tarmac. A 737 wheels down the runway, roaring and gaining momentum before lifting off into the sky.

Tom scowls at Bernie. "You're not supposed to be here. You know that. I don't even think *I* should be here."

The General returns, interrupting them. "So, Dr. Andrews, after reviewing your findings and given the current situation, we started constructing the southeast volcano coastal fence you recommended. But even as an expedited mission, it'll take us a week or more to complete it. And that's time we just don't have. So we've got a Black Ops Team on the ground, ready to launch a rescue for the hostages."

"I only have consulting experience. I'm no military expert, but it seems to me that they could explode more bombs if you attack them. I'll need some time to investigate the location of these explosives."

"Right, we've got a Jeep ready for you. You'll be joined by a bomb squad team and a military escort."

"Wow," Bernie says.

The General continues. "You'll be leaving for the volcano area in ten minutes. I have a meeting now. Good luck." He nods and strides across the tarmac to a military sedan.

Bernie and Tom look out west, in the direction of the mountains and the volcano. Shafts of golden, dusk colored sunlight pierce through the parting clouds as the rain abates.

"Sure hope they know what they're doing," Tom says, eyebrows furrowing. "They can't afford to make any mistakes."

Chapter Thirteen

"The Assault"
Barren Lava Fields, Kilauea Crater

Nightfall. The waxing moon rises, casting long shadows on a flat, otherworldly landscape. Clouds pass overhead while the twelve-man Delta Force Strike Team shifts from its prone position. Most soldiers carry M-4 rifles. One man carries an M-107 Barrett sniper rifle. Another lugs a MK-48 machine gun.

They advance with weapons drawn and scan the area through the night-vision goggles attached to their helmets. Outfitted in dark camouflage BDUs, helmets, knee and elbow pads, they blend into the monotone landscape. Only the dim, iridescent glow of the goggles marks each soldier. One by one, the Team rises, cautiously advancing, staggering across the rugged, rocky lava field terrain.

Brittle clumps of *a'a* lava rock crunch and crumble beneath the weight of their boots. In this sparsely vegetated field, they proceed, on high alert for the enemy. They crouch forward and move past patches of low grasses, shrubs, and lava rock piles, while they try to avoid the cracks and crevices. As they approach the end of the field, one of the soldiers halts. His pant leg catches on something. He leans down.

"Oh, shit!" he cries out. A powerful, bright, explosion drowns out his voice. His legs shatter. The bomb rips his face to the bone. He flies into the air and hits the ground, collapsing in a shredded, bloody heap.

The eleven remaining team members lie down in the open, weapons pointed forward. The field lights up as flares pop and explode by the tree line. A staccato gunfire bursts at them. With no visibility of the enemy, the troops can only return fire at the tracer rounds.

Between shots from his thirty round M-4 Rifle, the team leader screams into his headset microphone, "Fall back!" he yells to the Team. "Fall back!" Then he slinks backwards, like a lizard on its belly. He fires as he goes, while his team members follow suit. The bullets keep coming at them. They have no choice but to retreat, while taking deadly small arms fire.

"Damn it, damn it, damn it!" Sal drops into a chair and scratches the back of his head. "I can't bomb 'em and I can't call in artillery."

Headphone-wearing military technicians sit before consoles, listening to the strike team's frantic battle cries. The Jaggar Volcano Observatory, once a peaceful, calm setting, now buzzes with the activity of thirty personnel. Aides scurry between tables, while all other eyes are glued to the main computer screen. The heat generated images of the troops appear on the screen only to disappear one by one. Six soldiers are left.

"Get them outta' of there, now! Order the birds to strife enemies cover."

The technician orders the pickup. Sal barks at an aide. His gut wrenches while he watches three men drop back. From both the frontal and aerial views, the enemy is out of sight. The sounds of the conflict are far away. Above the hum of urgent conversations in the observatory, the technicians hear Sal's audible growl.

"How the hell did this happen?"

Chapter Fourteen

"The Memory of No Gun Ri"

An hour later, Kim Sung's soldiers return from the battle. A few have minor injuries, but none were killed. Some soldiers raise their weapons in jubilation while others cheer on, shouting victoriously.

Kim Sung observes the celebration. His smile broadens when Ho Dam approaches him. Ho Dam salutes and reaches out his hand. "Uncle, you were right. You know your enemies well," he blurts out.

"Yes," Kim Sung says. "They have predictable tactics. And they still don't know our exact location in the cave. Not yet at least." He releases Ho Dam's hand. "Good work."

Ho Dam turns to congratulate the soldiers. Kim Sung walks away, toward a corner of the command center. He has waited decades for this day, this moment. In his mind, the anchor-weight of that silence begins to lift, but he still remembers…

The lull of mid-day, interrupted. The villagers watch. Like gray bellied sharks, U.S. planes circle the sky. They look almost elegant with silver fuselages and wings displaying the United States Air Force insignia. Villagers point up, eyebrows raised and mouths agape. The sound of gunfire pierces the air.

Anyone is a potential victim as ammunition strafes the ground, striking villagers at every angle. People scream. A boy crouches as if to hide from the onslaught. Then bullets pockmark his cheek, ripping his face apart. A woman turns, only to find her back becomes a dart board for strafing and her pelvis splinters upon the gunfire's impact. An old man's arms sever from his torso like pulling bones from a mutilated chicken carcass.

As a boy, Kim Sung watches all of this. Its randomness. Its terror. Will it ever end? There is a pause when the planes stop. The day passes. Hope returns briefly.

But then the U.S. soldiers return and they have their plans. They direct the rest of the villagers under the bridge into a tall tunnel. Shouting. Yelling. There are protests and cries for mercy. The soldiers withdraw their weapons.

Some of the villagers cower and others panic. A few bolt from the crowd only to be shot in the back. Then, with all weapons trained back on them again, there is a dreaded silence and more waiting as the troops face the villagers down.

An old man starts screaming at the soldiers and others follow suit, moving toward them. Then suddenly the soldiers open fire on the old men, dropping them in their tracks. Chaos ensues as other villagers begin to rush forward or bolt away. The soldiers open fire on the rest of the unarmed villagers.

The sounds and echoes are terrifying, but the villagers have no time to protest. Hails of bullets rip through the bodies of the young and old alike, cutting them to shreds before ricocheting off the bridge walls. It seems to go on for an eternity. For the U.S. soldiers, these people are nothing. They're worthless. It's as though the soldiers are in it for sport. People run and hide. People scream. People die.

Amidst the melee, Kim Sung watches his sister run toward the back of the bridge tunnel, only to be blasted with a shot to the head. Pieces of skull splatter through funneled air. Their mother cries out. She grunts and wails like a wild animal. For a second, the rifle shots disrupt her cries, then a bullet strikes her shoulder and shatters her clavicle. She falls with her baby in her arms and cries to the heavens, to her ancestors, to Buddha, to the Catholic God the missionaries talked of, to anyone…but it's all for naught.

"Mommy, Mommy," Kim Sung whimpers.

He can see her. But, she can't tell where his voice is coming from and when she whips around to look, she faces another round of gunfire. A bullet strikes her chest. Her beautiful mother heart. Blood stains her white cloth dress, radiating like sun rays, like the red swirl of Korea's flag. She collapses in a heap.

From her arms the infant starts to roll away. Kim Sung wants to race to catch his brother in his arms, yet some strange gravitational force pulls him down and away to the ground. He is in shock. He has lost everyone. And yet he has to live.

An unearthly sound echoes. How can a mere infant roar like a savage beast?

Lost, lost, lost.

Kim Sung has to stifle his own cry of despair. He falls back to hide among the dead and dying villagers. The firing continues, but the survivors must stay quiet, playing corpse, as Kim Sung does. He feels his whole body tense up.

Later, he observes an American soldier pile the dead bodies on top of each other like stacks of firewood. As horrific as it is, the bodies keep Kim Sung hidden and warm. For one brief moment, he opens his eyes and peeks out, seeing the pale face of an American soldier – unshaven and sweaty. Oblivious and stupid. From then on, he hated that man and all American soldiers. He could never forgive or forget them.

Chapter Fifteen

"The Making of Salvatore Rosetti"

At six-thirty a.m. the Volcano Hotel restaurant clamors with the din of rattling cups and silverware. Military officers consume their bacon and egg breakfasts, while Army technicians set up communication equipment.

Colonel Sal Rosetti has just finished his meal. He sits alone in a corner booth. He didn't sleep well last night, waking in fits and starts while his mind replayed last night's disaster. A tragedy actually. He re-envisions the lights dying out on the computer screen. Those were his soldiers.

He sips coffee and numbly looks through the summer issue of Field and Stream magazine. It helps clear his mind as he views a full-page advertisement:

A RIVER RUNS THROUGH IT....
Experience Fly-Fishing at Its Best!
Summer River Expeditions in Montana
Book Now and Save!

In the accompanying photo, a handsome young fisherman in a khaki vest and a bucket hat, smiles ear to ear, holding up a freshly caught, large rainbow trout. Another smaller insert photo shows a lean middle-aged fly fisherman casting his line, with measured control, like a symphony conductor.

Ahh, trout.

This is the distraction Sal needs. He can picture the fish, leaping up waterfalls, colors of seaweed green, bright pink, and blue, peppery-spotted fusiform shapes that glisten in the afternoon light before they descend back into the torrent. He sees trout swimming through a river and trout lingering in a glassy lake. In his reverie, he can imagine a single prize beauty hooked on the line, mouth agape. His own hands grip the animal's wide, slippery, shimmering body.

Once upon a time Sal remembers looking up information on the Rainbow Trout. It's scientific name was *Oncorhynchus Mykiss*. A perfect name for a perfect fish.

Sal's fishing obsession began nearly fifty years ago, far away from Montana. Back then he was Salvatore Luca Rosetti, Jr. He lived with his family in South Philadelphia's Little Italy.

Sal's father, "Papa Sal," a second generation immigrant, would say, "It's like we're back in the old country. Everyone knows each other and each other's business." Papa Sal owned and operated the local store *Rosetti's Grocery & Deli*. "What else would I call it?" he joked.

Papa Sal would rise at four a.m., six days a week. His wife, Abagella, worked alongside him with Little Sal's older sisters – Teresa, Maria, and Sophia. The four children worked after school and often on Saturdays.

The small store was a cramped space, filled with every conceivable Italian grocery product. The customers complained about the temperature. In the summer it was too hot. The rusty fans only blew more heated air into the store and the sweaty clientele would open the deli's freezer for a cool rush. And with no heating radiator, it was bitterly cold in the winter. Families would snuggle up against each other and clutch minestrone soup bowls close to their chests.

"The cold keeps our supplies fresh," Papa Sal would say. "It also keeps the costs down. You not like the heat? You don't know what hot is until you've visited Sicily in the middle of summer."

"Ah, he so cheap he squeaks," Mama Abagella would say.

But the customers stayed loyal to the Rosetti family. They wanted their Grissini breadsticks and imported olive oil. They craved the family recipe homemade pizza, the baked bread, pastries, and sandwiches. Every day the scent of fresh cheese and salami permeated the store's dank air. Sal's oldest sister Teresa, the bossy one, ran the cash register and helped the customers. She knew what everyone wanted even before they ordered.

"Signore Crespi gets an espresso and chocolate cannolo," she explained to her younger siblings. "Signora Bartolo will have pesto sauce, capers, anchovies, and rigatoni pasta. Signorina Scarlatti always has two and a half scoops of pistachio gelato served in a medium cup."

Meanwhile, Young Sal worked in the background, keeping track of the non-perishable inventory of sauces, pastas, spices, wines, and a gazillion sardine cans. When he finally got his chance to work in the deli, he did it with all the bravado and skill he could muster. Impatient customers watched him make sandwiches and quietly applauded or critiqued him.

"Anchora, si oliva, anchora."

"No, troppo sale. No, no!"

He figured that if he kept up a good attitude, his father would let him run the cash register in a year or two. But his father disapproved of Sal's school performance. He was a poor student and a misfit. It didn't help that the local Catholic K-8 School was terrible. Sal detested the hierarchy of a thousand unspoken, arbitrary rules and regulations. Tucked shirts, tedious homework, yardstick slaps from hideous, cruel women dressed like The Penguin.

One day after school, his father, approached him. "I hear you are setting tacks on Sister Marinetti's chair." His father already knew about the day's incident. "Then you get caught," he continued, as if the discovery was worse than the crime. "How could you get caught? Schemo! Disgraziato!"

He grabbed Sal by the ear and pulled him outback by the store's dumpster. Before Sal could protest, the leather belt came down on his buttocks, with a fierce, burning sensation. He gazed up to the sky in furtive prayer. He choked up and started to cry, but he had to stifle it, knowing that tears would only infuriate his father more. This happened too many times. After each belting episode, it was back to work at the deli and carry on with the routine.

The Rosettis worked at the business from sunup to sundown, their only respite being Mass on Sundays at St. Mary Magdalen de Pazzi church. For Sal, church was just school continued. The homilies reminded him of the nuns' lectures, while the mindless sea of genuflections were reminiscent of his classmates' sheepish obedience to authority. He was ready to curse it all, but then there was Uncle ("Zio") Giancarlo.

Alongside his chubby wife, Leona, and his skinny daughters, Isabella and Daniela, Zio sat one pew behind Papa Sal's clan. Zio was a tall man, with long arms and sinewy fingers. Considering his height, he moved with grace. Dark, luxurious curls outlined his gentle face.

Perhaps he empathized with Sal's restlessness. Perhaps he wanted a son. In any case, when he softly whistled the *Agnus Dei* in young Salvatore's ear, it was a sign that Sunday would be a good day and even Papa Sal allowed this particular dispensation.

The church bells chimed at the end of the service and Zio whisked young Sal away in his old Cadillac, zooming down Philadelphia's Christian Street, across South Broad, to the banks of the Schuylkill.

With a view of the city skyline, they sat along the river, fishing lines cast. The excited Sal would ask Zio about his life. He was a second generation immigrant and considered himself more Sicilian-American than Italian. He had served in the U.S. Army during World War II. He told Sal of his military adventures and the young boy replayed each scene – soldiers landing on the beach, Zio taking cover under the dunes with a M-1 carbine in his arms, advancing to face the enemy, Zio's back injured from a friendly fire bullet. Sal was so wrapped up in Zio's story, he almost didn't notice when the fish bit on his line.

"Bravo, Salvatore, easy now, you no wanna' lose 'em," Zio would say as he leaned over Sal, offering tips on how to land the fighting fish. Zio would grab a net and scoop the thrashing animal like he was sifting sand. It was a Rock Sea Bass. Sal would marvel at its wild beauty and watch its silvery fins shimmer in the afternoon light.

"Catch a couple more of these guys and you feed your family."

"I wish," Sal would reply, knowing that his father would not be impressed with one bass. But he cherished those Sundays with Zio. It was the only truly happy time in his childhood.

Soon enough, the fishing adventures were less frequent. Papa Sal added more responsibilities to young Sal's schedule. He was intent on keeping Sal out of trouble and yet the more Papa Sal controlled, the more his son resisted. After a few arguments with Abagella ("But he so young," she would say. "Our baby, our only son." "He is also a big problema!" Papa Sal retorted), the Rosettis decided to ship Junior Sal off to military school in Washington, D.C.

Then, a year later, Zio died of a stroke.

When Sal heard the news, he felt as if his lungs would crush his heart. There was not enough breath to contain that deep cry. He did not even have a chance to say good-bye to his favorite person in the world.

Sal cried, silently, under the covers of the starched dormitory sheets and in the bathroom stall. He wept and punched walls and scowled at his peers. He watched his grades slip and the staff ignored his behaviors. So he realized, he had to stop with the nonsense. No one would come to his rescue. Nor could anyone offer real comfort. Instead of giving up, Sal would honor his uncle instead. He would carry on Zio's legacy and follow in his footsteps as a military officer, and then later, as a part-time fisherman. And Sal would do his damn best.

The first path was born of necessity – to be successful in the world and provide for a family. The latter identity was leisure, a stress release from D.C. life. Over three decades, Sal fished Chesapeake Bay, the lakes of the Northeast, the Atlantic and Gulf sides of Florida. Freshwater bass, snakeheads, sea bass, snapper…if it had two gills and fins, he caught it. He looked forward to his retirement days and expeditions galore.

Eyeing the Field and Stream ad, he dreams of an adventure in Montana. Fly-fishing would be a fun challenge. He reaches for his notepad, ready to jot down the contact information, when he senses something. *A new arrival at the restaurant?*

Accompanied by a soldier, two civilians mosey into the dining area. One of them is a young, chunky teenager in a yellow and purple aloha shirt. He keeps tugging at his shorts. The other one…*well*, Sal thinks, *he looks like a jerk*. Sal can't explain the "jerkiness" of the man, but the grin, the cocky head tilt, and the over-confident stance – these are tell-tale signs of a bonafide jerk. The soldier escorts the strangers over to his table.

Great. Just what I don't need.

"Excuse me, sir?" the man asks politely.

Okay, so he's an obsequious jerk. That doesn't make it better. Sal ignores him and continues to read, until the man slaps down a manila envelope on the table. Sal looks up and breathes through his nostrils, maintaining a blank expression. "You ever caught a steelhead trout?"

"No, sir," Tom says. "Can't say that I have."

"Do you fish?"

"No. I mean I went with my Dad a couple times. It wasn't really my thing." Tom glances to the soldier, unsure of where the conversation is going.

"Well, I can't say I trust a man who's never been in combat nor one who doesn't like fishing."

"The government sent me here to…"

"Yeah, yeah, I know. They think they're doing me a favor, as though I really need your expertise and you're Joe the volcano expert and everything. I suppose this is your sidekick protégé, too." Sal sneers before snatching up the manila envelope.

"Colonel, I have years of field experience. Specifically on Kilauea. I didn't expect to be here, so I'm a bit ill-prepared with all the protocol, but you guys called me. You need some expertise."

"Save your resume for the academics, please. I've heard all about you and right now, I don't need your help. If I do, I'll let you know." He pauses to pinch a toast crumb off his uniform, adding gruffly. "So in the meantime, kindly stay the hell outta' my way. Got that Professor?"

"I've been ordered to review every geological angle here, not to mention advise you."

"Advise?!" the Colonel slaps his hand on the table. He slides out from the booth and stands up. He's a head shorter than Tom, but he's an intimidating presence, stocky and built of pure muscle, with the disposition of an angry pit-bull. Tom back steps as Sal leans toward him.

"Okay. So please advise me on overcoming an enemy that's just KIAd some of my best soldiers and may shortly be killing the hostages, too? Well, come on, I'm waiting. I haven't got all day. What would *you* have me do, Dr. Andrews?" His voice rises to a higher key, booming throughout the restaurant. The servers and military personnel look on.

Tom flinches. Feeling every eye on him, he can only mumble, "I really don't know."

"That's what I thought. Now, stay the hell away from me. I don't need any of your theories right now. I can't stand this elitist bullshit." Sal turns to the soldier. "I'm heading back to command central. These two jokers are your problem now, so show them around."

Shouldering past Tom and Bernie, Sal heads to the door. He's about to exit the restaurant, when a communication tech hails him.

"Commander Rosetti?"

"Yeah, what is it?"

"Sir, it's *them*."

"What?" His brows crease and he races over to the tech's table. He grabs the offered cell phone from the man's trembling hand. "Put a trace on this call now," he says. "Who is this?" Sal whispers into the phone.

First he hears static and a rolling wave of white noise. Then a voice echoes, low and faint. The military personnel and technicians gather around, hovering over him while Tom and Bernie join the circle.

"Shhhh." Sal presses his index finger up to his lip and listens for a few seconds. The voice hisses at him in broken English for twenty seconds before the phone goes dead. Sal sweats and tries to control his breath. He glances at the radio tech. "Get a trace?"

"No," the tech says. "Just shy of that."

"Damm!" Sal slams the phone down on the table, nearly cracking its plastic casing. He turns, making his way to the door.

He marches across the lawn. Tom paces after him, followed by Bernie.

"Colonel Rosetti, please, stop!" Tom says. "I need to know what's going on. What did they say?"

"I don't want to talk to you right now." He forges ahead, undeterred from his trek.

"God, you walk fast," Tom says. He places a hand on Sal's shoulder. The Colonel stops abruptly and stiffens. Sensing the discomfort, Tom removes his hand. Volcanic ash floats on the air current between them, soft like dandelion fluff, dotting the back of the Colonel's jacket, gray-white specks of dust and flakes on a field of olive green.

"Sir, I need to know. What did the terrorists say?"

Sal glares back at Tom. "You don't need to know, but since you'll find out anyway…the KUF want media coverage here and a live broadcast, or else they'll start killing hostages. They're making this a TV event for their pumped-up United Korea fan base. I'll be damned if that's gonna' happen. I'd rather have a prostate exam from Mike Tyson. This place is going to be an absolute fucking zoo. So if you'll excuse me, I have to contact HQ and get them to bring in some force to keep the media in check."

Sal turns and continues across the dust covered lawn.

Bernie looks up. "So, I guess that means tonight's luau plans are off?" He holds up a colorful brochure and chuckles. "Trying to lighten the mood a little, sorry."

"Not a good time, Bern. Not a good time at all."

Chapter Sixteen

"The Detonation Site"

After breakfast, Tom and Bernie both head back to their room. The cabin is the converted Volcano Art Center and Gift Shop, a small, historic building, a hundred feet west of the Visitors' Center. Inside, Bernie notices the old photo display of the Art Center's timeline: its humble beginning as a thatched inn circa 1866, its fin-de-siècle glory when it was the former Volcano House Hotel (where Mark Twain stayed), its near destruction by fire in 1940, and an emergency stabilization in 1976.

"Due to highly active steam vents," Bernie says.

"You think this building is ready for the new century?"

"I don't know. Depends on how many more earthquakes it can sustain. But at least we're not that far away from Command Central. We're actually closer to Colonel Rosetti than most of his military forces are."

"Great," Tom says. "It's going to be a challenge to work with that guy. He's so old guard. Reminds me of my Dad. He might take a gander at the maps I gave him, but basically he thinks we're useless to this mission. Typical government crap."

Tom and Bernie stroll past the Hawaii-themed artwork and crafts. Like young children, they're careful not to touch anything that might look valuable. Oil and acrylic lava paintings hang on the paneled walls. Fine jewelry gift items are housed in locked glass cabinets. Inside one of the rooms, the military has provided two mattresses/beds for the visiting scientists and cleared a table for equipment, but otherwise the space has remained unchanged.

Bernie flops down on his mattress. He takes his shoes off and hoists one leg up. With his left ankle resting on his right knee, he picks at a toenail and flicks the dirt onto the floor.

"Do you have to do that?" Tom says. "It's disgusting."

"Huh?"

"Never mind. I'm just glad to be out of that scary Commander's hair."

"Yeah, he seems a bit stern," Bernie says.

Tom sighs and lies down on his bed, head sinking into the soft pillow. His feet dangle over the mattress edge. He looks up to a professional photograph of nighttime lava activity with flying tephra, volcanic scree, and streams of bright red against the night. It's better than any Fourth of July fireworks show. If he ever retired, he might consider photography as a hobby.

Growing up, Tom's father never encouraged hobbies that were non-sports related or deemed uncompetitive. Bob Andrews was a Navy Captain, a science teacher, and a high school sports coach. Football coaching was his real passion. He was more proud of the Palo Alto Vikings than his own flesh and blood family.

Nevertheless, he pushed Nick (the eldest), Liz (the middle child), and Tom (the youngest) to their individual breaking points. There were the long swims at Gray Whale Cove and timed mountaineering races on cliff paths. There were tests of endurance (7-mile runs), strength (weight-lifting) and psyche ("How long can you hold your breath under water?"), but only Nick, the football player, followed the exclusive military path.

Their mother was a quiet intellectual. When Liz and Tom went to graduate school, her effusiveness made up for their father's "mehs" of indifference. Of course, Genevieve Andrews was pushy in her own way. She became the driving force for achievement after Bob's heart attack and sudden death.

My dad was an asshole, Tom admits to himself. *But he shaped me into a rare breed of varsity jock-nerd, which is all but lost on these one-dimensional gamer Bernard types. A college freshman who reads comic books? Comic books! Ridiculous.*

Tom stares up to the termite-munched wood beams. His eyes are tired and he's ready for sleep, the rejuvenating jet-lag recovery kind. Then he hears the cell phone's annoying buzz.

"What now?" He sits up and grabs the phone, looking at the number. He grins with relief. "Hey, Suze."

"Hello, hello? Can you hear me?"

"I hear you. I'm at the Kilauea Park cabin."

"That explains the reception. I tried calling before and couldn't get through," Susan says.

"Where are you now?" asks Tom.

"At home. The military contacted me, but they were very brief and described it as an emergency situation. That's all. What's going on?"

"A lot is happening and I feel like it's all my fault." Tom slumps down again, the pillow forming a flying nun habit around his head. *An appropriate headpiece for this moment of sincere penitence*, he thinks.

"If you're referring to the River Mountain Cave, it's not your fault. You warned the government and they didn't listen. So the onus is on them, really. Now they need help. And you are very needed. But I should be there with you. You know that. You gave me your word."

He's unsure what "word" she's referring to, but he doesn't dare ask for a reminder. Mention of the River Mountain Cave unhinges him. To discover the rare, radioactive vitrellium element and then blindly turn that information over to an enemy – it's the worst case scenario.

"I was an idiot to have my passwords in the laptop case. Maybe I'm getting more forgetful these days. I guess I never thought a band of hired thugs would be hiding out in the jungle, primed to steal our private information."

"Yes, that's right, *our* private information. You need a helper this time, too. If only for emotional support."

"It's far too dangerous here, hon. The entire subsurface is riddled with fractures. Terrorists planted explosive devices in some of the fissures and abducted a busload of tourists. They've already detonated one bomb. If they ignite anymore, this entire area will crack like an egg. So just stay put."

"I'm serious, Tom! If I don't come, it'll be our marriage that will crack. I'm not asking for your permission."

"Stop and think about this for a second. Terrorists with guns, high-explosives hidden in lava fields or fractures, a potential natural disaster. Please, stay home."

"To do what? Tend the cactus? Call me egotistical, but this is also one of the biggest assignments of our careers. I'm not about to just sit here, while you're off playing Thor Heyerdahl!" Susan pauses to calm herself. "Look, you promised me that we'd work together, that we're a team. I need to be with you."

Tom looks around and sees Bernie staring at him. He frowns and waves him off. "This is not your concern."

"What? What did you say to me?" Susan says, now indignant.

"Sorry, Suze, not you. A fly on the wall. Bernie's eavesdropping."

"Bernie is with you at the Park? Then I should definitely be there. He needs someone to look after him."

"And I guess they think I need an assistant. The Commanding Officer is a bulldog, real pain in the ass. He has experience, but the dude just lost part of a commando team in battle. After the reception I got from him this morning, there's no way he's going to allow any other civilians on board."

"Rubbish! I'm your wife. I'm a geologist. What's it going to take? Are you going to make me wait until you're dead and I have to ID your body?"

"C'mon, don't be morbid."

"Well, it sounds like that's what we're dealing with here. A life and death situation. Besides, I already bought my ticket. So tell the officer in charge I'm coming."

"Susan, please don't…"

"It's final. It's decided." There's no anger in her voice now, only cool resolve.

Tom sinks his shoulders in defeat. "I've never won an argument with you in the past. Why would this be any different? How did you get a ticket?"

"I know people."

"All right. I'll try to get you clearance, but I have a bad feeling about this whole situation and having you here could make things worse."

"Three heads are better than two."

"Three heads? Oh, yeah Bernie. Well, if you're going to fly over here, do you think you can bring some extra clothes for us?"

Susan stifles her laugh. "Mama Susan's got it."

After quick goodbyes, Tom sets the phone down.

"Real smoooooth," Bernie says.

"Not another word."

"Okay."

Tom stares up and out the window for a moment, watching the sunlight escape out from a mass of downy clouds. He misses his wife – her smile, the lavender honey scent of her hair, the warm, inviting breasts that he wants to nuzzle in, her belly, her luscious hips and buttocks.

"Don't get too comfortable," Bernie reminds him. "We're supposed to do field inspections this afternoon."

"Yeah, I know. I'm just gonna' nap for a bit."

"Okay, Dr. Andrews."

"That's right, 'Dr. Andrews.' I like the sound of that."

Tom's eyelids grow heavy. He closes his eyes and imagines the flash of Susan's long legs and her eyes sparkling green and he's walking toward her…he feels her radiance completely, until his breathing slows down and he conks out into a deep sleep.

A half hour later, Tom wakes up. Bernie is arranging equipment on the table.

"A Comm Tech called," Bernie says. "We're all clear to examine the detonation site. They're going to send an officer to escort us. We have to go through a checkpoint to get there."

Tom pats down his fluffy, bedhead hair. "Thanks for organizing the stuff."

"I got your GPS receivers, check. Inflation tilt meters, check. Time to pack up the bags, boss."

"Hmm. Not too sure who's playing the boss now." Tom takes off his sandals and puts the government-issued hiking boots on. He glances at his canteen, full with water.

"Yep, I took care of that. A good boss is always a good helper, too," Bernie informs him.

"Thank you. You're starting to grow on me…maybe…"

They exit the cabin and walk down the front door steps. Waiting for them in a parking spot is a Jeep and military officer escort/driver. Tom sits up front and Bernie hops in the back seat.

"It would be cool to have Dr. Susan here," Bernie says with an innocent gaze.

"Please don't remind me. She's acting all crazy and stubborn about this. I rather her not be in harm's way."

"Well, if I had a wife, I'd let her make her own choices. Only seems fair."

"When you get married, you'll understand," Tom says.

"I hope to someday."

The Jeep winds around Crater Rim Drive, heading south past the Volcano Observatory, stopping at a military checkpoint. They turn off-road. The military escort drives over the lava field terrain to the site of the first detonation. Followed by the escort, Tom and Bernie carry their inflation tilt meters and GPS receivers.

"This is a MEMS driven tilt meter," Tom says to Bernie. "Calibrated for temperature variation, accuracy, and performance. It will show the swelling of a main magma chamber, as well as the draining of a chamber and the eruption at an adjoining vent."

"Changes recorded with the electrolytic sensors," Bernie says.

"Yes."

Bernie begins to unload the rest of their equipment as Tom checks the meters.

"I've been wondering for a while…how could you tell where the bombs detonated?" Bernie says.

"Sometimes you just see it of course. Or data from INSAR satellite," Tom says, turning to help Bernie unload more equipment. He sets up an EDM (Electronic Distance Meter) which is used to measure the distance to fixed targets on the flanks of the volcano, a general surveying tool for eruption areas.

Bernie bends down to examine tephra, the coarse fragmented lava rock produced by the explosion. "This is pretty exciting, being at one of the most active volcanoes in the world."

"And to a degree, one of the most unpredictable. Fortunately, the flows are usually slow and meandering. But with high-explosives planted in the area we could have a different matter on our hand all together," Tom says.

They measure the inflation tilt, while plumes of smoke exit from vents on the surface.

"There's definitely a higher inflation reading here," Tom tells Bernie. "But, we can't get an accurate temperature reading with our thermograph, because some of the heat is residual from the explosives."

Bernie looks around, stretching his back. "To think some of the military was injured or even died here."

"Yeah, it's a real tragedy. For their families too, God help them. It's good to hear your concern, though. I wasn't sure if you were some kind of robot, emotionally detached from the real world, save for your phobia of the dark."

"I'm not too scared of the dark. I'm scared of *sleeping* in the dark. There's a difference you know."

"I guess so."

"Inherently, the dark doesn't scare me. It's just that it energizes my senses rather than relaxing them. I was diagnosed with Asperger's when

I was a child. High-functioning, highly-verbal autism. People have said I seem to be cut off from my emotions, but it helps me analyze situations better than a lot of quote 'normal people.' Often I underreact and then sometimes I overreact. I have what they call 'special interests.' Many scientists are Asperger types. Did you know that, Dr. Tom?"

"No, but it makes sense. Thanks for letting me know. I'll be on the lookout for any signs that I may be a fellow Ass-burger. Right now, I need you to hold the EDM. We have to take some measurements of distances for my geochem guy back in Arizona. With the help of satellite-based sensors, he can determine the composition of the tephra and detect the sulfur dioxide and ash content of the plumes to verify that these eruptions are different."

Thirty minutes later, they finish their examinations, load up their gear, and jump back into the Jeep. The driver swerves, snakelike, to avoid the large fissures on the bumpy lava field.

"Got some deep rift zones here," Tom says.

"I see," Bernie says. "And when the magma flows sideways, it can trigger earthquakes and eruptions along its flanks."

"That is correct," Tom says while his cell phone rings. "General McGregor, hello." Tom pauses to listen to the General.

"Yes, Sir," Tom says, "We finished at one of the detonation sites. So far, we can conclude that the blasts were powerful enough to induce sizable earthquakes. There is also the possibility that more explosive activity could happen along the area where the East Rift Zone meets the Southwest Rift Zone. I'll get you the coordinates as soon as I confirm my findings, then you can start searching for more explosives."

The call ends.

"Everything still okay?" Bernie says.

"We're still breathing," Tom says. He looks straight ahead, as the escort driver accelerates across the rough terrain and up toward the main road. "It's a good time to keep emotions in check. Maybe I'm an Ass-burger too."

"It's AsP-berger. Sheesh, get it right."

Chapter Seventeen

"A Crazy Dream"

Later that evening, Susan sets her ticket on the foyer table. Quietly, she thanks her friend Lydie. Through family, Lydie has military connections, ways of overriding the airlines which she doesn't go into detail about. (Just "I got you covered hon" and Susan can't afford time to ask questions).

Each moment seems both fleeting and eternal. Susan can't sleep, so she revs up into super organizer mode. She packs Tom's clothes in her own suitcase and then places Bernie's clothes, personal items, and a few selected superhero comic books in a carry-on bag. Still energized, she tidies up each room, as though preparing for guests.

She even goes through financial paperwork and the kitchen's spice rack before she jumps into the nightly routine, taking a couple extra minutes to exfoliate her skin. The face washing feels cathartic. She also wants to look fresh and flawless for Tom, presenting him with the "dewy" look that the fashion magazines always advertise.

This is all presuming he is safe and alive. There were no calls after that early afternoon talk. He didn't mention the number of bombs the terrorists planted, nor how destructive the bombs might be. He only reiterated that he didn't want her there.

How am I expected to stay calm? she thinks.

The bedroom is quiet. The A.C. is off and a window is open, which allows for the curtain to rise and fall as a sliver of moonlight illuminates the walls. Despite the anxiety, she is exhausted. She feels as if small weights are attached to her eyes. They become heavy. Within five minutes, she's asleep, dreaming...

She's inside the Volcano Hotel Restaurant, but the leather chairs have been replaced with 1950s style red vinyl booths. The worn wood floor is now polished, black and white checkerboard tile. "Great Balls of Fire" blasts from a shiny new jukebox.

Susan sees Bernie at the other end of the restaurant. She calls out to him, but her words are inaudible, drowned by the blasting rock and roll music.

She makes her way through a crowd of young people dressed in fifties attire. Is this some kind of costume party? Approaching Bernie, she sees that his hair is slicked back and he's wearing a yellow bow tie, with a plaid button-up shirt. He sits alone in a booth with a huge bowl of peppermint ice cream in front of him. The chocolate mint chunks are enormous, some as large as jasper geodes. Bernie picks at the ice cream with a chisel and small hammer, focused like a true geologist. He begins to pound at the chunks. Susan stands over him and asks what he's doing, but he ignores her, fixated on the task at hand.

He hacks away. Kraaah…krrrraaaahh. Tiny chocolate fragments, no more than a millimeter in length, chip off the ice cream block and fly in all directions, with some pieces striking Susan's face and shoulders. She doesn't expect the minuscule shards to hurt, yet they do. A burning-cold sting. She backs away and raises her hands to shield her face.

Bernie is still chipping away when she turns and sees a young couple seated at another booth. The girl adjusts her scratchy and uncomfortable British school uniform, as she babbles in an indecipherable language to her guy friend. She stops talking. Both the girl and boy stare up at Susan. Their eyes are emerald green, pixilated, like old Pac Man computer cartoons.

"What are you?" Susan asks. They don't respond. Susan looks down at herself. Her breasts heave, pushing out from a gingham check apron. She has a name tag on and there's a notepad and pen in the apron pocket. She pulls out the pen, as if to take an order, when a screechy collective voice disturbs her.

"FEED US! WE'RE HUNGRY!" They scream. The teenage boy hollers at her in a Cockney accent. His eyes are wide, eerily green like the rest of the customers, and he doesn't blink, but rather stares Susan down. She drops the pen and pad and backs away toward Bernie. She yells. He doesn't respond, still too engrossed in the ice cream hammering.

The calls of "FEED US!" become louder and louder. Customers rise from the booths and walk to Susan. They make their demands. They raise dishes and bang on them with forks and knives. She turns to the exit door, but when she tries to run, she encounters a strange resistance, as though *she's moving underwater against a current. With her legs paralyzed, she swings her arms and torso forward, until at last, she breaks into a sprint, pushing through the door.*

She sweats and pants, trying to catch her breath. Suddenly, her whisper morphs into a shout. The cement beneath her feet is burning hot like melting lava rock. The ground gives way. The earth splits, fractures, and opens up around her to reveal a flow. The flames could devour me in an instant, *she thinks.*

She leaps from broken rock to broken rock, avoiding the lava torrent. The magma pulses at an increasing beat. All around her, the lava rises. A tide of fire. Channels of scoria and bubbling stone. Inescapable. She runs until she comes to a dead end, teetering at the edge of the open caldera. Then the ground vibrates and shudders below her. It crumbles and she's plummeting into the caldera, toward a certain death.

"Nooooooo!"

But just as she is about to hit the lava pool at the bottom, she feels an intense pressure under her armpits. She hears a whoosh sound. Now, she's flying high above the lava. She turns her head to catch a glimpse of familiar blue sleeves and an iconic red S ensconced in a diamond shape.

"Superman?"

Then she sees Bernie's face above her, smiling with confidence. He spins her around and she is parallel to him.

"Don't worry, Dr. Susan," he says. "Just keep holding my hand. I gotcha'."

But as they gain altitude, he loses his grip. She cries out. He shifts and struggles, clawing at her, but she slips from his grasp and falls, hurtling to the fiery hell.

"Oh God, dear Lord." Susan rolls off the bed, onto the floor. Her legs are trapped in a swaddle of duvet cover and sheets. She places a hand over her heart. Within a minute, her breath is able to slow down. Thankfully, it was only a dream. But what could it possibly mean?

Chapter Eighteen

"Somewhere Over the Caldera"

Across from the Kilauea Lodge and Restaurant, Sal Rosetti sits at his desk and sighs. It's four in the afternoon and the sleep deprivation has hit him.

The outside air temperature gauge reads a comfortable sixty-eight degrees, but inside the office, it's warm and stuffy, inducing a grogginess despite two cups of coffee. He's been up since daybreak – checking in with Washington, looking at the satellite images of the volcano, reviewing military reports, and filling out his own reports. He stands, stretches, and opens the window levers behind his desk, allowing a light breeze to pass through the cramped office. Rusty cabinets, useless furniture, and a towering stack of papers surround him.

He sits down again. Methodically, he reviews a stack, adding his signature to the bottom of each page. He places a page in a pile on his right side.

The Done Pile.

He pulls out his trout keychain and gazes down to the shiny silver etched with realistic details – six-fins, flaring nostrils, gills. The key chain, something between gag and sincere gesture, was a gift from his son Kevin. They don't talk much. Not from any falling out, but the agreed mutual "busyness" of living different lives in different places. Kevin resides in northern California and works in the tech world that "you would never understand, Dad." ("Try me," Sal says, but his son ignores him.)

Sal remembers that it will be Kevin's birthday next week. That should count for something. And Sal prides himself for not naming him Salvatore III. The cycle ended with Kevin. No belts, limited insults. Still, he wishes he could be a better father. He wishes Margie was here.

Marguerite ("Margie") passed away ten years ago. He keeps a dated picture of her in his wallet. It's from 1976, July 4, 1976 to be exact, the bicentennial celebration in D.C. In the photo, Margie is sitting on a wooden bench by Gerbera daisies. She is wearing a red, ribbed shirt and dark blue jeans, her hair styled in Farrah Fawcett waves. She looks sweet and carefree. That's what she was. His lovely, generous, nurse wife. She was an amazing mother too. She was joy. She was light. He recalls the timbre of her sunny laugh and her extraordinary eyes, blue green, flecked with amber gold. Margie was a timeless beauty, never ostentatious.

The photo was taken years before the ovarian cancer diagnosis. At least there was a chance to say goodbye, but he misses her with a fierce desperation, every day and especially during these quiet, reflective times.

There's a knock at the door.

"Come in," Sal says.

A young military aide enters and salutes. "Sir, we have a visual on the bus. It's located on the northeast side of the Caldera."

"Northeast side? Closer than we thought."

"Near the area where Dr. Redland's map suggested."

"I never doubted her," Sal admits. "But we had our orders and I don't care for the Johnny-come-lately types."

Sal straightens up in his chair. His motion, combined with a delicate wind, propels a paper to the floor. The aide bends over and picks it up.

"I'll take that," Sal snatches it out of his hand. He turns back to his desk and sets the certificate down. The title reads Official United States Army Notice of Death.

He murmurs to the aide, "Let's go."

They walk single file down the hallway, through the foyer, and outside the building. It's a one-story historic lava rock construction with nine-foot tall columns supporting the covered entryway. In the shaded entrance, the porous texture looks sponge-like. Moss and small staghorn ferns sprout from rocky edifices. A garden frames the building and walkways host a variety of ferns and yellow ginger blossoms. Their fragrance sweetens the voggy air. His Margie would have loved this. Flowers enlivened her as though they were family.

Sal's reverie abruptly stops when he reaches the end of the walkway. "Crap," he utters.

A news' crew hurries to unload cameras, cords, microphones, and a phalanx of boxy lighting and sound equipment from their van. Sal stands next to a long-haired, bespectacled Gen-X technician. The man sits on a plastic crate and checks his video camera.

"What the hell is this?" Sal says to the aide.

"They arrived about an hour ago, Sir. They have official clearance. I thought you knew."

"I did. But I wasn't expecting this to be such a hullabaloo." He grimaces. "Do they even know what happened?"

"I assume so, Sir. We've had to follow the terrorists' demands."

The technician spins around and points the camera lens at Sal. A red record light blinks like a warning siren.

"Put that down!" Angry and red-faced, Sal shoves the camera away. "What's with all this extra equipment on the lawn? If this crap isn't moved, we'll start moving it for them." To prove his point, he picks up a speaker and sets it in front of the van. "Can I ask you guys something? What's this perverse obsession to sensationalize every moment? Really?"

The media crew looks dumbfounded.

"Oh, just forget it," Sal mumbles.

When Sal arrives at the restaurant, he sees the press has also set up film and recording equipment alongside his men's stations. He picks up a headset and binoculars and signals to an aide to put a headset on.

"I'm still part of this op. I'll be out on the deck," he says to the aide.

At the overlook railing, he peers through the binocular lenses, taking in the panoramic view of the crater, before he assesses the situation. The tour bus sits on the edge of the Kilauea caldera. Two Army Black Hawk helicopters circle above the vehicle like protective mother birds…or maybe a murder of crows waiting to scavenge the bus remains. Sal tries to stop his mind from going there, but it's inevitable.

Two Boeing CH-47 Chinook helicopters approach the front of the bus, hauling a thick, gigantic net suspended between front cargo hooks. The CH-47s are the workhorses of helicopters, with twin engines, tandem rotors, and the capability of reaching 200 miles an hour. They can handle the bus. Pilots lower the net into position in front of the bus.

"Commandos ready on fast ropes. Orders sir?" the aide asks.

"Drop 'em. Now." Sal says.

Two commandos drop from a Black Hawk helicopter. They swing from lines and descend onto the bus, as though they've practiced the routine a thousand times.

"They got this," Sal whispers.

The soldiers pull out pry bars and jostle the tops of the closed, dark-tinted windows on both sides of the bus. A second Black Hawk moves in, dropping off two more commandos.

A soldier calls into Sal. "Windows aren't opening, Sir."

Sal waits and watches them try to pry open the windows. "Break them in. Command. Permission to break windows."

"Roger that."

One of the commandos gives a thumbs-up to his partner. Together, they smash the bus windows and glass shards fly in all directions.

"What do you see?" Sal says. There's no answer.

Then, suddenly, the bus roars to life. It accelerates, flinging all the commandos off the rooftop like useless toys. They hit the ground, a couple feet from the caldera's edge. Fortunately, they are protected by pads, gloves, and helmets.

Then a cameraman shouts, "It's moving!"

"No shit!" Sal yells. He watches the commandos scramble away as the bus launches into mid-air, wheels spinning. The bus nose-dives into the net and slips downward. The front bumper and undercarriage catch onto the helicopter. Suspended in the sky, it hangs between the Chinooks. The weight drags the net down, causing the helicopters to lose altitude.

"This is not good. Damn it. This is not happening," Sal says. "We need a visual on the passengers in the bus," he calls out to the helicopter pilots. "Get the bus safely to the ground. Maintain altitude and bring it over the rim."

"Roger, that. We'll give it a go."

Slowly, the helicopters rise upward with the bus dangling between them like a gigantic dead fish on a line. The bus rises up as the choppers accelerate and speed toward the rim.

Gazing through the binoculars, Sal feels his blood pressure rise. A knot of trepidation twists in his stomach. "What are you guys doing? You're not going to clear the rim! Drop the net, drop it now!" he shouts.

"Roger that," the lead pilot orders his co-pilot and the second Chinook. "On my mark...ready, set..."

But before the bus is released, one of the Chinook helicopters shudders, vibrating with ferocious intensity while the bus slams into a lava rock ledge outcropping on the caldera rim. Windows explode upon impact. Chunks of glass and metal shatter, glittering in the sunlight like jewels.

The impact causes a shock wave to pulse upwards to the one Chinook still attached to the net. The helicopter spins and whirls. A horrible squeal emits from it, like a pig that knows it's going to be slaughtered. Louder and louder. The Chinook falls, spiraling out of control. It tilts and veers off, rotor blades close to the ground. It crashes, exploding against a cliff face in a hail of violet-orange rubble.

"Oh my God!" a newswoman cries. The onlookers gasp.

Sal clutches the railing and strains forward, his knuckles white with tension. He watches the explosion while the net loosens from the Chinook. The bus tumbles down to the caldera in another smashing blast.

The other Chinook struggles and wobbles upward to clear the rim. It then hurtles ahead, nose cone close to the ground, front rotor blades shredding bushes and trees. Then, as the helicopter finally stabilizes and gains altitude, the main rotor blades hit a lava rock hill. Sparks glimmer.

The Chinook swerves and careens into a woody area, smashing into the ground. A massive fireball erupts and engulfs the helicopter. Above, the sky gags with smoke.

Sal's teeth clench, his eyes narrow. He slams the radio headset down. He takes a circuitous route back to the office. He is beyond cursing out loud or blaming the stupid people that were assigned to this mission. Numbness spreads over his entire body, moving from his bowels to his brain and back again. A sickness spreads over him.

Eight men dead and the hostages in the bus, plus a downed Chinook. I'm the idiot in this mess.

In his mind, he sees the bus slipping again. He visualizes the poor, panicky hostages inside, their cries muffled by the noise of the chopper rotor blades.

Why didn't they fight? Smash the windows? Try to escape? Anything? Were they drugged to a stupor? Or already dead? How did this happen?!?

It's gruesome to envision rotting cadavers, but drugged or gunned down has to be a more peaceful exit than being violently hurled through the air, slamming into a cliff face, and falling 300 feet into the caldera. Either way, it is what it is - an overwhelming defeat, the worst failure of his entire life.

When he arrives back at Command Central, he is alone. He enters his office, opens the mini-fridge, and guzzles down a club soda wishing it was hard liquor. The carbonation washes over his insides, offering a temporary panacea.

This damn mission! Everything that could possibly go wrong, has.

He closes his eyes and wipes a hand over his sweaty brow. The sickness abates, yet the numbness remains. He's been in the military, without any breaks, for over thirty years. But this mission is a curse, like the crazy Sicilian black magic he heard about as a kid.

He stares out through a window at the tropical foliage. Forest greens, blood red purples. A voggy mist permeates through twilight dew. The fragrance of ginger and jasmine that was once intoxicating now cloys at him. The phone rings, and for the first time in his career, he lets it go until the answering machine picks up.

"Rosetti? Are you there? Commander Rosetti?" It's General McGregor, right on time. "If you're there, pick up."

Sal plops in the desk chair and stares at the phone. His stomach churns. He might just throw up. General McGregor probably wants to meet in person, but why bother?

Then the order comes, words reel out with the expected formality, "It is my unfortunate duty to inform you, Colonel Rossetti, that you are relieved of your command. Repeat, you are ROC. I'm on my way, to personally assume command."

Chapter Nineteen

"Fire at Will"

Between the Volcano House Hotel and Colonel Sal's headquarters, a busty brunette reporter stands on the lawn, fiddling with the microphone attached to her lapel. She puckers carmine pink lips and bumps her hair up for a volume lift. White, volcanic ash flakes settle on her navy blue blazer while she talks to the camera.

"Hi, I'm Katie Richards, from Channel Ten News Emergency Hour. We're here at Hawaii Volcanoes National Park, but today has not been your typical day in paradise. It's been an afternoon of terror that has gripped the Big Island as military helicopters failed in their attempt to rescue American hostages. Of the forty-six hostages, we can only presume there were no survivors. And just last night, another failed rescue attempt left six U.S. Special Forces members dead in a battle with the Korean Terrorists."

She eyes Sal walking from his office through the parking lot. "Hold on, the commander in charge of the operation is heading our way. Let's see if he's willing to share any more information with our viewers."

Katie and her three-member video crew make a beeline across the lot, catching up to Sal.

"Commander, can we please have a few words about this situation?" she says while thrusting her microphone out in front of him.

He walks faster. Despite Sal's training and her goofy kitten heels, Katie matches him step-for-step with the practiced endurance of a super recruit. They walk alongside one another, adjacent to a large rectangular koi fish pond. Katie holds the mic out further, directly under his chin.

"Get that damn thing away from me!" Sal blurts out, swatting at the microphone.

"But Sir, a quick question first. Exactly how many of your soldiers were in those helicopters that went down?"

"I'm not authorized to answer your question. Besides, I'm not in command of this operation anymore, so get outta' my way!"

As the words leave his mouth, Sal waves her off forcefully. His arm swings into an arc, catching her blazer, and knocking her back. She stumbles, dancing a clumsy do-is-do, until she falls, with a splash, into the knee-deep fishpond. Frightened fish dart in all directions. Her heels float up to the top of the water's surface like miniature life rafts. She sits upright in the brackish koi-water, the back of her Ralph Lauren skirt soaked, hair matted in mermaid waves. Her mouth cleaves open in devastation.

"Oh crap," Sal mutters, halting in mid-step. He crouches down and offers her a hand, but it's too late. There are tears in her eyes and a scowl on her once cheery face.

"Sorry, my dear," he says. "I'm still a soldier, not quite your knight in shining armor." He helps her to her feet, then steps back, and resumes his walk to the restaurant, as a cameraman continues to film him.

Inside the Lodge, the military is busy as ever, but the news media has disbanded to another location.

"They left a few minutes ago," a female military aide tells Sal.

"Not enough morbid excitement for them, I guess." He sits down on an ergonomic chair. "We were too slow to act. We had the bus coordinates, everything."

"Sir," the female aide calls out. "The General is on the phone."

"Well, all right." He picks up the phone, covering the mouth piece. "Quiet in here," he commands the personnel. The cacophony hushes down to a low din. "Yes, Sir," he says into the phone. "I got your message and I understand... But Sir, if you do that...Yes Sir, copy that."

He frowns and sets the phone down. A minute later, he sees Tom walk in, his hands covered in dirt from the expedition. Sal straightens up and raises his voice to address the whole room. "All hostages are presumed dead. An assault of attack birds will arrive within an hour. They'll destroy everything near the bus site and the cavern."

"Are you really sure this is the right course of action?" Tom blurts out, drawing attention from the military personnel.

"Look Professor," Sal says, "if you want to talk, we gotta' take it in another room."

Tom nods yes. Together they walk outside the Volcano Hotel shop. Sal sits down on a bench and peers at Tom. For a second, he sees his son Kevin in this young, goofy scientist. Tom is in the same age range, probably five years older. Both men have childish grins that belie any serious mood and eyes that tend to stare in perpetual wonder. They both have the same wiry muscular build and confident, carefree demeanor.

"You're going to have to give me more time," he says to Sal. "Work with me, Colonel."

"I'm trying. I've been reviewing your maps of the volcanic activity, the lava tubes and caves, trying to think of other ways to surprise the terrorists."

"Then do it. You can't send in gun-ships," Tom insists.

"Not my call, son. I've been relieved of command."

"I thought that something like that might happen. But I think McGregor is making a big mistake. They can retreat too easily. If you start firing, it will only bring the enemy that much closer to their goal."

"And how would you know?" Sal says.

"I can't speak for the psychological motivations of these guys. But I do make observations for a living and I've studied this volcano for years. There are countless tunnels they can hide in and that gives them a tactical advantage over us. They're hiding out. If we're aggressive, they'll ignite more bombs for sure. Plus, they have this whole revenge thing going on. You can't underestimate that."

"Not a bad assessment," Sal offers. He gauges Tom's close distance for any signs of agitation. But the scientist is calm, with no trace of hot-headedness, only the determination to get his way.

"There's got to be another strategy besides sending the gun-ships. Isn't there someone you can convince? Some other General who'll listen?"

"You don't get it, Andrews. I'm done. I'm toast."

"Then you know what will happen?" Tom says.

"I know perfectly well. Why do you think I've been trying to avoid this situation?"

Sal pictures the explosions and volcanic chaos. He sees the cliffs of the Big Island's South Coast crumbling into the ocean. True, he's witnessed life and death, but never in conjunction with a natural disaster. His mind jumps to the reporter from this morning's incident.

Katie, what-was-her-name? Not good form to push a woman. But then, how could she understand? And how would this clueless, myopic scientist, who's spent his whole life chiseling rocks and reading seismographs, get it either?

"We need more time. You can't just ignore this and give up," Tom whines.

"Look," Sal says, his deep voice becoming hoarse. "I come from a long line of military leaders. We're resilient as all hell and we don't give up easily. But, I have to follow the chain of command and obey my orders."

"You officers are so good at giving orders. But real leadership comes from character, not rank or position. Come on! Step up, take control, tell them. Insist they stop this order."

Sal glares at him. "You're way out of your league! You've got no frickin' idea how a military operation works and you don't know what it's like to lose half of a Strike Team, two helicopter crews, a busload of war veterans and their wives!"

Flushed to ire red, his face contorts. "Try and wrap your head around that. Life, death, duty, honor. Maybe someone who's seen death, maybe a *real* doctor could understand. All your theories, computers, and geocache toys don't mean shit in real life."

Tom shrugs his shoulders. "Well, maybe you're right. But I'm not the one who keeps making mistakes."

"I'm going to pretend I didn't hear that, Andrews."

The young man is grinning.

What an asshole! Sal thinks. *He wanted to say that. If only I could throw a punch at him and get away with it. Maybe it would clear the air between us. A blow to the face or at least throw a large heavy object at him.*

Tom paces back and forth, averting his focus from the Colonel. "Do you know if they've actually recovered any of the hostages' bodies from the site yet? The bus could have been empty. The hostages could still be alive. Did your commandos or you see them in the bus?"

"Negative."

"Then maybe, they were never in there to begin with..."

"That is something to consider...okay, maybe we are on the same page here." He's not sure how, but this nutcase may have convinced him of another possibility. "We'll have to get McGregor on board. You think I'm tough? That guy's radical."

When the General arrives, via a Black Hawk landing on the lawn, he's wearing a helmet and uniform. He's relieved Sal of leadership, but keeps him on as an unofficial second in command. The General ignores Tom's plea not to attack and refuses to hear any more talk on the matter. Sal and Tom follow the General back to the observation deck at the restaurant.

Standing among the military personnel at the viewing deck, Sal monitors the flight path through binoculars. Tom stands at a respectful distance nearby, while General McGregor gives orders via radio headset.

"Attack positions."

The vog haze mutes the late afternoon colors. A squadron of six AH-1W Super Cobra helicopters race across the sky, speeding over the Kilauea caldera. The Cobras are light in the wind despite their heavy artillery. They are built to seek out, kill, and destroy. They are armed with air to ground, laser-guided, heat seeker missiles, including the Hellfire missile, with its fire-and-forget capability.

The Cobras also carry sidewinder air-to-air missiles and 70mm rockets. They are equipped with an advanced precision kill weapon system (APKWS) and a three-barrel, 20mm Gatling gun that can be fixed in position. The pilot can aim the weapons and fire simply by looking at a target.

Under the command of McGregor, the Super Cobras line up in front of the cave mouth, about a mile away from the observation deck. They hover above the caldera floor, below the rim, and far enough away from the cavern that their missile explosions won't ricochet back at them.

"Bogey team, you are cleared hot. Fire at will," McGregor orders.

"Copy that."

Sal watches through his binoculars as everyone on the deck looks out in anticipation. The familiar scent of nervousness begins to overwhelm Sal's body. He takes a few deep breaths, resigned to the facts. It's not the best solution, but it's a permanent one. Then after tomorrow's debriefing, they can probably pack up and go home.

"Weapons, locked and engaged," the lead pilot's voice blasts back to the General.

"Fire at will," the General calls again.

"Copy. Steady now..." the lead pilot says, "Aim..."

A hush encompasses the crowded deck.

"Wait!" the lead pilot calls out amid crackles of static. "Hold your fire! Repeat, all helos, hold your fire! Stand down."

Tom approaches the railing, shoving his way through the military personnel who exchange curious glances at each other.

"What's going on? Talk to me!" McGregor shouts into the radio.

With binoculars wedged under his bushy eyebrows, Sal scans the landscape, focusing on the area at the mouth of the cave. Something moved. His fingers dig into the knobs, re-focusing. He blinks to clear his vision and then sees it.

Korean soldiers have pulled back a huge length of camouflage fabric from the mouth of the cave. He focuses in on a line of veteran hostages. Their wives cling to them at the cavern entrance. Two soldiers hold them at gunpoint.

The pilot replies over the radio. "Sir, it appears the hostages are alive and still being held. They're in the cave mouth standing in front of the KUF soldiers."

"These guys know what they're doing," Sal says to himself. His voice cracks as he lowers his binoculars.

Stunned, General McGregor sees the hostages too and raises the radio receiver to his parched lips. "Mission aborted! Repeat mission aborted! Return to base."

Chapter Twenty

"Howard & Irene"

The American helicopters circle back to their station, while Ho Dam's men rally up the hostages. He gives his troops the "okay" to drop the camouflage back over the cave mouth.

Flanked by soldiers, James and the other hostages walk back inside the cavern, re-adjusting their eyes to the darkness. The sight of the U.S. helicopters was a relief, James thinks, even if the initial tactic was aggressive. The military knows they are alive and so amidst hunger, thirst, and oppression, there is a glimmer of hope. In the recesses of the dimly lit cavern, after this horrifying ordeal, the veterans and their wives try to relax, hands still zip-tied in front of them.

James is tired, his mind shifts between dreams and reality. One moment, he hears his wife's sweet voice calling his name. He can feel her warm, soft skin and he can almost taste her fruity perfume. Then, the next second, he opens his eyes and perceives the dozens of exhausted veterans and their tearful wives. The Korean soldiers have removed the blindfolds and the hostages look bewildered as ever.

James inspects their faces until he locates Howard. *There's something special about that old curmudgeon.* James keeps coming back to the man. Perhaps it is Howard's inner strength and his stubborn streak, combined with a tenderness towards Irene. Despite the situation, Howard kindles a fighting spirit. He rests in his wife's arms while she strokes his thin gray hair. James watches them and listens to another conversation.

"So, that's why our bus was targeted?" Irene says in a raspy, dehydrated voice.

"Apparently. Back during the war, the Koreans went through hell. Four U.S. invasions in three years. We were beaten back, winter would set in, and then the reinforcements would arrive and were able to push the fight further north. Complete destruction.

"We ravaged their country, with bombardments and napalm. Racked the entire peninsula. It must have devastated them. We were green soldiers back then, kids really. We made too many mistakes. North Korea has their fair share of blame, but it was our training ground for 'Nam, which was a pretty violent war as you know."

"You can't blame yourself. You were so young."

Howard reflects on her words for a second before looking up into her eyes with a mischievous glint. "How 'bout now? Do I still look young to you?"

"Handsome as ever," she says while she kisses his forehead.

Their hands interlock, gnarled fingers fitting together like puzzle pieces. Irene's attention drifts to their youthful past. She closes her eyes, bowing her head.

"You remember when we met, Howie?"

" 'Course I do. Can't forget that day ever…"

"I'd love to hear about that special day," James speaks out, easing forward. "Something cheery while we wait in this smelly, dank cave."

"Yes, that's a good idea," Irene smiles nodding at James.

"Ah, shucks," Howard says. "You may think I'm hallucinating from lack of food. But okay, here goes. Let's see. I was eight years old. I was in second grade. Irene was six, almost seven, and in the first grade. She was the new girl at Oak Street School in St. Louis."

"We were only kids," Irene says with a giggle.

"Yeah, but I knew a looker when I saw one. Chestnut-auburn hair and the prettiest face. And those dimples… So there she was in her white blouse with a rounded collar. She wore baby blue ribbons in her hair to match the dress. She was so beautiful and I fixated on her. And I said to myself, in my mind of course – 'for the life of me, I am going to get one of those ribbons!'

"Back then the boys and girls had separate recess areas with boundaries enforced by our teachers. Those teachers were such bores. Tyrants and idiots sometimes. But you didn't mess with them, unless you had a screw loose, like me. Ha, ha!

"Anyway, the recess teacher's back was turned to me. She was reprimanding a girl who cut in front of another playing hopscotch. Shy little Irene was waiting her turn next to them, momentarily distracted by a pair of turtledoves sitting in the tree. How 'bout that, turtledoves? A pair of them. Guess what else? One was on the boy's side of the schoolyard and the other on the girl's side. I only realized it later, but it was a sign for us. Those birds were like Rennie and me, but at the time I had a specific mission.

"Like a jack rabbit, I sprinted toward her and for a moment stood behind her without making a peep. I caught a whiff of her gorgeous reddish hair. Oh, wowie, kazowie. Sweet as honeysuckle. Enthralling. They say your sense of smell is strongest at seven-eight years old and I think I knew then, that yep, she was my girl. So, like a wild tomcat, I marked her, right then and there.

"Then *Whoosh!* I pulled on one of her grosgrain ribbons and spooled it around my hand. She cried out, because it pulled her hair and she was caught by surprise, but I paid no mind. I turned and ran like all hell. Laughing at my success, all across the schoolyard, down the hallway, and back toward my classroom, where a couple kids ratted me out.

" 'Howie was on the girl's side!' A classmate of theirs squealed in delight. Another yelled, 'He did it!' I was runnin' and runnin' and then I had to slow down to round the corner and I ran head first into our Principal's old knees.

" 'Whoa, there! What have you got there, Mr. O'Malley?' he said in a deep voice. I was dumbstruck. I ended up with two weeks of detention and had to return the blue ribbon, but it was well worth it to hold that treasure for a few moments, to inhale the aroma of her lovely hair. And when I gave the ribbon back, I introduced myself to the most amazing girl ever. In time, she learned to like me too."

The hostages laugh, some to the point of an earsplitting guffaw.

"Looks like we all need cheering up," James says, enjoying the momentary relief.

But then he overhears Ho Dam stirring about in another cave. Perhaps this is psychological torture. Or worse, bonding. No one is beyond Stockholm Syndrome at this point. They are relying on their captors for survival and any rebellious move could mean death. The hostages continue to wait in the holding area, when they notice a light flash on. It's the blinking of a video camera.

"Going live!" Ho Dam shouts. The flashlights turn on, including one that looks like a powerful spotlight on Ho Dam. He marches among the hostages with a 9mm pistol in his hand. He looks around and flashes a sinister, gratified smile, until he settles on Howard. "Him," he states, pointing.

"No!" Irene gasps. Three soldiers yank her husband unto his unsteady feet and tie his hands together. "Please," she continues. "I beg you, please. Don't hurt him."

She reaches for Howard's hand, but a soldier raises the butt of his rifle ready to knock her down. Cringing back against James, she can only watch as the soldiers forcefully drag Howard across the cavern floor. He struggles, his skin flayed by the rocky outcroppings.

"Make sure we have this footage," Ho Dam orders. "We have a signal here to send this video."

Howard pushes against the captors, twisting his zip-tied hands back and forth.

"Let her watch," Ho Dam says to the camera wielding soldier. "I want to see her reaction on film." A soldier brings Howard around to face Ho Dam while the cameraman starts recording. Like a seasoned reporter, Ho Dam positions himself in front to deliver his well-rehearsed news –

"For your U.S. Imperialist aggressors and their insolent war crimes against my people…" he states. "For the atrocity at No Gun Ri and the murder of our people…"

The soldier holds Howard's right side. He reaches over and grabs a section of his shirt. With a hard yank, he tears Howard's shirt open to reveal a patch of gray chest hair.

"No! Oh, God, please no! Don't do it!" Irene screams, her voice echoing in the cave. She lunges toward Howard until a soldier blocks her. All the while the cameraman swings between Ho Dam, Howard, and the terrified veterans.

Howard raises his head to meet Irene's eyes. "You're as beautiful as the first day I saw you. I love you my darling." His strained voice is only a whisper.

"I love you, too," she says. "I'll always love you." She is quiet for a moment. In a flash, she sees Howie as a rascally young boy, then as her courtier. She sees him handsome and happy on their wedding day, and Howie's delighted face when their children were born. A proud father of a son and daughter.

And she sees them together as they were before all this happened – traveling, having fun, loving, laughing. Then the sobs begin again.

Ho Dam turns to Howard. The cameraman waltzes between them, as Ho Dam raises the gun to chest-level. "You want to die honorably? So now you will." He fires a single round into Howard's heart.

The seconds seem to last forever as Howard falls to the floor and dies. Irene cries out and collapses onto the ground.

"Damn you, son of a bitch!" James yells. He rushes to catch Irene. The soldiers raise their weapons at him, but he ignores them, holding Irene in his arms.

"Leave the bus driver," Ho Dam instructs them. "Take the body outside."

Together three soldiers lift Howard's bloodied body and shuffle to the caldera edge. Two other soldiers hold back the netting that covers the cave mouth. Ho Dam stands in front of the wide expanse of the caldera drop-off. Light silhouettes him and frames the clouds of sulfuric vog that rise up in plumes. Next to Ho Dam, the camera zooms in on Howard's face, his eyes open in frozen shock, lips parted in prayer or plea.

"For not giving into our demands and for trying to rescue the hostages. This man has paid for your mistakes," Ho Dam says in a somber tone. He signals to the soldiers and they heave Howard out and away, into the caldera.

Back in the Volcano Park briefing room, Tom narrates how lava tubes are formed. Sal and General McGregor listen at the back of the Jagger Observatory room. Tom uses a laser pointer to draw attention to a digital map of the caldera.

"Right here, you can see the magma and gases building up in the earth's crust from below at the hot spot. Here is the magma load under Kilauea, which exceeds millions of cubic feet."

Sitting at a computer, Bernie types in a command, pulling up a series of heat-images displaying the movement of underground magma as it turns into lava flows.

"Flows cut across and down the volcano, with some emitting from vents on its flank," Tom continues. "Meandering downward like a river or stream toward the sea. After a flow decreases, the exposed top layer cools and hardens into a crust. While beneath it, the lava may still continue to flow, eventually forming an elongated channel.

"Once the flow stops completely, it then discharges as it reaches the sea or other lower elevations. Then hollow tubes are left behind. Layers upon layers of sediment can also be deposited on top of the tubes, concealing them, turning them into underground tunnels that can run for miles."

McGregor shifts in his seat. "So it's possible that the enemy infiltrated one of these hidden tubes prior to our arrival, mapped out the area, and set up their command center? If so, then it's possible for us to locate and find the hostages through one of the lava tubes?"

Tom looks askance at the General. "More than possible, Sir, *if* we can find the correct tube. We saw the soldiers in a cave at the caldera's edge. We know they're hiding there. It's just a matter of locating the tube and accessing it, without alerting them. Finding a secret passage of some kind."

A knock on the door interrupts the conversation and Sal shouts, "Come on in!"

A military aide enters, glances around at the irritated faces, and salutes. "Sir, we've just received a transmission from the terrorists. Is this your computer tech?" he asks, pointing to Bernie.

"Yeah," Bernie nods as the aide passes him a memo.

"What is it?" McGregor demands.

"It's a URL link to something," Bernie says with a confused look.

"Type it in," Sal groans.

Bernie follows the orders, fingers flying over the keys until a low-resolution video plays. "I can't hear what they're saying. I'll try to fix the audio here. Wait a sec."

The video resolution is poor, with blurred bodies moving out of sync, flashes of colors, until the camera focuses. Sal points out Howard dangling between two Korean soldiers. A few seconds later, the soldier pins his arms back, exposing his torso. Ho Dam points a pistol at his chest.

The video footage distorts, but the audio track surges, on full blast, and the shouts of the by-standers rack through the computer speakers. A round of shots splinters through the airwaves. The video appears again with the tossing of Howard's body.

"Ah crap!" Bernie says. "They're killing the hostages."

Chapter Twenty-One

"Susan Arrives"

Hilo International Airport

A rain cloud settles like a thick blanket over eastern Hawaii. The airport is a crowded one-way mass of anxious locals and tourists clamoring at the TSA security checkpoints with as much carry-on luggage as possible. Wading through the throng in the opposite direction, Susan pushes her way past panicked adults and crying children.

Most people are worried, some are amped-out, high on their natural adrenaline, while others have opted for a cigarette or marijuana buzz-calm, which the airport security has briefly permitted, if only to tame the masses. All it would take is one holler to stir the sea of humanity into a raging storm. Everyone is trying to get out, except Susan.

Tucson – LA – Honolulu, with a longer layover there than expected, then a small commuter plane to Hilo. She felt nauseous on board the bumpy flight and worried at the sight of only two fellow passengers. But what should she expect? Military personnel were flying to a terrorist threat zone. Almost twelve hours later she's arrived, amidst chaos.

Making her way out of the main terminal, Susan heads straight to the car rental kiosks. Upon approach, she slows down... *Not now. Please.* But of course this would happen and she didn't even think about it. All the kiosks are locked up and dark inside. Notes posted on the doors and shuttered windows instruct customers to drop their rental keys in the locked metal boxes.

A desperate recklessness grips her as she tries to squeeze her hand through the slot to reach for any key. Nope. She turns to the surrounding street, empty and silent, absent of any moving vehicles.

"Bloody hell," she curses under her breath. Back home, she had tried calling every friend and acquaintance she knew on the Big Island, pleading, "All I need is a ride. Or just leave me the keys to your car. I can't explain the situation, but Tom needs me..." No one bothered to call back. They probably thought she was crazy.

Frustrated, she leaves the kiosks and heads toward the terminal's public parking lot, eyeing the empty cars. She's never broken into a car or done anything illegal. Right now she wishes she knew how to hotwire a car, wishes she'd pay more attention to her derelict cousin Will's antics.

She pulls on the driver side latches. They're all locked. Rivulets of sweat stream down her forehead. *This is ridiculous. What was I thinking? Maybe I should just go home. Why am I even here, risking my life?*

She fumes, turns around, and realizes she's standing next to a red 1978 VW Bug. It's out of place among the new sedans. She eyes the word **LADY** stylishly painted on the side amid black polka dots. *Old banger. I know this car!* She lifts the driver's side door handle and pulls the unlocked door open, its rusty hinges creaking. Peering inside, she sees a note taped to the steering wheel.

Aloha Susan - The keys are under the driver's seat. Please be nice to my LADY. I hope she can help you out. Mahoe, xxoo

"Good old Mahoe. I should have known he'd come through," she says to herself. "Lady Luck."

She had left him a voice message, a last ditch effort to connect with someone on the Big Island. And he pulled through. He had been their Hawaiian volcano guide/consultant years ago and was truly one of the kindest people they knew. A pure Hawaiian, blessed with genuine aloha spirit.

A tear of relief moistens her eye. She hurls her luggage in the trunk and climbs into the driver's side. Reaching underneath, she pulls out a small, wooden-tiki figurine keychain with glittery green eyes like the pixelated eyes from her dream. Strange coincidence, she thinks, shaking her head. She shoves the key into the ignition and engages the clutch. The old Bug fires up and she heads southwest on Highway 11.

Driving several miles up the Highway, the altitude rises, the air cools, and a light misty rain falls, darkening the volcanic gray asphalt to pitch black. Susan's ears pop. She turns on the wiper blades and focuses on the desolate road ahead. She sees the remains of a wild boar, a hit-and-run victim, festering on the side of the highway. Its guts glisten, skin baked in the heat. *Poor thing. But maybe it's better that way. Sudden death by car versus an actual slow, burning death from molten lava.*

The climate shifts from humid tropical to cool and temperate. The roadside environment hasn't changed much since their last trip here, five years ago, except now it's nearly deserted with neither a residential car nor tourist rent-a-car in sight.

She thinks back to their honeymoon on the Big Island, but as usual the restful getaway was eclipsed by Tom's research and their wild expeditions. She remembers slipping a dozen feet of rope between gloved fingers as she lowered him into the caldera. Acidic smoke bit at his nose and eyes. The sulfur dioxide had mixed with the day's drizzle, creating an acid rain so strong that it ate away at the metal frames of his glasses. Then they hiked countless miles across barren lava fields in order to get close to live lava. No doubt it was exciting, but not romantic.

Here they are again, in paradise. *To track down…terrorists?* Susan is ready to scream, to thrash her lungs in a guttural cry, but she's beyond tired. Her stomach is empty and her bladder is full, while her mind wanders in various directions.

She rolls down the manual window. It's cooler outside, maybe sixteen degrees centigrade, she guesses. *When will lay Americans finally realize the ease and beauty of the metric system?* Even her sister-in-law, Liz, uses the metric system to teach high-school chemistry. Liz lives and works in Brooklyn, a place that Tom never visits because urban means people, crowds, noise, and connectivity. His top dislikes include development, traffic, congestion, crime, and pollution. "Too many rats in a cage," Tom says about cities.

Susan will counter. "But what about the concerts and museums and all the fun activities?"

He ignores her comebacks.

And now, here I am, she ruminates. *I left a good job and dear friends in California. I left the beautiful Pacific Ocean. For what? To live in a remote, desert compound so Tom has the time off to hurl himself into caves and volcanoes and win awards for his Mom?*

No one else questions him. He's just "doing his thing" or "being Tom." He hasn't bid adieu to a career and he doesn't have to negotiate the stares of his friends, asking, telepathically and sometimes verbally, "What are your future plans, Susan? Starting a family soon?"

It aggravates her too much. People want to see a woman "be it all" or "sacrifice it all." No in between. She'd like to punch those imbeciles.

As the rain increases its intensity, obscuring her visibility, Susan also questions the immediate plans. *Do I have any? I mean, what am I doing?* She clutches the steering wheel, wrist tendons stretched and aching, while the Bug chugs uphill to the entrance of the Volcanoes National Park.

The military have set up a roadblock and an armed guard stands in front of it, trying to stay dry and warm under a parka. She slows to a stop next to him and rolls down the window. He approaches her, taking a second to glance over the car. He leans over her driver's side door and frowns.

"I know, I wasn't expecting a VW bug either, but with all the rental agencies closed, I didn't have much choice." Susan chuckles nervously and releases her fingers from the wheel.

"Sorry ma'am, but we're not allowing any civilians into the Park at this time."

"I understand, but I'm with Dr. Thomas Andrews, research consultant for Commander McGregor."

He eyes her suspiciously. "I'll need to see some I.D."

Susan opens her day-pack and pulls out her wallet.

"No one alerted me to your arrival."

"Tom probably forgot with everything going on."

"Do you have clearance from the Commander? If so, I'll need to see that paperwork."

"Yes, I do." She hands him a faxed document. McGregor's signature sprawls across the bottom.

Using a flashlight to inspect the paper, the guard steps back to get a better look. Rain drops coalesce on the lapel reflectors of his polyester hooded parka, creating a watery, spider web array. A sliver of halogen light from the guard booth flickers unto his face. He's young, slightly fat-cheeked, with blond stubble and a broad nose, eyes hidden underneath his cap.

Susan figures he's new to the job protocol, trying to appear official.

He holds up his radio to make a call. "Paperwork looks fine ma'am. I just need clearance from my commanding officer. Excuse me."

Susan watches the guard pace in front of the entrance while he murmurs into the receiver.

"Okay, you're all set," he says when he returns. "Good to go."

She shifts out of neutral, hits the accelerator, and eases off the clutch. The VW cruises down the southeast Crater Rim road, passing ranks of 'ohia trees and ginger plants. She can't help but imagine terrorists lurking behind foliage, ready to attack. Fragments from her nightmare return and at once she sees the Pac-man faces in the restaurant and the spewing volcanic fire and then her own body, consumed by fire.

"No," she says. "Can't think about that."

It's eerily quiet here. She had expected a buzz of night activity with barricades and military helicopters flying overhead and legions of guards. The military must be re-strategizing a plan of attack. Or maybe they have to be absolutely quiet. She drives past the Visitor's Center, headlights on low, until she reaches Tom and Bernie's assigned lodging at the Gallery.

She pulls into a parking stall and turns off the ignition. For a moment, she relaxes in the car, satisfied to have finally arrived. The moon illuminates a parked Jeep, brightening the surrounding rocks, trees, and shrubs. There's a stillness and peace at night, even with the chaotic reality of the situation.

She grabs her luggage and approaches the lodging. The door is unlocked. Leave it Tom to have the door unlocked during a crisis. She steps inside and walks into the main room and turns right into the bedroom corridor.

Bernie sleeps on the couch, snoring in notes that could be mistaken for a show-tune. *What a charmingly, geeky dude he is.* She sets her luggage on the floor and takes a moment to pull the loosened blanket back up to Bernie's chin.

Sleeping below a volcano painting, Tom is curled up on his side. His eyelashes flutter, cartoon long and black, the envy of women. His face is sweet and boyish. Until now she doesn't realize the degree of loneliness that can infiltrate her mind. Despite all the frustrations she experiences in marriage and the fact that she could be content by herself, she just couldn't leave him. She loves him too much.

She removes her pants and shirt and unfurls the covers to climb into bed, encircling his arm around her for that perfect snuggle fit. He mumbles, then smiles. His body comforts her, but the space in her heart cavity continues to expand open like a horizontal free-fall. Tiredness overwhelms, yet even at the moment of drifting off, a particular desperation returns.

Do you still love me, Tom? Not just when you're playing superhero and rescuing me from jungle vultures, and not just when you're loving your own kooky life, but now? In these moments of deep peace, when your mind has turned off, can you say that you really love me?

Chapter Twenty-Two

"One Wise Old Hawaiian"

As his early morning caffeine buzz wears off, Mahoe Makaweli catches a glimpse of himself in the rear-view mirror. At seventy-five years old, his brown skin is leathery and wrinkled, teeth yellowed from hand-rolled cigars and Kona's "jet-fuel brew." White hair sprouts from his mutton chops, but his eyes sparkle with youthful curiosity and his laugh resonates with a warmth that has not abated in decades.

He watches the bird ornament tied to the rear-view mirror bounce to the rhythm of his old Toyota pick-up truck. The vehicle chortles up the highway and rattles over cattle guard crossings. Mahoe's seven-year-old grandson Keoki wakes up next to him and shakes off his grogginess.

" 'Ey sleepy head," Mahoe says. His voice is smooth like honey and he speaks in Hawaiian Pidgin English, a creole used around family and close friends.

"You know," he continues, "right before you was born, your grandmuddah and I stay up hea' and she buy 'dis honeycreepa' ornament for you."

He touches the bird ornament and Kook looks up at it.

"So, Keoki, I says to her, 'Dat boy not gonna' play wit' dat. He gonna' look at it one time and that be all.' But sho 'nuff, you love it. Baby hands just grabbin' it like some wild bird catcha' and you pluck out feathers. I say, 'He gonna' make one kapili scepter for the ali'i chief.' Heh, heh."

Mahoe pauses. "You no mine if I smoke, eh boy? Jus' one cigah?"

"No Granpa," Keoki says.

Poor little Keoki, Mahoe thinks. *A sweet boy whose life has already been marked by tragedy.* Mahoe's youngest daughter Malia had Keoki at thirty-six. He was her first and only child before she died in a car crash. Keoki was only three and thankfully he was not with her. She was alone in her car, driving home at night from a friend's house.

A 200-pound wild boar wandered onto the upper highway in Kamuela, an area known for its lush, highland grass and cattle ranches. It was dark and the feral pig was covered in black hair. Malia was driving 60 mph when she swerved to miss the animal. Instead she hit a sturdy eucalyptus tree, one of many that line the road in that area. She hit the trunk head-on, breaking her neck. She died instantly.

Keoki's father was never in the picture, so Mahoe and his wife Kaleho took Keoki in and adopted him. The boy was what locals called an "opihi (limpet) baby." Like limpets stuck on rocks, Keoki could not separate from Grandpa Mahoe, his hanai (adopted) father.

When the extended family heard the news to evacuate the Big Island, Mahoe's sister, Auntie Jo, tried to take Keoki to the airport for their flight to Seattle. Keoki kicked and screamed, until Mahoe stepped in to try and resolve the situation.

"I promise I take care of 'im," Mahoe said. "And we be safe, you no worry, sistah. We fly out once we take care of dis' business. We still don't know if dis' a false alarm."

In the panicky moment of sorting children and luggage, Auntie Jo finally relented and gave Keoki up. Mahoe could only hope his crazy plan would work...

While the truck winds up the road, Mahoe lights a thin, hand rolled cigar, and exhales. A sharp cherry scent proliferates through the vehicle. He rolls the window down, but smoke rings still dance in the air. The rust-barnacled truck rounds a corner and approaches the guard shack at the Volcanoes National Park entrance.

A guard steps out of his station and Mahoe waves at him. The guard frowns and signals to slow down, but instead of de-accelerating, Mahoe steps on the gas – *klunk, klunk* – the truck rattles as it rides over the speed bumps. Keoki and Mahoe don't have time to see the shock on the guard's face or his angry fist raising.

"Granpa, da' soldier like stop you," Keoki says.

"No can. We gotta' talk to whoever stay in charge."

"Da' guard will call someone."

"I no care, we take our chances, boy."

The truck hums along until Mahoe sees a barricade of four military Jeeps, with eight armed soldiers. He slams on the brakes and skids to a halt. The soldiers advance, aiming at Mahoe with M-16 rifles.

" 'Dis is a bit overkill," Mahoe says with a sigh.

"Put your hands on the dashboard!" one of them orders, shouting at them. "Now!"

"Uh-oh Granpa, we in big kine trouble," wide-eyed Keoki sputters out.

The stern-faced soldiers walk around the truck. They keep their weapons trained on Mahoe. One of them opens the driver's side door.

"Sir, get out of your vehicle now and keep your hands above your head."

Tahoe slides out, keeping his hands held high. They turn him around, placing his hands up on the hood to frisk him. The passenger side door flies open and a soldier pulls the startled Keoki out of his seat.

"No hurt my grandson now. He a good boy."

Should have listened to Auntie Jo. Should have never followed Keoki out to the street to say good bye. You can't give an opihi baby a chance.

As a soldier taps Mahoe down, another officer peppers the old man with questions. "Why didn't you stop at the roadblock? Are you carrying any weapons?"

Mahoe turns his head to face his inquisitor, tweaking his voice. "I need to talk to your commanding officer about an important mattah."

The officer pulls out Mahoe's wallet and turns him around.

"Who are you?" he asks Mahoe.

"My name's Mahoe Makaweli and *this* is my grandson Keoki," he explains, softening his Hawaiian pidgin. "I was born and raised here. I work as a Hawaiian historical researcher and teacher at University of Hilo. I know about the geothermal systems that make up the island as well as the location of hidden lava tubes in the area."

Keoki pipes in. "Yeah, my Granpa know plenty 'bout da' volcano, mistah."

The superior officer takes one last look at the I.D. in Mahoe's wallet before passing it back to him, eyeing him suspiciously. "Maybe you do, and maybe you don't, but either way you're coming with me. We're going over to headquarters."

Mahoe complies and gets in the passenger seat of the military Jeep. Keoki sits in the back with a soldier. The Jeep rumbles down the road. Keoki surveys the landscape. Mahoe straightens up in the seat. If his wife was still alive, there'd be hell to pay. Of course, she'd never allow Keoki and him to go on such a dangerous escapade.

Mahoe's interest in the volcano started decades ago when he was a child. The government banned 'Olelo Hawai'i, the Hawaiian language, when the U.S. annexed Hawaii as a territory in 1898. His grandmother Makanani Wailea Kawena was raised as a devout Christian, but she honored Hawaiian culture and recounted the traditional stories about her ancestors and Hawaiian mythology to her descendants.

As a child, the tales of the awesome Madam Pele, Goddess of fire, intrigued Mahoe. As the ancient tale goes, Pele is the resourceful wanderer, traveling from island to island until she settles in the Halemau'mau crater. In one story, the jealous Pele kills her sister Hi'iaka's mortal lover. Hi'iaka grieves over his death. In her sadness, she impulsively digs a scar into the Kilauea crater, which looks like geological collapse.

Science explained what was evident, but stories provided a richness to reality.

After supporting his young family as a mechanic, Mahoe went back to college and graduate school to study Hawaiian culture and science. It was a journey that seemed so natural, he couldn't question it. Years later, he became a resource consultant for scientists interested in the Hawaiian traditions.

He knows the military won't listen to stories. Nor are they likely to view personal experience as relevant to their operation. But if he can get Susan or Tom to convince them...

The Jeep pulls up to a building.

"General's in a meeting," the superior officer says to Mahoe. "You'll have to wait."

"We can wait. I assure you officer, we mean no trouble. I'm here to 'kokua,' to help, you folks." He looks around at the line of Humvees and Jeeps. The air is hot and sulfurous. Turning his attention to the landscape, he sees a flash of reddish gold hair and a medium-tall, curvy form gliding toward them.

"Susan!" he shouts out to her, happy to see a familiar face.

"Yes. Here, in person," she says. "Officers, I know Mr. Makaweli. I've worked with him for years."

"He doesn't have any paperwork," an officer says.

"I can attest that he is credible and that he is here to help us."

"Da' Lady Bug treat you right, Dr. Susan?" he asks, instantly comfortable with her.

"Perfect. Thank you. Do you still drive it?"

"I don't drive that ol' junka' anymore.' I had give it to my niece, Leilani. I tell her, Dr. Sue is coming from da' mainland. She had to leave of course. No need for automobiles."

One of the officers clears his throat. "Hate to interrupt you two, but we have a security issue here. I have to check with headquarters to make sure Mr. Makaweli can get clearance."

Susan fails to hide her scowl. *Give it a break,* she wants to say, but she chooses to focus back to Mahoe. "Is the rest of your family safe?"

"Most went to Washington State, east of Seattle. Plenty safe dere."

The last time she saw Mahoe, he was with his large extended family – four sisters and three brothers (those who were still alive from the original 13 siblings), and children, grandchildren, and great grandchildren. There were nieces, nephews, and cousins too. Susan couldn't keep track of all the names. Everyone was huddled up at the mountain cottage, sipping hot chocolate, playing cards, and cracking jokes.

"I'm glad they're going to be safe," she says. "But what about your grandson and you? This is a potential catastrophe." Her eyes flutter with nervous energy.

"I think we can try stop them before that happens. If the commanders will listen to me and the military works quick, we'll be safe. We got an exit plan if not."

The officer returns. "You're clear, Mr. Makaweli."

"It's true. I do have information that could help."

"That's great and we'll try to get you in front of the commanding officer," the officer says.

"I like talk to 'im right now."

"That may be difficult," the officer says. "He's super busy right now. And, frankly, he's stubborn as a mule."

"I used to train mules, long time ago when I lived on a ranch," Mahoe says. "My grand-son ova' dere, he say I'm one old mule. We can do stubborn."

Susan watches Keoki totter over to his grandpa wearing a plaid shirt, jeans, and worn-out cowboy boots. Dark brown locks frame his heart-shaped face. Pronounced dimples bookmark his perfect white teeth.

"He's a beautiful boy," Susan says. "You're not worried about him being here?"

"What good dat gonna' do? He'd be safer with ohana, yeah, but he like stay with his Tutu Kane. You may think I'm crazy, but we gonna' stop those terrorists in their tracks. As for Keoki, don't let his age fool you. Sometime he pick his nose and act like a keiki, but he's smart as a whip. I can't get anyting past 'im. So bettah' watch out."

He turns aside. "Eh Keoki, this is Mrs. Dr. Andrews. I can call her Dr. Sue, but she's Dr. Andrews to you, okay? Act nice."

The boy giggles, eyes widening. "You gonna' save us from bad guyz? If you a superhero, where's da' cape?"

"It's in the wash, love."

"How you foget' dat? We gotta' save da' island!"

"You're right about that, Keoki." Susan turns to Mahoe. "He knows what's going on."

"Pretty much."

"That's a lot for him to take in."

"No worries, he can handle. No doubts or fears for Keoki. Bettah' to have da faith of one child, ya' know."

"I guess so."

"Dr. Tom around?" Mahoe asks.

"He should be here any moment."

She wants Mahoe to divulge his knowledge, but perhaps the secrecy is a protective measure. She recalls when he escorted Tom and her on a night expedition out to a remote lava flow. It was a long hike over rough terrain, and there was the darkness to contend with, but Mahoe never complained. They spent hours taking photographs of the flow and surveying the area. Susan remembered how he rattled off various Hawaiian myths as he assisted them in each task with precision.

He didn't have to rely on technology; he was a true citizen scientist of his environment, hyper-observant and very knowledgeable about the island. He knew which vents to look into at what time and for how long. His volcano knowledge did not just rely on charts, data, or statistics and although he was familiar with scientific methodology, he operated beyond the realm of facts and figures.

Mainland westerners might react with skepticism or guarded awe, but in Susan's opinion, Mahoe was a one-of-a-kind geological prophet. She had never met anyone like him.

"Susie," she hears her husband call out. She gestures for Mahoe to wait by the Jeep as she walks up to meet Tom halfway. He's cleaned up, dressed in a spiffy aloha shirt and khakis. His wavy hair is loose and tousled, an errant strand falling over one eye.

"You look nice, love," she says.

He greets her with a hug and kiss, and then abruptly pulls back. "You really shouldn't be here. It's way too dangerous."

"You keep saying that. Fact is, you shouldn't be here without me. So here I am." She grins and walks with him over to the Jeep. "You remember Mr. Makaweli?"

"Of course. Our Hawaiian consultant from the summer expedition." He leans forward and shakes Mahoe's hand. "Great to see you again."

"I have plenty good kine data that can help this operation, Dr. Tom."

"Great. Mr. Makaweli, could you give us a moment?"

"Sure 'ting."

Tom leads Susan off a few yards to the other side of a building. "And exactly why did you bring him here?"

"I didn't. He came by himself."

"The higher-ups aren't giving me the time of day. What makes you think they're going to listen to an old dude? The mainland military is not exactly known for their aloha spirit or sense of inclusion. We're in the middle of a frickin' national emergency here."

"Well, from their string of failures with this mission, it sounds like they could use some different tactics. I think we should at least give him a chance," Susan says.

"Is this one of your 'woman intuition moments?'"

"So what if it is? You're going to have to trust me."

"They won't be on board," Tom says, shaking his head. "It's old school, boys' club, by-the-book protocol."

Susan looks over his shoulder at Sal and McGregor. Her eyes widen and her voice drops to a whisper. "They're right behind you."

Stunned, Tom whips around.

Sal muses. "That's right, we do have our protocol, but a woman's intuition? Now that's a subject that's always fascinated me. How'd we ever win a war without it?"

General McGregor stands next to him, cracking a smile.

"She's like this before coffee," Tom says.

Susan rolls her eyes. *Thanks for defending me, Tom. Maybe if the military listened to intuition they wouldn't be in such a mess? Jerks.*

The bizarre visages of the General and Colonel temporarily distract her from Tom's remark. She watches them with curiosity. The General's face is haggard, yet dignified, a map of many weathered storms and seasons. She doesn't know what to make of the eye patch. It's almost comical, but frightening to think of the reality. *Did he really lose his eye in battle?*

The Colonel is almost a foot shorter than the General, yet somehow more threatening. He's stocky, square-jawed, and built like a pit-bull. He exudes an air of protectiveness and inner strength, until she glances at his wild, furry eyebrows. *They look like they might crawl right off his face...*

While she's thinking this, she addresses them in her most polite British voice. "Thank you both for your leadership. Now, I also want to introduce you to someone."

"Suze," Tom says, trying to deter her. He sets a hand on her shoulder. She brushes him off and waves Mahoe over.

"Gentlemen, this is Mahoe Makaweli, a very knowledgeable volcano consultant. We've worked with him before."

"Yes, sirs," Mahoe says, toning back his pidgin slang. "I can tell you what you need to know once we take a seat. These old feet are growin' tired."

McGregor nods. "All right. Lead the way. Please, remember, time is of the essence."

Mahoe shuffles off with Keoki beside him. The others follow and circle around Mahoe at the picnic bench.

The vog settles in as sulfur fumes rise from the caldera. South and east of the grassy park, lava fields stretch out to the horizon and thousands of fissures run across the surface, interrupted by jagged saw-tooth rocks and sprigs of stunted trees, weeds, and ferns. Military men and women walk around the premises. Susan spots a squad of armed soldiers moving in formation along a nearby path.

"You've got three minutes," McGregor announces.

Undeterred by the General's gruffness, Mahoe leans back and kicks his legs out.

"Ahem," Sal taps his watch.

"I get one old story that could help you find the lava tube entrance. I'll speak clearly, so you understand."

"A story, huh?" Sal says. "Continue."

"One day, long time ago, when I was one boy about Keoki's age, my ohana and I stayed in our cabin close by. One morning I went hiking wit' my dog Laka. He was a collie mix, a *poi* dog or what you call a mutt. Anyways, I was hiking in the forest and Laka started barkin' and he runs right off. I call after him, 'Laka, Laka, where you going?'

"But he no listen. So I follow his tracks to a lava tube hole hidden in the bush. I know he was on to something. I follow him into the lava tube, crawlin' on my hands and knees a few yards and then the lava tube opens up! It was about fifteen feet tall inside and just as wide. It was incredible. Most tubes are small and narrow. I had heard of these big tubes, but neva' had seen or been in one."

"All right," the General says "secret entrance to a lava tube. Got it. But we need you to speed up the story here."

"Okay, I keep walkin' and callin' for Laka, 'til I get near da' tunnel end and I see a light coming out of one *puka*, a small hole. It's about two feet above ground. I start pullin' away chunks of lava rock.

"Laka had gone in there. So, I crawl in and enter a big cave. It was warm. I could smell sulfur and see molten lava. I hear Laka barking. I run over to him and wrap my arms around him. And then I look across and see that he is barkin' at one big ol' boar."

"What does a wild pig have to do with a terrorist hideout?" Sal interjects.

"That was what Laka was afta.' Makes sense, yeah?" Mahoe speeds up his storytelling pace. "So I tell Laka, 'Dat's one big pig, but we gotta' get outta' here, so let's go home.' We crawl through the lava tube and back up da' tunnel. We was about half way out when I start feeling all dizzy kine. I look down at Laka and he stay moving real slow. So I stop and sit next to him, then I lay down and fall asleep.

"I don't know how long I was out, but when I wake up Laka is barking again. I look up and think I'm dreamin.' But no! Right there in front of me was one super tall lady, dressed in red and gold, wearing one long, flowing dress. Her hair was long and black, but she was so beautiful."

"A woman in a dress? In the middle of Kilauea's lava tube system?" Sal scoffs in disbelief. His eyebrows furrow as he glances to McGregor. They shrug shoulders at one another.

Mahoe continues. "It's true. The woman was towering over me. She seem like maybe ten, twelve-feet tall. I look in her eyes and see flames of fire! She's glowing, all orange and red. Den I knew who she was. She spoke to me, with a voice like thunder.

'Get up, go now!' she say. Me and Laka, we run for our lives outta' of dere. When I look back, she had changed into a huge flame of fire, like one big fountain of lava! I know for sure who she was – don't know why it took me so long…"

Mahoe pauses, his eyes gazing in reverie.

"Well, who was she?" Sal says.

"The Guardian of the Volcano. Madam Pele."

Sal scoffs. "Really? I don't mean to be insensitive, Mr. Mahoe, but this sounds to me like you were hallucinating from the noxious fumes. I can't buy into mythical malarkey. Whatever it is, or was, it's not the type of intel we're looking for."

"I can assure you, Commanders, it's no malarkey. I tell you da' truth, believe it or not, I saw her with my own eyes. And I know the location of the lava tube that leads to those caves. It can only be that one place where the ceiling is so high and open. It's the hidden entrance…so small, you can easily miss it. I'm sorry that I don't say the exact location. It was years ago, but I can show you the general area."

Sal shifts on the bench and glances sideways for second. "Well, the element of surprise could work in our favor."

"Look, I get one map," Mahoe says, taking out a crumpled page.

It's a sketch of twisting and interconnecting tunnels that reminds Susan of a subway map. She holds one end of the map as Tom, Sal, and the General look at it.

Tom squints. "I'll be the first to admit, my own geological maps of Kilauea couldn't pinpoint the exact location of the terrorists' lair."

"It's quite detailed," Sal chimes in.

"All right then," the General announces. "You have one hour."

"To what?" Susan says.

"Find that damn lava tube."

One bloody hour?

Susan can't believe it. She watches military personnel escort Mahoe and Keoki toward the truck. Mahoe walks slowly, shoulders hunched, while his grandson buzzes around him like an energetic fly, chattering away.

"Keoki also want to give you some-ting," Mahoe calls back to Tom and Susan.

The boy runs back to the couple and holds out a small leather bag for

Tom. Hesitantly, Tom takes the bags and examines the contents – a dozen shiny red berries. "Coffee?"

"Sacred ohelo berries," Keoki says. "You throw 'em in da lava for good luck and maybe Pele will protect you. And don't worry about me, Doctors. My Granpa' and God gonna' keep me safe. We gotta' leave now."

Keoki turns and scurries back to his grandfather. They stand there for a second. With their matching smiles and twinkling eyes, Susan sees the clear genetic link. *Yet how can they remain so calm?* They wave goodbye, in the same rhythm, hands slightly cupped, smiling. The warm casualness of the Hawaiian culture always appealed to Susan.

"Take care, be safe, and thank you," she says as she waves back and restrains a quiet cry.

Tom is nonplussed as he explains to her that a military official is picking up Bernie and driving him over to the Thurston lava tube. "Or I guess we could just leave him in the cabin with his comic books."

"The Thurston lava tube is huge. We could use his help," Susan says.

"Yeah, okay." They step up into the Jeep. Tom takes out his cell phone and starts dialing. "Jer?"

"Lord help us. Why are you calling him? We know where we're going."

"I just have to verify some info. It'll only take a sec… Jerry, I need you to look up some data on the Thurston lava tube. I have this strange map from our Hawaii consultant."

Susan overhears loud rock music blasting on Jerry's end of the line. She knows he's probably in his small, messy office, surrounded by piles of empty energy drink cans, his feet perched on the table. Maybe he's playing darts or computer games.

"No Jer, I don't want to hear about the underwater caverns off Greece," Tom says. "Look up the shield volcano file. I'll wait. Yes, I know about the collapses…you're saying there was one in the 1950s. Sealed off the lower main section? That's all we need to know. Thanks, bud."

He hits end on his cell phone and glances over to Susan. He brushes his hand against hers. "It's good to know that we should start in the lower section," he says. "Even still, it might be near impossible to find it."

"And we don't have much time," she says, sighing. Under her shorts, the upholstery feels hot and itchy, only ratcheting up the anxiety even more.

The Jeep stops for a large convoy of troop carriers and supply trucks. Eight Marines disembark from a vehicle and unload their supplies.

Susan squeezes Tom's hand. She wants to believe him. She wants to respond with a joke or some light-hearted, witty comment. But in all truth, she's never been so scared in her whole life as she is right now.

Chapter Twenty-Three

"Tainted Blood"

In a smoke filled cavern, Kim Sung faces a rock wall, where he has set up a shrine. A gold Buddha figurine shimmers by candlelight and incense burns with a pungent aroma.

His devout grandparents were Buddhist practitioners. From them, he learned the sacred teachings of the Eightfold Path – Right View, Right Thought, Right Speech, Right Action, Right Livelihood, Right Effort, Right Mindfulness, Right Concentration.

So how did he reconcile peaceful Buddhist philosophy with being a military man? He couldn't. But no man is free of hypocrisy. Korean Christians, claiming allegiance to God and Jesus, set fire to Buddhist temples and decapitated statues. Some of the Muslims were terrorists. Communists preached equality, yet their leaders were tyrants.

The Buddha himself came from a family of warriors and the study of the Vedas included knowledge of close combat fighting, archery, swordsmanship, and horsemanship. To follow the path of Buddha-dharma is to bear up under hardships in the search for enlightenment. Discipline, courage, honor. Virtues of a serious Buddhist practitioner are the same qualities needed for a strong valiant warrior.

So Kim Sung meditates, tapping into awareness and preparing himself for the next step. The light flickers and he senses disruption. Ho Dam enters the cave.

"Are you done yet?" Ho Dam says. "We're ready to strike."

Calmly, Kim Sung pivots around and looks at him. "No, not yet. Please sit. Join me in meditation."

"Do I look like I have time for candles and prayers?" he says while he raises his arms in exasperation. Low candlelight swathes the tension in his angular face.

"Sit," Kim Sung orders.

"You're wasting time."

"*Time?*" Kim Sung says, raising his eyebrows. "You know nothing of time or patience. I have waited over fifty long years for this day, but you have stolen our victory." He stares at Ho Dam. "You are *beulsun*, tainted blood!"

"You can't throw that word around. You are a coward!"

Kim Sung turns away and looks back to the wall, maintaining his calm. "Who gave you authority to execute that hostage?"

"No one had to! Retribution for our massacred families. You were there. Have you so easily forgotten?"

Standing up to stretch, Kim Sung nods with disapproval. "You've jeopardized this entire mission. Your stupidity has caused the Americans to send reinforcements. Now they will attack."

"Let them," Ho Dam says with a shrug. "We'll execute the rest of the hostages and detonate the bombs."

"No, you are not speaking wisely. We must start surrendering hostages in exchange for safe passage home."

He waits for Ho Dam's spitfire response, but there is none, only the weighty lull of silence. Then Ho Dam laughs loudly. His giddy snorts reverberate through the cave and ricochet, echoing off the walls.

"You're an old fool! That's exactly what the Americans want."

Kim Sung chooses not to speak, focusing on the altar. With his back to Ho Dam, he'll offer another prayer, a thousand prayers if necessary, for his impulsive stepson. He cannot take this personally. Once upon a time, he was also impatient fool. Only through prayer and meditation was he able move through those feelings and quiet his mind.

"You're not going to say anything?" Ho Dam asks.

"What can I say? You've disobeyed my order. The consequence speaks for itself. I am relieving you of your command."

Kim Sung senses movement, closer and closer... he whirls around and blocks Ho Dam's punch with his left arm. Simultaneously, he clamps his right hand on Ho Dam's neck, digging fingertips into soft flesh. The prayer beads dangle from his left hand. He raises the beads before Ho Dam's startled, frightened eyes.

"You are still so weak," Kim Sung says, disgusted. He pushes the younger man away, releasing him to stumble backwards.

Ho Dam grumbles in a hoarse voice. "You're crazy." Crouched down and hunched over, he coughs to regain his breath. "All your talk of peace and you want to fight me!" He rises to his full height, clenching his fists and shaking his head.

Kim Sung is unfazed by the temper tantrum. "And *you* are still an immature child."

"AAAhhhh!" Ho Dam screams and lunges toward him. Kim Sung ducks and Ho Dam flies past him, smashing into the altar. A candle extinguishes.

"*Gyeorugi!*" he declares, jumping to his feet again.

"So be it," says Kim Sung. "Gyeorugi. We will spar. Now, set your gun down."

Ho Dam unclasps his pistol from his utility belt and sets it on a rock ledge.

"*Charyot*," they say in unison, announcing the spar. They stand at attention and bow to each other. With hands raised, they circle around, moving slowly in calculated steps.

Suddenly, Ho Dam lashes out, throwing the first kick, a side kick. Kim Sung blocks it. Ho Dam throws another kick, a high one aimed at the face, only to have Kim Sung effortlessly obstruct it again. Four Korean soldiers rush into the cavern entrance and stop to watch this strange entertainment.

"Commander Kim Sung is winning," one soldier quips to another.

Ho Dam overhears the gossip and catches his breath. "Get out of here, you idiots!"

They move back, but continue to observe the spar. The duo swing back and forth like a menacing pendulum. Ho Dam unleashes a furious assault, a spinning wheel of limbs, but Kim Sung blocks every punch and kick, holding his prayer beads in hand. He is up against the wall when Ho Dam throws a fist toward his face.

Kim Sung tilts his head, allowing the fist to fly past him and slam into the rock wall. Ho Dam yelps. Kim Sung leans back and waits. A vestige of candlelight flickers on his dark skin, his nose and eyebrows outlined in shadows. Ho Dam clutches his sore fist and straightens his posture. Then Kim Sung leaps forward. He throws a powerful kick to Ho Dam's unguarded stomach. The force sends Ho Dam reeling backward and dropping to his knees.

Show him that I am serious, Kim Sung thinks. *Just enough to end this nonsense.* He steps behind Ho Dam and wraps the prayer beads around his neck. With his foot pushed against Ho Dam's back, he pulls on the beads.

"Now you will submit." He pulls the beads tighter and Ho Dam gasps. "It's never too late to pray," Kim Sung says with force.

Ho Dam shakes his head. His eyes roll back. He's losing consciousness, slipping away.

Kim Sung releases the tension and kicks the middle of Ho Dam's back, sending him flailing into the gravel. He lies there for a minute before wiping tears from his eyes. Then he kneels, spits the dust from his mouth, and staggers upright. He massages the red, bead-inscribed impression on his throat and stares vehemently at the soldiers.

"Seize him," Ho Dam says to the guards.

The men hesitate, questioning who they should give allegiance to, while Kim Sung is bent over picking up pieces of the wrecked altar.

Ho Dam clears his throat and manages to blurt out. "He is a traitor. No better than the Americans. We answer to a united Korea, not to this old bastard. He wants us to surrender. If we do, we will be imprisoned and die there!" Ho Dam reaches for his gun and he points it at the soldiers. "Do it. Now."

Submitting to the new orders, the three soldiers escort Kim Sung into the hostage cave. He walks with his head bowed toward an unoccupied area and he sits down on the ground. Confused, the hostages look at him, careful not to stare either. Irene is lying on her side, whimpering, while another woman sits next to her, offering comfort.

Kim Sung raises his head to her. "I am sorry for what happened to your husband. I did not order his execution. Perhaps you don't believe me, but I know what it's like to watch your loved ones die." He feels a sharpness in his ribs, pain that time has still not healed.

"I do believe you," she says before turning away.

Arnold Dillon, a reedy-looking man, stands up and walks over to Kim Sung. The guards take notice, but he appears too weak to do anything dangerous. "I thought you might be hungry," Arnold says in a southern accent, offering a bowl of rice to Kim Sung. "It's hardly cooked, but it'll do."

"No thank you." Kim Sung swats it away from him. The bowl flies out of Arnold's hand. It clanks on the ground as the rice scatters like a spray of tiny white bullets on the dark gravel, startling some of the hostages. "Sorry folks," Arnold sighs in frustration. "Ain't much good anyway.

All the while, Kim Sung tries to keep his mind on his breath. Yet he finds that his mind is wandering. The meditation was fruitless. Memories return.

No Gun Ri Bridge.
His brother, shot in his mother's arms.
Then the slaughter.

The dead, piled under the bridge, soon start to smell in the heat. He's buried under stacks of men, women, children, babies. And quietly he waits all night, making sure the soldiers are gone.

In the morning, his voice groans from beneath the bodies. Kim Sung writhes and pushes, extricating himself from the human mass of death. He crawls out and stumbles over the corpses. He's frightened and breathing hard above the blood soaked earth. He straightens up for a moment, taking in the gruesome sight. Bodies, transitioning from life to death.

Kim Sung backs away, shaking his head in horror and confusion. He falls over a body and stifles a scream. It's a young woman, maybe nineteen or twenty years old. Her eyes stare back at him, round and large as onion bulbs, frozen in permanent panic. Her lips are pursed as if to say "no." Somehow her face is unblemished, white like porcelain, innocent, but her body is covered with blood.

I am sorry, he wants to say, but his voice is raspy and dry. "Sorry" won't do any good anyway. He stumbles, walking as fast as he can, in the opposite direction that the U.S. soldiers went. At least he has that much sense. Where are the other survivors? He slept little through the night, but managed to doze off, knocked out by sheer exhaustion.

He is delirious and doesn't know where he's going. He has no home anymore. Yesterday he had a family – a mother and siblings, but now they are all dead. And he is alone, an orphan and a refugee.

He walks up to the road, shading his eyes from a harsh morning sun. What happened? He's like a monk, focused on the present, telling himself there is no permanence. Certainly, the past has been obliterated. As for the future, he cannot say.

His ears still ring from the gunfire and the screams of the victims, but he can also hear crickets murmur and songbirds chirp. Then he hears another soft sound. A crying infant. Alive. How many times did he hear his baby brother cry and ignore him? So why does it startle Kim Sung now? It is the only sound of human life he has heard for many hours. He turns left, toward the source of the cry.

First, he sees a woman lying under a tree, dappled by the shade, leaf silhouettes dancing on her. She could be asleep. She is another survivor and she'll wake up soon, he tells himself.

He nudges her, but upon closer inspection he sees it – the blood seeping from the top of her forehead, gravity fed liquid, running like a tributary down the side of her face to her breasts and into a stream that pools in her lap, then across her loins before wrapping around her thighs and staining her white cotton dress a purplish red. Her face is still, expressionless. She is not moving or waking up and doesn't appear to be breathing.

She loosely holds a small, moving bundle, shifting in her arms. At some point she was clutching this bundle, perhaps at the literal point of death, when her spirit left her body. Just like his mother did earlier.

Kim Sung bends down and unwraps the bundle. It's a healthy infant child. He smiles at the new life and picks up the crying baby and cradles it in his arms. A little, newborn baby boy, just like his brother was. The infant's dark hair is thick, his head oval-shaped, eyes wide and searching. Kim Sung holds the baby close. He stops crying. Cradling the baby, Kim Sung crosses the path to the upper foothills.

For miles, he walks with the baby in his arms. He stops for breaks and prays for water. Just before sunset, he reaches a hidden mountain village. The farmers end their shift and the women sweep away the summer dust. It's the end of the sowing season. Children chase butterflies. It is quiet here, undisturbed by any military presence. It's like his own village, miles away. Or like his village used to be.

The baby starts to cry again – these cries are different – weak, but urgent. Impatient for sustenance. Maybe I've made a mistake? Maybe I should have just let this child die? Or maybe someone in this village will show us mercy? He tries to soothe the hungry baby and yet Kim Sung needs soothing himself. Water, food, a bath, rest, real sleep. In his famished, delirious state it looks as though the village homes swell and shift like mirages.

A slender girl (a mirage too?) hangs laundry on a line. Her mouth puckers in a whistle that he cannot hear. She peers up, stares at him, and he knows she is talking, but he can't make out what she is saying. Thirst overwhelms him. She nods, fervently, then scurries back into the house. A few seconds later an older replica of the girl appears, her mother no doubt. The mother gestures for him to come inside, saying, "We will help you." Kim Sung hands her the child, then he falls back, fainting in the dirt.

Kim Sung stayed in the village with the baby, caring for him as if he were his own younger brother. It felt good to have a brother again and a safe haven. A home again. The child and Kim Sung both grew up in that village until they were both young adults.
Eventually, he fell in love and married the young laundry girl. Her mother passed away a few months after their wedding, and so with the help of villagers they raised the baby boy. They named him Heo Dam (Ho Dam), "heo" meaning advocate, "dam" meaning gall. He certainly lived up to his name.

"Yes, he did," Kim Sung nods, whispering to the cave walls. Ho Dam has always been a strange one, obsessed with the cause, emboldened by the tragedy, although he was only an infant when it happened.

Perhaps Kim Sung had told him the story way too many times. He blames himself for that. Still, there is something else. It's as if some intangible, malevolent, demonic energy had sunk talons into Ho Dam when he was just a boy. The wounds did not heal as he grew up.

Kim Sung first attributed it to typical male teenage hormones. But Ho Dam never grew out of that aggressive phase. He had been heartless and thoughtless in the worst ways, hurting small animals and picking on children who could not defend themselves. As an adult, it seemed he was always teetering on a precipice between cool impatience and hot anger.

Kim Sung denied it for many years, but this latest inexcusable act of aggression caused him to realize something. Though he hates to admit it, his adopted child is *beulsun*, "tainted blood." The only thing he can do is stop Ho Dam, even if it means hurting him. He can't allow him to continue on this path, ravaging and killing, in a misleading crusade for vengeance.

Chapter Twenty-Four

"Coastal Cliff Stabilization"

Layers of vog intensify the sunset colors on the Big Island's southeast coastline. A U.S. Navy Carrier Air Wing (CVW) operates offshore. The CVW consists of squadrons of aircraft from fixed-wing aircraft to rotary aircraft. Organized from central command, the CVW conducts air operations, dispatched from a nearby USS Aircraft Carrier.

CVW provides the air cover and support capabilities for the Carrier Strike Group (CSG). This CSG consists of a wide array of air, land, and sea vessels that descend and work on miles of the towering, volcanic coastal cliffs. Guided Missile Cruisers, a Destroyer, Merchant Marine ships, and Military Sealift Command ships accompany the aircraft carrier. Their mission – to reduce cliff fall-out, by stabilizing the cliff faces with anchors and wire mesh fencing, thereby mitigating the effects of any potential tsunami.

U.S. military helicopters and jets fly to and from the carrier to the coastline. The Marines work closely with U.S. naval forces. Their military personnel, amphibious warfare ships, and tactical aviation squadrons, known as Marine Fighter Attack squadrons, are stationed aboard the carrier.

The Marines utilize their fleet of Harrier II Jump Jets – jet-powered attack aircraft capable of vertical/short takeoff and landing operations. The Harriers are versatile, with helicopter-type hover abilities. They function from improvised bases, such as car parks or forest clearings, without requiring large and vulnerable air bases. Like large wasps, the Harriers hover, firing stability anchors onto the cliff faces.

It's a massive joint effort with synchronized systems, logistics, people, vessels, vehicles, and aircraft. Soldiers repel down the cliff, attaching thick cable lines to the anchors. Helicopters, laden with cargo, lower rolls of metal wire fencing and crates of supplies to the military personnel and merchant marines on the cliff tops. With D-9 tractors, the team guides the wire rolls to the edge. Then they attach the metal rolls to cables and secure them to the bluff.

From above, the men and their machinery look like busy insects, skittering on the cliffs. The 1,000-foot-tall coastal cliffs dwarf the soldiers and only a small, half-mile section of the cliffs has been fenced off. The rest awaits coverage. A daunting, Herculean task to be completed.

Chapter Twenty-Five

"The Lava Tube"

Twert-twert-twert...

Signals from the terrestrial sonic depth scanner-sensors echo off the lava tube walls. Newly acquired by the U.S. Military, the devices were developed for the mining industry by a Swiss company. Tom, Susan, and Bernie wave the sensors along different areas of the cave, trying to detect any substantial cracks and weak spots, the potential openings to a lava tube. Headlamps focus light while the three of them crouch and rise in the damp, cool recess.

"How much time do we have?" Susan asks Tom.

He stops and glances down at his watch. "Ten minutes."

"Can I look at Mahoe's map again?"

"Good luck making any sense of it."

He hands her the map and she looks down at the circuit of black lines. She reads the phrase *secret tube* next to a thin, meandering line.

"The map is worthless," Tom says. "I mean, yeah, there's some thought put into it, but it's not helpful."

"I'm afraid you may be right." Sighing in frustration, she hands it back to him.

"I like Mahoe. He's a good guy. But he's getting old and probably a bit senile," Tom says as he rolls up the map. Bernie asks to use it.

"You sure, kid?" Tom says. "We've only got a few minutes left. I'm going to have to alert the military. You guys can keep at it, but I have to report in. There's no cell service here. Gotta' head up."

Susan nods to him. She paces back from the cave wall and clucks her tongue against the roof of her mouth. To some degree, she's used to this. It's usually a trial and error process. But they've never had to work against a cataclysmic ticking clock.

Is it even worth it? Couldn't the government just throw some money at the terrorists and call it a day? Does our military even need to be involved with Korea anymore?

"American hegemony," she grumbles to herself. If Tom didn't get paid, or if the work was boring, she wouldn't tolerate this frustration. She walks further back into the tube. She calls out for Bernie, but he's nowhere to be seen.

Then she notices his tattered backpack, now darkened with volcanic soot. Next to the pack is his abandoned scanner. Her headlamp light darts back and forth between two adjoining walls.

"Bernie, where are you?" she says as she shines the light around in circles. "Please, don't disappear. This is the last thing we need."

"BOO!"

"Whoa!" She lurches back and looks down.

There he is, jutting out of a hole near the ground, his head, face, and shoulders covered in black, lava rock dust.

"You scared the dickens out of me," she says.

"It's dark in here. I've got a light though. And no nightmares…or would those be day-mares? Anyway, I'm pretty sure this is the hidden entrance."

"How did you ever find it?"

"The map." He pauses. "It may look confusing, but it's really not. It's a simple scale. Mahoe didn't label it, but it was easy to figure out. I thought the opening was close to ground level because of its relative low position on the map. Didn't even need to use my scanner. Sorry for scaring you. The darkest hour is just before the dawn, right? We can hope for the best."

"I hope your optimism pays off. We need to hurry and let Tom know." Together, Susan and Bernie scramble back up to the main entrance of the Thurston tube.

"We found it! Bernie found it."

Tom's mouth drops. He shakes his head in disbelief. "I guess we better call the Colonel."

Minutes later, Sal and the platoon arrive, looking out of place in military garb among the delicate staghorn ferns and flowering ginger. Sal wears his BDU, knee and elbow pads, a helmet, and body armor. He straps a rifle over his shoulder and secures a pistol at his side.

He then hands Tom a Kevlar vest, ballistic helmet, and night-vision goggles. "Sorry, there's no insignia on your vest."

"I'm not that kind of doctor anyway."

"Right." Sal gives him a communication set. "Don't break it."

"I've been fiddling with gadgets since I was a kid." With assistance from the technicians, Tom readies himself.

Susan watches on, her stomach churning with anxiety. "Do you think this is necessary, Colonel? I mean, he *is* a civilian."

Sal doesn't answer and Tom ignores her stare while he buckles the vest. "Tom, you're acting as if this is just another day, like it's no big deal," she says.

"I agreed to it," he says, still evading eye contact with her. "We have to stop total destruction from happening or we lose, big time."

"Why you? You've done enough. They have the information they need. So, maybe a delusional part of me imagined that this would be all peace and love and sunshine in Hawaii, but that doesn't mean we should be *here*, in this cave, close to the terrorists."

"I have to get the troops acquainted with the cave. A scout mission to set them in the right direction. I'll turn around and come back after that. By the way, I was reluctant to come over. You were the one chompin' at the bit."

"So I could be with you!"

Tom leans over to kiss her cheek, encumbered by the new uniform. She is too tired to protest the advance. Moreover, his breath is surprisingly fresh and his embrace comforts her. Years ago, when she was a romantic school girl, she read wartime stories of people falling in love when the stakes were high, regarding each moment as a precious gift. Even at the time she considered it too sentimental and dramatic. Now she realizes there's truth behind it. This could be the last time they see each other.

She turns away, crying. A military tech offers a "sorry, ma'am" condolence and escorts Bernie and her back to the base camp.

Tom re-focuses. He directs Sal and the twelve men Special Ops team to the entrance. Undeterred by the uniforms' weight, the Ops follow him and Sal as they get down on all fours and shimmy through the passageway. The ceiling's basalt lavacicles chip off and crackle above their heads. The floor is rough, created from decades of volcanic activity.

But nowhere near a flow, Tom thinks, reassuring himself. It is wet and cool inside the tube. Some of the military men make wisecracks about being in a volcano birth canal ("She gonna' push us out?"), meanwhile Tom only sees the particular details: a pale moth flies toward the headlamp's light. Down below, a tubular helicite rises from the cave's floor like a twisting branch. Helicites are delicate and it's possible that unintentional contact could scrape them off, thus endangering the cave ecosystem. It's no use mentioning this to the soldiers. They wouldn't understand.

Beep-beep-beep.

He hears Susan's voice echo through the communication headset. "Tom, do you read me? Hello?"

"Hey, I was just thinking about you."

"Really?"

"No, I was actually thinking that I haven't devoted enough time to observing cave micro-flora and fauna."

"Of course. Now you promise me you'll turn around when you can, yes?"

"Roger Dodger. I mean, I promise."

The tunnel opens up to a wider passage. Sal and Tom rise to their feet. The platoon leader and squad follow three paces behind them.

"You still there?" Susan says.

"We might lose communication. If you start fretting, lovey, think about our last vacation."

"That was our honeymoon, years ago."

"And it was one of the best times of my life."

Tom gets on his hands and knees again to crouch under a low overhang of stalactites. "When this is finally over," he says, "we'll take a couple weeks off to go on a real vacation. No conferences, no expeditions."

"No research?"

"Yes."

Suddenly, a loud rumbling fills the cavern.

"Tom? What the hell's going on?"

His communication cuts off. Tom and the rest of the men sprawl onto the ground. Rocks and dirt pummel them while they lunge forward and scramble for cover. Tom covers his head and rolls under a ledge. Behind them, the passageway collapses. Bombarded by debris, the platoon members scramble backwards.

The quake subsides, dust settles. With his headlight flicked on, Tom looks to the surroundings. The tube is still open in the direction they are heading, but the passageway behind them has sealed shut, separating them from the team. Sal lies on the floor, eyes closed, helmet knocked off his head, forehead smeared with his fresh blood.

"Colonel?" Tom gives his headset a shake before he yanks it off. He kneels down, on level with the unconscious Sal. "Wake up! C'mon."

Tom positions himself behind Sal and lifts him up, trying to rouse him. "You're breathing, sir. You're alive. Wake up now."

Sal's head falls into his lap. He groans and then opens his eyes. He pushes Tom away. "That was...that was weird."

"You mean being in my lap? No time for military homophobia-paranoia."

Sal stands up. "Ah no, I'm dizzy," he says as he stumbles over the debris, rubbing his head and covering his wound. He grabs Tom's shoulder to steady himself.

"Are you okay?" Tom asks. "Do you want a bandage for your bloody forehead?"

"I'm fine. No, I don't need a Band-Aid right now," he mutters.

"It's not been verified, but we can assume there's been another detonation, which resulted in an earthquake."

"Before we take another step," Sal says, "I'll need to contact HQ to get an update on the orders."

"Your headset is wasted. I know mine is. Communication could be completely down."

Giving Tom an irritated look, Sal grabs his rifle, shakes the dust off it, and takes out a replacement headset from his backpack. He turns on the headset and makes attempts to connect to the base camp. "Big Dog to Lucky Lady, come in, over, over. Damn, it's just static."

"The obstruction from cave-in debris interference may have cut off our radio contact."

"You're probably right." Sal pauses. "The Medevac team will arrive to pick up any injured platoon guys, meanwhile we're stuck here 'til they dig us out. It'll take 'em hours to clear that. We can sit here and wait or continue on and try to find the enemy's locale."

"Your call, Commander."

"We better keep moving." Sal picks up his dented helmet, adjusts his headlamp, and starts walking across a clutter of loose rocks.

Tom exhales. "My wife's going to be beside herself. Sorry, Suze."

Tom steps through the tunnel. He can hear his own heartbeat. His breath slackens, boots crunching on the volcanic rock pebbles, while the rusty odor of the Colonel's drying blood wafts in the stale air. The tube narrows. There's a source of light up ahead and he feels the air warming before they approach a deep, glowing channel ten feet below them.

"Lava?" they say in unison.

"I didn't expect to see it so soon," Tom says.

"Your guy's Madam Pele. Here she is."

The heat is intense and through its haze they see bubbles coalesce on the surface, loosening rocks on the banks and carrying the rocks down into a winding, molten stream. They walk parallel to the lava stream, until it curves and cuts across, intersecting their path. Standing back, away from the throbbing heat, they observe the area above the flow. Their headlamps light up the cavern walls.

"There has to be a way around this," Sal says. The ceiling above them is low, amplifying the heat.

Tom assesses the dilemma. The ceiling surface is smooth and there's nothing to cling onto, so even if they had the appropriate climbing gear, the task would be impossible. Their own suits protect them from residual heat, yet there is no way to traipse through 2,000-degree lava.

"We'll have to turn around and find another route," Tom says. "It's a maze, but we'll find something."

Sal searches the bank of the stream across from him. He lets out a long, measured breath. "It's not an Olympic jump. Maybe only eight or nine feet across. I think we can make it."

"The body armor weighs a lot. This isn't a high school track meet either. We're not going to get a little grass stain if we fall," Tom says.

Sal back-steps, calculating the distance. In a manner of seconds, he runs ahead, leaping over the stream and landing solidly on a flat, protruding rock a few feet above the flow. He then jumps to the other side.

Tom shouts out. "Way to go, G.I. Joe!"

"I showed you how it's done. It's easy. Don't slip."

"Can you throw me a rope or something?" Tom hollers. Sal continues his trek down the next section of the tunnel, away from the flow. "Tough love, huh?" Tom mutters. "Guess, he still wants to play his macho game."

Tom steps back to study the jump. The rock he needs to reach is no larger than a couple feet across, its surface semi-flat for landing, if he hits it at the right angle. There are a few smaller, closer rocks jutting out above the surface, but from his vantage point they don't look stable. Through the heat, he can tell that there is no uniformity in the rocks' formations and no clear pattern to guide his jump choices. From one direction, he could be safe, landing on the right spot, with the proper momentum. *But, if I overshoot or undershoot or hit the wrong side? I'm burned. Literally.*

Even falling for a second into a shallow section would be painful. If he survived, he'd be maimed with third degree burns for the rest of his life. And if the river is deep, he would sink into it and melt into the molten lava. The stream would then carry away his entombed remains to some undetermined shore. His bones would embed into the molten rock, which would harden. Then, maybe, in the not so distant future, a geologist or rock enthusiast might unearth the fossilized human remains.

Poetic justice for a volcanologist? In a philosophical way, it would be kind of beautiful. But in reality, it is a hellish death, and there's Susan to consider...and the mission...and that damn Rosetti with his taunting smirk. Rosetti's about to go it alone, in his own bull-headed style. He's probably trying to be some big hero to make up for his recent failures.

"I can do it, I have to," Tom whispers.

He thinks of other courageous members of his family – his dad driving at Nascar, his older brother base jumping in Yosemite, his sister hang-gliding in New Mexico. Then there's his strong-willed, dominant Mother, and Susan herself, who has surprised him with her adventurous side.

Taking a deep breath, he sprints toward the flow and leaps over the lava. Spanning the flow, he hits the main rock. He sidesteps, losing balance, before he jumps over to the next rock. He lands again, but almost topples into the lava. The heat smolders his pants and boots.

How the heck did Rosetti do this so quickly?

"Adrenalin Andrews and steady he goes."

With another breath, he leaps up and away to the other side. He stands on the edge of the embankment. His heart pounds, his feet spin out, and seconds seem like an eternity. He scurries up the embankment and slides back down the slope of crumbling rock. He yelps before hurling himself further up onto the bank. Sitting down, he claws at his shoelaces and throws the partially melted boots aside. He touches the hot cotton of his socks and whines. Those have to go, too.

Dousing his foot with water from a canteen, he watches steam rise from his skin. There are no serious burns, only patches of red blisters on the top of his left foot and singed hair on both legs. Mostly, it's the burning smell that is annoying.

He picks up and examines the melted rubber on the boots' soles. The arch of the left boot is warped. The shoes are still usable, but they would kill his feet. He grabs his Teva hiking sandals from the pack, puts them on, and then ties the boots to the backpack. He sighs, stands up, and hurries to catch up to Sal.

The Colonel is sitting, his back against the tunnel wall, exhausted, yet trying to hide it. "Nice to see you made it, Andrews."

"Thanks a lot for your help at the crossing. My foot was cooked, char-broiled."

Sal's grin shifts to a look of disgust. "You might think I'm some sick son of a bitch. You may even hate me. But ya' know what? I don't care. It's like what I tell my men, you're not dead yet, so quit acting like it. When you're faced with an enemy that is bigger and meaner than you, you're gonna' thank me that I pushed you so hard."

He turns and spits, as though punctuating his remarks. "The smart ones listen to me and tough it up. The others, the wise-ass, soft city boys like you, sure as hell wished they had."

He scowls and looks Tom up and down, before turning his heels to walk forward.

Holding back a retort, Tom follows him. *Great. I'm stuck in an underground oven with the Sadistic Drill Sergeant from Hell.*

Chapter Twenty-Six

"Super Bernie"

The seismograph reads 8.0. Voggy heat undulates around the campground area. A thick coat of ash has dusted everything in view from the trees and ferns to the geologists' tools. The Medevac Team carries injured soldiers to the temporary, white-tent "ER."

Despite the relative safety above ground, Susan panics. She's never seen so many bloodied, mangled bodies. One soldier grimaces in pain as he hobbles, carried between two of his teammates. Another man reclines on a stretcher, still and quiet as stone. Another barely looks like a man. His arms and legs are crushed, hanging like a scarecrow's make-shift limbs.

That could be Tom.

She fumbles with the radio headset and curses. It's pointless to even entertain the idea that she could reach him. Bernie appears calm, waiting under the meager shade of an 'ohia tree and checking the seismograph readings. "Four point five, three point zero," he calls out. "It's lessening. So, have you heard from Tom and Sal?"

"Nothing," she says. Spotting one of the uninjured soldiers, Susan decides to flag him down. "Sir? I know you need to get back to the command center, but do have more information about the Colonel?"

The soldier mumbles "no." Then she sees that General McGregor has also just arrived and he's speaking forcefully with a radio contact advisor. She hesitates for a moment, until an image of Tom flashes in her mind. He's bloody and mangled, with gravelly pebbles scattered across his face, his violet blue eyes flickering in and out of consciousness. She visualizes a band of Korean soldiers holding him at gunpoint and torturing him...no, it's too gruesome to dwell on...she'll have to speak with the General.

She watches him as he dismisses the radio contact personnel. This is her only opportunity. She rushes up to him and taps him on the shoulder. He whips around, lifting one eyebrow up in surprise. He towers over her and he's massive, like a tank, with that wide, imposing jaw and a spear-shaped nose.

She stutters. "General, Sir, I apologize for interrupting at this chaotic time, but have you heard anything from the Colonel or my husband?"

"We haven't."

"Are they still planning to carry out their mission?"

"I never gave that order. But Rossetti is a zealot of sorts."

"Tom as well." She takes a deep breath.

"Look Ma'am. We have a team that's going to clear the tunnel. Until we gain radio contact with them, we can't do anything." He grunts and tugs at his collar. Then he sighs and softens his tone.

"We'll devise a rescue plan should they need it and I will definitely have you notified. In the meantime, I suggest you go back to your cabin. I can tell you, in spite of the many accidents on this operation, Colonel Rosetti is a very capable combat leader and wouldn't do anything to endanger your husband's life."

"Accidents happen," she says.

The General reassures her again, though his one good eye avoids her. He signals to a soldier. "Private," the General announces, "please escort Dr. McCarthy Andrews and Mr. Wilkes back to their cabins where they'll be out of harm's way."

Susan obliges, but she's no longer concerned about hiding her grimace. *Hell with them.*

It's almost ten p.m. Splotched with watermarks and slaked in powdery ash, the cabin's bathroom window is an opaque glass. Susan splashes cold water on her face. She ignores the conga line of thirsty ants that marches down into the sink. The ants will need their fill too.

She senses a chill in the air and wraps a shawl around her shoulders. She resigns herself to making a cup of tea, wandering over to the hot plate that Tom set up in their room.

Despite present circumstances, it's a comfortable place, decorated with professional art. There's a detailed painting on the wall of an i'iwi bird, with its colorful plumage and downward curved beak. Next to the bird painting is an enlarged, framed photograph of the volcano at night, showcasing its brilliant violence in a display of purple, orange, red, and yellow lava explosions.

She pours bottled water into the kettle. Then she sees it. A folded piece of notepaper next to the hotplate. She picks it up. A hand-scrawled message reads –

I'm so sorry to sneak out tonight, but I want to try and help Dr. Tom. I studied Mahoe's map again. There could be another entrance, just east of here that might meet up with his route. Please don't worry about me.

Also - I borrowed your GPS and promise not to break it.

Love, Bernie

"My God, no!" she rubs her forehead. *Is he insane?*

She should call the military, but no, he'll just get farther away. There's no time for dilly-dallying. She throws on baggy clothes, boots, and a jacket. She grabs a flash light and the Jeep keys, then hustles outside. It's getting dark and the temperature has dropped by about ten degrees. The car's leather seat is cool on her bottom. The steering wheel feels like a slippery, coiled snake. She starts the Jeep. Keeping the headlights on low, she barrels off into the night.

He could have taken a shortcut toward the east rift zone. That's the only way that makes sense. He couldn't have gone far. She might be able to intercept him in just a minute or two. She crosses her fingers that no one will stop her. The Jeep slows, as she turns right onto a dirt road. Looking to the side, she sees rumbling in the bushes. A sense of relief and joy washes over her, until high beam lights pierce the relative darkness.

"Hello?" she says, still blinded and startled by the light. She cries out her window. "Is this some kind of a checkpoint? I have a permit."

The driver door flies open. Susan has no time to react, while gloved hands reach in and yank her from the Jeep. Gripped by terror, she accidentally bites down on her tongue as she's thrown down with force onto the ground.

"Owww. Hey, who are you? Let me go!" she demands, tasting her own blood in her mouth.

Her eyes adjust and she makes out the forms of three masked soldiers, all aiming automatic weapons at her. The man she assumes is the leader steps forward. She blocks the light with her arm and can only see the outline of his body – taut and muscular. He shouts something in Korean and raises the butt of his rifle above her head, about to strike at any moment.

She lifts her arm higher, anticipating the sound and pain of clashing metal against her skull. But the blow never comes. Confused, she looks up to see another figure rush forward, flying through the soldiers, portly yet confident.

Now, with features darkened, only his eyes stand out, like white radish bulbs in a freshly tilled field of garden soil. His crooked teeth seem to glow as a grin spreads across his painted face. He has a red bandanna around his forehead.

"Bernie?" she whispers.

Then the lead soldier hurdles over her, in a wide parabolic arch, with the Rambo-like "super hero" wrapped around his neck. Bernie screeches. Landing on the soldier, he slams him into the rocky ground. They wrestle over the leader's rifle. The other soldiers rush in to pull Bernie off.

Susan's mind races. *Three-against-one. What chance does he have? I've gotta do something fast.* She crab-walks to the edge of the road and grabs two fist-sized lava rocks. She stands, heels in the dirt, firmly planted, and screams, "Hey!"

One of the soldiers straightens up and looks in her direction. She hurls a rock at the side of his head. A direct hit. He yowls and stumbles over.

Two years of playing ultimate Frisbee on the graduate quad was not a colossal waste of time after all, she thinks. Boldness surges through her body and she lunges forward. The second soldier turns around as she swings the other rock at his face. He yelps and collapses backwards, unconscious.

In a flurry of arms and legs, Bernie and the lead soldier continue to roll away and grapple for control of the rifle. Susan searches the ground. She turns to pick up a discarded AK-47 from the unconscious soldier.

The lead soldier rolls on top of Bernie and twists the boy's wrist. He now holds the rifle and raises the butt above Bernie, ready to bash his head, until Susan auto fires a burst into the soldier's back. She recoils, watching a fountain of blood stream from the man's body while he falls off Bernie.

Then Bernie tumbles out from under him and grabs the other rifle. He points it at the two rock-struck soldiers. One of the soldiers snarls and leaps up at Susan, grabbing her from behind by the hair. She groans as he whips out a combat knife. Tears funnel down her hot cheeks while the knife is poised under her chin, right above her larynx.

Still, keep still.

A single shot rings out and the soldier crumples. Susan's legs buckle and she falls, the knife lightly scratching under her chin.

She looks on in disbelief, catching her breath. "You shot him in the head. You could have killed me, too."

"I know, sorry about that. Crazy luck, I guess," Bernie says as he jumps to his feet and points the gun at the last soldier left alive. A large, red goose egg has risen from the bloody gash on the man's forehead. He comes around, groggy, moaning and rubbing his head.

"We better tie him up if that's all right with you," Bernie says.

"Good idea," Susan agrees.

"There's some rope and duct tape in my backpack. Keep an eye on him."

Susan levels her rifle at him. Bernie steps into the bushes to retrieve his pack. Together they tie the sitting soldier to a tree, taping his mouth shut and wrapping his hands behind him.

"That was totally incredible, Bernie. Thank you for saving my life, too."

"I'm not sure how we did it. Perhaps it was a surge of adrenaline and cortisol combined with increased levels of my testosterone as a call to action, and your oxytocin bonding for needing to help me. Mind you, I have access to that type of bonding as well, and you may have had some testosterone release as well."

Susan laughs. "That's a good assessment and it sure seemed to work. Since we're out here, we may as well find the lava tube entrance. Do you think it really connects to where Tom and Sal might be?"

"Possibly. There's only one way to find out. We gotta' look around. These guys weren't hanging out here for nothing."

"We might run into more combatants."

"Can't assure you that we won't. But according to Mahoe's map, after the entrance, the tunnel goes in three separate directions, with the center tunnel being the largest. I'd venture to say that the terrorists had to take that route considering their number of hostages."

He pulls out a flashlight and shines it on the copy of Mahoe's map. The lines look like branches of a family tree on its side. Like a circuit maze or some imagined brain of a robot.

Susan gazes back to the tied usp soldier. There must be five Eagle Scout-worthy constrictor knots around the man's wrists. His mouth remains gagged, courtesy of Bernie's bandanna. He's not moving any time soon.

"All right Master Bernie, super ninja, let's roll.

Chapter Twenty-Seven

"Stop the Killing"

Late at night, shifting in and out of a feverish sleep, James imagines he's back home in Hilo on a usual rainy Saturday morning. He sees the plush, round chair that faces his master bed. It's a vintage chair with termite-scarred legs and faded Hawaiian print pillows. He's sitting up in bed, strumming the guitar. In the living room, the T.V. hums low, while rainwater batters against the roof's eaves. From her cramped room, daughter Micaela sings some pop song he's never heard of.

He smells bacon frying in a pan and he can't wait to taste the smoky, sweet meat and nibble the velvety, over-easy eggs and warm, buttered toast. He sees his beautiful Hawaiian-Filipina wife, Kainani ("Nani"), saunter into the bedroom – casual, sexy – the way she can be when she doesn't fuss over a little plumpness on her bottom or worry about their daughter's social life (or lack thereof). Nani's skin is creamy brown. Her smile, radiant and soulful, yet accessible. Her eyes dance with life. She winks at him and whispers that she is going to treat him to a tease before breakfast.

"Really?" he says, feeling a surge throughout his whole body. She pushes the guitar out of the way and hops on him, unsnapping her white lace bra with finesse. Her breasts heave against him. He kisses her neck, tasting faint traces of coconut butter lotion. Her scent drives him wild. He throbs, ready to be inside her…

Upon awakening, James confronts a totally different reality. The cavern reeks of sulfur and all-too-human odors. A urine scent lingers. The hostages have had no choice but to relieve themselves in the cave's corners. Some shiver with the effects of dehydration and the onset of starvation. Couples cling to one another for warmth.

James has given up trying to be a hero. When Howard was shot, that was it, as though the leader, their brave wolf, had left the pack. No one else could take his place.

James watches Irene. Earlier, she was screaming at the guards, but now she shifts between frantic motion and paralysis. She moans softly to herself like a lunatic. Tears collect in the creases of her dirty face and stream down to her cracked lips. Her hair is matted down with sweat and black dirt. She brushes a hand on her dust-covered dress. Howard's blood has already dried up on her clothes, flaking and crumbling, and she seems to take an odd comfort in that. The blood is more than a reminder. There are traces of him, his DNA. The blood is Howard.

The hostages can't sleep. They stare at the cavern walls and pass the time watching a dim lantern glow cast shadows around them. Some play games to occupy their time.

"I see a butterfly," a hostage mutters.

"No, it's two cats dancing," another says.

They are only trying to keep sane, James thinks. *How much longer can they play that game?*

Then James sees Kim Sung stand up and move toward Irene, ambivalent to the guards' stares. Kim Sung would probably not do anything violent, but James cannot trust him either. A mere unkind word could break the poor woman down or send her into a fit.

Kim Sung clears his throat. He reaches his right hand out. "Your husband has not died in vain," he offers. "How can I say this?" Kim Sung pauses, distracted by the cave's shadows while he searches for the right words. "He made me realize how wrong I was."

Irene looks up to him.

"Innocent blood cannot be avenged," he continues. "Only forgiven." He hands her a cloth to wipe her tears. He sighs, then turns and walks back to his corner. James watches her blot the tears. She is too good for this world.

In a nearby cavern, Ho Dam sits on a lightweight collapsible chair, chin to chest, trying to doze off. The explosives went off on time. With his men guarding the entrance, there's no way the U.S. military could get to the hostage cave without detection. The Americans will give in to his demands, or they will follow their own procedures and many more will die. But in spite of his tiredness, Ho Dam's mind cannot fully rest. He remembers Kim Sung's story. He told Ho Dam so many times that it burned into his brain. They were both orphans. They had nothing to live for, but each other and the hope for justice.

He shakes his head and whispers Kim Sung's name, then he raises his head. It's time for action. He rises and gestures to a nearby soldier holding a video camera.

"Let's do it," he says.

They walk into the hostage cave. Ho Dam waves his arms to get the hostages' attention. "*Your* government still refuses to simply acknowledge the atrocity of what they did to my country during the War. Now, you will pay for such unspeakable war crimes. And *your* blood will pay the debt to my people."

He signals to the soldiers to grab six of the veteran men and drag them away. Their wives protest, but the soldiers promptly hold them back. All the while, the cameraman films the unfolding drama.

"Forgive them," James says.

"What did you say?" a soldier barks at him.

"He should just forgive," James replies.

The soldier scowls and without a second thought kicks James in the gut. James doubles over, choking on his own fetid breath. He watches the women being held back, as they yell in dissent.

Ho Dam smiles, emboldened by the sight of the terrified hostages.

"You carried out your government's brutal orders, murdering unarmed and defenseless civilians. Killing my people with bombardments, napalm, air strikes, and firing squads! Our homeland was a testing ground for your Vietnam War.

"It's all a part of your government's tactics. You look for countries with precious resources, recruit the ignorant that are willing to fight, and then murder the innocent. Again and again, you do that. To fuel your economy. So your people can have all their little luxuries. Their fluffy toilet paper and air conditioned cars. Business as usual for the American capitalists. Collateral damage for political gain. Now, you will pay for these crimes. I am being gracious. It's more than a fair trade."

Kim Sung sits silently in his corner, ignoring the rant.

Ho Dam stares down Kim Sung. He continues on his tirade. "You think I am a radical, don't you? Well, I was raised on the American media. I went to the international schools. And you know what I realized? Even those goody-two shoe, Teach for America, hate Western capitalism types were racists too. They really despise us.

"We work harder than them and we are often smarter than they are. We are a threat. So what's the problem with blowing away a few, old American veterans? Their country should consider it a favor that they won't be a burden on their tax system with their medical expenses or filling up their nursing homes. I'm a custodian, really, just doing a little clean up…"

"Please, God, stop this insanity," James whispers, standing off to the side, but Ho Dam ignores him.

"I think it's…what would they call it? Apropos to execute Americans in a national park? Creative idea, no?"

The soldiers line up the six veteran men in a firing squad fashion. They raise their rifles, poised to aim and shoot. The women cry and wail. One woman breaks away and runs toward her husband until a soldier strikes her on the face. Like a pack of aggressive dogs, the guards surround her, ready to strike again when needed.

James gets to his feet and cries out, "Stop!" A hot anger tightens his limbs. "They've all been through enough," he says.

"Trying to be an American hero, fat man?" Ho Dam says. "It's too late for that. Maybe you should have thought twice about working for a company that's supported by war-mongers. And now, Mr. Big Shot Bus Driver, you have the special privilege of watching some of your passenger friends die."

The soldiers pin down another woman and hold back several veterans. Amidst the confusion, Kim Sung quietly walks past the distracted soldiers.

Eyes shining with bloodlust, Ho Dam steps before the camera and stares into the lens. "By refusing to acknowledge Korea's tragedies, or make restitution, the United States of America is responsible for the deaths of these veterans. I speak for my country, when I say…"

"You don't speak for anyone but your sick self," James shouts.

"I speak for Korea, united against the American aggressor!" Ho Dam raises his arms, gesturing for the soldiers to aim their guns at the line of hostages. The veterans brace themselves for the inevitable.

"Ready!" Ho Dam cries out. "Aim…"

"No, stop!" The voice of Kim Sung echoes against the walls. Ho Dam turns to see Kim Sung hurl himself in front of the firing squad, waving his arms, face flushed with agitation.

"The killing must end now!"

"Shut up! What the hell are you doing?!" screeches Ho Dam. "Step aside old man or you will die, too."

Kim Sung ignores him and instead turns to the squad. The guns' barrels point right at him, like a twelve-eyed militia monster. His hands tremble, but he stands firm and strong.

"Lower your weapons," he says. Confused, the soldiers hesitate. "Drop your weapons, now!" The soldiers lower their weapons and stand at attention. There is a collective sigh of relief from the veterans.

Ho Dam stomps up to Kim Sung. His voice ramps up to a scream. "Get out of here! Or I'll order them to fire at you."

"Like those American soldiers were ordered to fire at us, fifty years ago?"

"Yes," Ho Dam says with a devilish grin. He turns around, ready to give the signal when Kim Sung grabs his arm. He tries to shake off Kim Sung's unyielding grip.

"Boy, you need to know what your mother said to me before she died."

"What? You told me she was dead when you found her. I know your entire story by heart." Without taking his eyes off Kim Sung, Ho Dam gestures to the cameraman. "Stop filming please." The cameraman lowers the recording device.

"But it was not as I told you," Kim Sung says, as he leads Ho Dam off to the side, away from the veterans and soldiers, but still within earshot.

"You're crazy. Delusional," Ho Dam says.

"No, it is time for you to know the truth. I never said anything before. I wanted to forget all about it."

"Alright. Make it quick."

"After I picked you up from your Mother's arms, I stood there for a moment, holding you, amazed that you were healthy and beautiful, not a scratch on you. You started crying so I tried soothing you. But then, I felt a tug on my pant leg. I shuddered. I was petrified. Was it a ghost? Knowing my state of mind at that time, I would believe anything."

"I don't have time for ghost stories."

"Listen. When I looked down, I saw that your Mother was still alive, just barely, but breathing. She looked up at me, her eyes begging me. Her eyes were so beautiful in their last light. She was trying to speak and I could not hear her, so I bent down to listen to her."

"She is gone. She cannot come back," Ho Dam says in anger.

"No, listen. She smiled ever so slightly, happy to see her son, *you*, alive in my arms. She raised her hand and pulled me closer to herself. My face was next to hers as she whispered in my ear, 'Care for my son,' she said. 'Like he was your own. And please, promise me, you'll stop the killing.' Then she fell back, closed her eyes, and died. I swear to you, those were her last dying words to me."

Kim Sung faces Ho Dam. Pouches hang under Ho Dam's weary eyes. Stress and anger have prematurely aged him. And fear as well.

"I never spoke to you of this," Kim Sung says. "Because I didn't want to stop the killing and that was wrong. Please forgive me. I wanted vengeance on the Americans. It drove my entire life; it fueled my anger and resolve. I was nothing without my fight for vengeance. It was a cold and bitter unforgiveness, that I held my entire life. I waited for so many years for that moment to get back.

"But now, that it's happening, I realize how sick it is and how wrong I was. I fulfilled the first part of my vow to your Mother. I raised you like my own son, or dear brother or nephew. I cared for you as I would my own child, even though I was young. I loved you, as I promised your Mother I would. And now, I must fulfill the rest of the promise."

Kim Sung looks back to the squad and levels a steely gaze at each one. "No more killing. Allow these men to return to their wives. We will surrender if need be."

The squad looks to Ho Dam for confirmation. But he only bows his head and closes his eyes as if deep in thought and he does not respond. Kim Sung gestures to the soldiers to lower their weapons. He turns and signals the other soldiers, guarding the women, to move away.

The wives and their husbands rush to each other, faces beaming with tears of joy, smiling like the first days of their trip, before the takeover. Their relief overwhelms Kim Sung to the point that his own eyes brim with tears.

To Ho Dam, he says, "Your mother and our ancestors are pleased with us this day." He reaches and pats Ho Dam gently and lovingly on the shoulder. He continues speaking to Ho Dam. "Yes, this is a good day. Thank you, my son. We are truly free now. The guilt and weight is off of both of us."

Most of the soldiers have moved back to their stations, but some linger around, waiting for a cue from one of the leaders. Their loyalties split.

Indeed, Kim Sung is the main leader, but he has abandoned the orders of his own superior. Kim Sung begins to walk away, inhaling the air with a tranquil expression. *There is hope for Ho Dam and for all these people.* And then he hears…

"Kim Sung!"

"Yes, my son?" Kim Sung calls back. He doesn't turn around to see Ho Dam's pained face, nor does he catch the sourness in his voice. When Kim Sung spins around to face Ho Dam, two shots ring out like a blaze of fire.

"I'm not your son!" Ho Dam shouts as Kim Sung clasps at the wounds in his abdomen, in disbelief. "And I will keep on fighting. I take my orders from Commander Lee and we will have our demands met." He holsters his pistol. Wiping the sweat from his brow, he strides out of the hostage cavern.

"What have you done?" Kim Sung cries. He slumps to the floor, holding a cracked rib. Blood gushes out unto hands. He knows he only has a few hours left and he is no longer able to fight back. The betrayal and the deep sadness – these are worse than any physical pain.

Ho Dam rushes back to the command center cavern, pushes a technician aside, and opens a glass-covered console. He carefully lifts out a detonation activator, then turns around, holding it out to his men who have followed into the cavern with him.

He speaks with pride. "Today an old leader has been dismissed. Now, we hold victory in our hands." His men raise their weapons and give a resounding cheer.

Chapter Twenty-Eight

"Another Lava Tube"

Susan and Bernie follow a trail that leaves the side of the road and meanders through the brush. A million thoughts bombard Susan's mind – *Will the U.S. military detect us? Will we be caught by terrorists? Are Tom and Sal okay? Will we find them? Did I really just shoot someone?*

She has never used such violent force, let alone firing a weapon and killing a person. There's the pain of moral remorse, but also an odd sensation of accomplishment. *Is this Superhero Syndrome?*

Perhaps, as Bernie said, humans are more controlled by the hypothalamus and pituitary gland than we thought. She can attest to the battiness of her current mid-30s, a time that she anticipated would be more focused on her career and raising a family, but is instead divided between gardening obsessions, competing with Tom's Mom, and scheduling volcanology escapades.

As they hike along, she notices Bernie's hands are shaking.

"Is it too dark?" she asks him.

"No, that only happens when I try to sleep. The moonlight is nice. I was thinking about how we just made it out of that last encounter. It could have gone badly."

They stop in their tracks. Susan motions him to get down next to her. She points up ahead to a cinder cone hill, lit up by the rising moon.

"That looks like a guard up there," Bernie says.

"If he sees us, he'll contact the others. Stay low," she says as they both crawl closer to him.

Once they arrive near the area, still hidden by foliage, they see a lone, bored Korean guard standing at the top of the cinder cone hill, flicking cigarette ash into his own miniature cone.

"Are you sure we should be doing this?" Bernie says.

"No. But there's only one guard there. We already handled three guys. I say, we scope out the situation and then we'll go back for reinforcements."

"All right."

"Okay, here's what I'll do. I'm going to divert his attention, try to get him to come this way. You wait here," Susan whispers to Bernie, "Then when he gets next to me, clobber him with your rifle butt."

"Can't I just shoot him?"

"No, Rambo, we're trying not to kill anyone, and a rifle shot would alert others. We need to do this undetected."

She sets her rifle down, unfastens the top buttons of her blouse, and adjusts her bra, pushing up her cleavage. She stands and hikes up her shorts to reveal soft, inviting flesh.

Bernie's eyes widen. "That's definitely a distraction."

"At this point, I'm not beyond the proverbial tease. Let's just hope it works. Stay down and be quiet. Wait 'til I signal you."

He agrees and then scrambles away, taking cover behind some shrubs.

Susan steps out into the open approaching the guard. "Hello there," she calls out, waving to the guard. "Is this the way back to the Kipuka trail?"

The guard raises his eyebrows, tosses his cigarette, and strolls down the hill toward her. When he approaches within a few feet of her, she steps to the left, nodding at Bernie. He leaps out from behind the shrub, swinging his rifle at the back of the guard's head, connecting with a solid hit. The guard falls forward.

"Out cold," Bernie says.

"All right, good job. Now let's tie him up."

They tie up the guard's hands and feet with what's left of Bernie's rope and duct tape. Finished, they grab their rifles and Bernie's backpack and bolt off. They scramble up toward the lava tube entrance and look into the small tunnel, shining their lights into it. The tunnel veers to the right and downward.

"You know, Dr. Susan, we make a pretty good team," Bernie remarks as he crouches down. "Two green lights in a row."

"We got real lucky. Now I need you to go back and notify the military and get help."

"What? I thought we were in this together."

"This may connect to the hostages or Tom and Sal. They're up against thirty soldiers or more, so we'll need back-up."

"But I'm not entirely certain this tunnel connects and I can help you…"

Susan grabs him by his shoulders and looks straight into his eyes. His sweaty, dirty forehead has crinkled into rows of long furrows, his acne drying out from the sulfurous air.

"This is not up for debate. My husband may be in some serious trouble down there and I'm not going to risk both of our lives trying to save his. I need you to go get us help."

Bernie gulps. "But, you might need my help, too."

"Bernard...no. Absolutely not. We need reinforcements. We need the military here. Do you understand that?" she says while she pulls on his shirt sleeve and shoves him away. "Now, go back and get them. Hurry."

"Yes, Ma'am." Bernie nods. Reluctantly, he turns and walks down the hill, kicking at pebbles as he goes.

Susan points her flashlight down into the inky blackness of the lava tube. As far as she can see, it looks narrow, an experience to incite claustrophobia. She could deal with Bernie having a fit about not getting his way, but she's not sure if she can handle crawling through the passageway for very long. Maybe it will open up.

Balancing the AK-47 against her shoulder, she lowers down and scooches for fifty feet, before she passes into another lava tube. She is able to stand now. She walks through the cool tunnel a few hundred yards until she sees a faint light up ahead.

She turns off her flashlight and peers down to the end. There's an open cavern below. Crouching, she moves behind some boulders and looks into the cavern. She sees hostages and four armed guards.

Clambering further ahead, she stops and lies down on her stomach behind a cluster of jagged rocks. It's so quiet in the lava tube. She can hear the murmurings of the soldiers. She fears her own breathing could be a give-away, but they don't seem to hear or notice her. She watches them, trying to think of the next step of the attack.

I wasn't trained to do this. Maybe I should just wait here for Sal and Tom.

She hears gravel dislodging. There are footsteps behind her. She pivots around, weapon drawn, as a heavy body flops down beside her. Startled and desperate, she swings the rifle toward the body.

"No. wait, stop," a squeaky voice says.

"Bernie! What are you doing here?" she scolds him, still careful to keep her voice at a low level.

"I had a change of heart as they say. I was afraid you might run into the terrorists and I can't leave you alone."

"As though you can help," she mutters.

"I did help the last two times. Look, I know you must be mad at me, but I had to follow you, because I've got a plan that just might work to free the hostages."

"No, Bernie. You need to get us back-up."

"I'll toss something over there, and when they turn, we open fire on them."

"That's a stupid idea."

"Why?" Bernie insists. "All our diversion tactics have worked so far. These guys are sheep. Followers. We can take them. There's only four guys, just one more than the others we surprise attacked."

"That's only the four we can see right now. But once we open fire, others are sure to come running in, and they could start shooting the hostages. You shouldn't even be here. I told you to get reinforcements. What's the matter with you? Am I gonna' have to hold your hand and drag you out of here?"

"No, I'll go, but I was just thinking that…"

"Sh-h-h, get down."

Susan's eyes follow new movement near the hostages. She lowers down and watches. Followed by a cameraman and a dozen of his armed soldiers, Ho Dam enters the cavern. Shadows pulse along the cave's walls.

Ho Dam stands in front of the hostages and faces a camera. His thick, black hair sticks straight up like a porcupine. He gesticulates with aggressive hand motions, but his legs move gracefully. He stops and speaks directly to the camera.

"At this moment, I hold in my hands, death for anyone near this volcano. It is the detonator that will activate a series of irreversible events that no one can stop! We are about to rewrite history. We may be remembered as military martyrs, men who died in honor, serving a united Korea." He waves the detonator.

"Hold this, Doctor Sue," Bernie says while he hands Susan his rifle. He takes a deep breath, exhales, and stands up.

She tugs at his pant leg. "Wait, what are you doing? Bernie get down!"

Where is the impulse control? Is he supposed to be on some kind of medication? Then she remembers the comic books that he reads non-stop. It must be a yet-to-be diagnosed personality disorder.

"Please Bernie, you're making a big mistake, get down! This is beyond stupid."

He isn't listening. He raises his arms and lets out a high-pitched battle cry. Then he rushes forward, leaping down the path toward the guards. Susan hunkers down. She's powerless to try and interfere with the situation. Closing her eyes, she fears an inevitable tragedy.

The Koreans look up at the boy, startled. They aim their rifles, but Ho Dam raises his hand to stop them from firing. Bernie advances upon them, landing in various martial arts stances and crying out with every jump. Once he's in front of them and on level ground, he continues his cries, strutting toward the leader. Finally, he stops in front of Ho Dam. Bernie bows low and then assumes a fighting stance posture. Within seconds, he breaks into a series of kicks and jabs, slashing the air with his limbs before he stops in a balanced fighting position.

In the uncomfortable silence, the soldiers stare at him. Ho Dam's chuckles burst into loud, hysterical laughter. The soldiers exchange curious glances at each other and lower their weapons, while they try to suppress their giggles. Then Ho Dam stops laughing and shakes his head, raising his hand for attention. His men stop laughing and point their weapons at Bernie. Ho Dam pauses.

Susan can't tell what Ho Dam might do to Bernie. He could instantly stab him with the large combat knife strapped to his side or even strangle the poor kid. Or maybe he would do something far worse, some act of violence or torture beyond human comprehension.

But Ho Dam doesn't react. Instead he steps up to Bernie, with the cameraman still filming him.

"You have got to be the funniest thing I've seen in a long time!" Ho Dam belts out. His eyes shift around and his smile slips into a grimace. "Unfortunate for you though, little fat boy."

All the soldiers point their weapons at Bernie's head.

Ho Dam looks at the camera, spitting out words. "You stupid Americans. How dare you send me this poor excuse of a martial arts fighter! Is this some kind of racist joke? Some ploy? Surely, he'll also die with his blood on your hands."

Susan watches Bernie and she begins to shake in place. She wants to scream out, but she is too paralyzed by fear. She clutches her rifle. *I can't leave him and the hostages to that madman. If I don't do something now, they'll all be dead.*

"Since he's made it this far," Ho Dam says, "I'll play your game. I'd like to see if he really knows how to fight. So I'll give him a chance. If he can defeat even the smallest of my men, I'll release him and allow him to live."

With all the soldiers and Ho Dam's attention on Bernie and the camera, Susan scampers over to a nearby ledge where she can get a better view of the action, while still hiding.

Ho Dam turns his head and shouts to his men. "Young Cho!"

His men part, allowing a short and youthful soldier to walk past them. The soldier takes off his paramilitary cap to reveal a shiny bald head.

"Young Cho," Ho Dam orders, "Destroy this idiot."

Young Cho stares at Bernie and flashes his silver, capped front teeth.

"Are you ready, pudgy boy?" Ho Dam says.

Bernie quivers. He nods and raises his hands in a Tae Kwon Do stance. The two begin to circle around each other, shoulders hunched, eyes fixed in a mutual stare. Then Bernie charges. Young Cho simply side-steps, leans over, and extends his leg. Bernie trips over it and tumbles to the ground. But he regains composure and quickly jumps back to his feet.

"Stupid belly," he utters while he scrambles back into position. Young Cho grins when he gets an 'okay' to fight from his commander. Bernie charges again and leaps into a roundhouse kick, aiming for Cho's stomach, but the small, sturdy soldier grabs his leg and slams him down, twisting his calf like he's wringing a soaked washcloth.

Bernie cries, "Uncle, ouch! I give up!"

"What does that even mean?" Cho asks, laughing with evil intent.

"It means stop, 'cuz that really hurts!"

"But, I'm just getting started..."

"Pleeeazze...."

Cho releases him.

"Thank you," Bernie says with desperation in his voice. He rises slowly, bowing in a proper surrender.

Young Cho bows too, showing off an elaborate dragon tattoo on the crown of his head, the ominous symbol of the KUF army. As Cho lifts up, one vertebrae at a time, he suddenly unleashes a flurry of rapid jabs at Bernie's flabby mid-section. Dazed from the blows, Bernie can't even react. Arching his leg, Cho sends a final kick to the temple, toppling Bernie down with a thud.

"No, no, no." Susan's whole body quakes. "Get up, Bernie."

Ho Dam signals for two soldiers to lift the unconscious boy to his feet. They hold him up by his arms as Ho Dam hands another soldier the detonator. He slaps Bernie across the face, grabbing him by the back of his hair.

"Fool, how did you get in here?" he yells to the semi-conscious Bernie, yanking his hair several times. Ho Dam slaps Bernie again and again, until he finally becomes conscious for a moment. Then his eyes roll back and he passes out.

"He's worthless," Ho Dam says. He pushes Bernie to the ground and takes back possession of the activation device from one of the soldiers.

Queasiness overwhelms Susan. Acid churns and boils at the back of her throat. *I'm watching Bernie being tortured and I'm too scared to even move.* Terrifying images flash through her mind: Bernie's fingers being torn off, his head dunked and held under a vat of water, a burning rod searing the delicate skin on his arms, a sword piercing through his neck...

No! Don't think about that. That's not going to happen...it can't...

With an unpleasant gulp, she swallows the burning acidic fluid. She preps her rifle. With it cradled in her right arm, and Bernie's weapon slung across her shoulder for easy access, she slides forward.

She takes a deep breath. It's a fake calm, but it's all she has. She jumps up into a wide stance, sending bursts of flying bullets at Ho Dam's feet.

"Ah-Shi-bal!" he curses.

"Drop your weapons or your leader dies," Susan shouts. She advances steadily at them. "Drop your weapons and set the remote device down." Her AK-47 points at Ho Dam's head. He hesitates. She can see a tiny pool of sweat collecting above his upper lip. "Do it!" she yells.

Ho Dam signals his men to drop the weapons. He sets the detonator down, though it is still within his reach.

Susan scoops up the detonator and nudges the unconscious Bernie on the cave floor, keeping the gun trained on Ho Dam. She watches Ho Dam's eyes twitch, one focusing on the periphery, the other looking down at the detonator in her hand. There are dark circles under his eyes, but he looks younger than she had imagined.

Stay calm, breathe, she tells herself. She knows the military isn't going to arrive any time soon. She states the only demand that makes sense. "Release the hostages."

"Are you serious? Do you really expect me to do that?" he spits out. "I have orders from my commanders. The U.S. has not even made an attempt to negotiate. Do you think I'm a fool?"

Ho Dam winks to the side and a soldier rushes from behind, pouncing at Susan. She swings the rifle on her left side around and fires, cutting the soldier down at point blank range. Ho Dam leaps toward her and she bangs the muzzle of the other AK-47 on his forehead. He stops, frozen in rage, nostrils flared and breathing deeply, his gaze fixed on her.

But she's resolute. She props up her flashlight and shines it on Ho Dam. "One more move and you're dead."

"I should have my soldiers shoot you already," he says. "But you intrigue me. You know that you won't leave here alive. That's for sure." His pupils shrink like two angry black pinpoints. He bites his lower lip and gestures to the soldiers. "Okay. I will do an exchange. Release the hostages!"

"You're all free to go now," Susan adds.

The hostages look on in disbelief. First, a young kid doing martial arts (or some version of it) and then a beautiful British woman. It's not what they expected. They race out, as fast as they can, while Ho Dam simmers with anger.

He hisses. "Do you really think you'll actually succeed?"

"If I don't, then you'll die with me." She shoves her rifle nozzle closer to his head. "Now turn around, slowly," she says.

"I care nothing of my own life," Ho Dam answers. "I am committed to our cause. I can assure you though, you won't win. *You* still want to live." He speaks with a calm tone and turns toward his soldiers.

With the rifle, she pokes his back. "Maybe I don't. Want to live. The door will close on both of us. So be it."

She looks down at Bernie. There are pink slap marks around his face, flushes of color against translucent skin. He's gaining consciousness, but surely the reality of not being a superhero has hit him. He rolls over and looks at her in disbelief. "Dr. Sue. What happened?"

She lowers her voice and bends down to him. "Just some natural hormones kicking in, like you said." She reaches to grab him by his shirt collar, like a mother cat grabs a kitten's scruff, quick and matter-of-fact. But in her distraction, she lowers the guns.

Ho Dam signals to his team of soldiers.

"Noooo!" Bernie and Susan yell in unison. The soldiers jump on them, wrap their arms around her, and pull the weapons away. Bernie tries to fight them off, but they easily pin him down, tackling his weakened body back into submission. Ho Dam smirks while some of his soldiers take turns pummeling the new hostages with their boots. He motions to the rest of his men to hustle up the passageway after the veterans, shouting his order.

"Go after them. I want them all back here, now!"

Chapter Twenty-Nine

"Adios GPS"

In the middle of the night Sal and Tom arrive at an impasse – a landslide covers the tunnel in front of them. They bend down to push and toss the loose rocks aside, looking for an opening. Tom sets down his backpack and pulls out his sonic depth sensor. After a quick reading of the sensor's diagnostics, he points to the wall above them.

"There's an opening up there, maybe about ten to fifteen feet thick, maybe more."

"This'll take a while," Sal says.

"We'll have to start lifting the rocks, one at a time."

"I didn't see this cave-in on that old man's map. By the way, do you have that?"

"No," Tom answers.

"What?"

"I gave it to Bernie. But I memorized most of it and mapped it out, sort of, mentally."

"All right, whiz kid. We're going to need some *physical* strength now, so start lifting."

They pull at the rocks, hurling them behind. After twenty minutes of strenuous work, Tom feels his chest tighten, his breath quickening in short, staccato beats as he pants.

"Rosetti, I need to take a break…"

"Okay, but not too long."

Tom stumbles. Dizzy and achy, he finds his backpack buried under the discarded pile of rocks. He pulls it out and searches through it. He locates his water bottle at the bottom of the pack, next to a few smashed protein bars. Carefully, he brings the metal canister to his lips and takes a big gulp. He leans back and lets the backpack hang open when he hears a metallic *chinking* sound. Something fell out.

He looks down. Headlamp light reflects off the face of a silver gadget. He picks up the object. It's the GPS, his mother's gift, smashed. The digital counter flickers from zero to eight and back to zero. He crouches down and turns it over to read the inscription: "With Love, Mom."

She used to write the same phrase, accompanied with a smiley face, on his school lunchbox napkins. She also wrote it on the letters she sent him in college and graduate school. The sentiment was real, but the hold was tenacious and inappropriate. She is still way too overbearing. A coddler, a control freak.

Susan knows that of course. He misses her right now, especially when she first wakes up in the morning, yawning like a lioness, with a ruffled "mane" of hair, grinning with a perfect mouth and bright white teeth. Translucent green eyes, red-golden hair, warm skin, gentle swell of hips. And he loves watching her work – catching errors in citations, reviewing abstracts. Once upon a time, she wrote papers on the glaciogenic deposits in Death Valley and the intrusions in the granitic rock of Yosemite. It's true, she was willing to give up her research in California and said it was worth it to be with him, if it was *just* him, no mother-in-law judgments or intrusions. She had her own way of being overbearing, but she had a point.

Susan, I want you to be happy.

I miss you and I love you.

"Hey Andrews, come on!" Sal hollers, breaking Tom from his trance. "No time for daydreaming. Give me a hand. I think I'm almost through."

Tom stands and lets the GPS roll out of his hand. He raises his foot, hesitating for a second as though invisible tentacles are holding down his boots.

No, it's time to move on. Adios.

He stomps on the device and smashes it into smaller pieces. "Love you Mom, but I gotta' cut the cord," he says quietly. He readjusts his shirt, throws his backpack over his shoulder, and scrambles up to Sal.

Together they push aside the last few rocks and crawl through a short, narrow passageway. They stand and find themselves in another long lava tube.

"Whoa, what's that?" Tom says. They look up to see a throng of people heading their way, marching in the dark. Sal positions his rifle and shines light in their direction.

"Please don't shoot!" James hollers, raising his tied arms to cover his eyes.

Tom is shocked to see the haggard faces of elderly men and women. "I'm American," he says, lowering the flashlight to illuminate his own face. "And we have extra flashlights for you," Tom calls out.

"Thanks, we're trying to stick together. It's slow going," James says, breathless and nervous. His aloha shirt clings to his body with a filmy sweat.

"Good," Tom says. "By the time you guys get to the other entrance, the military will have cleared the passageway." He hands to flashlight to James.

"But we have lost communication with soldiers," Sal says. He pulls out a knife to cut James' zip ties. James uses the knife to cut the ties off the others' hands. The veterans echo a chorus of thank yous.

James says, "The other half of your team has just been captured."

"What? Wait a minute…the other half?" Tom stares at Sal then back to the crowd. "How many were captured?"

"Just two of them. It was actually quite bizarre. Not sure how you do things these days. There was a kid, about 17, doing bad Kung Fu imitations and a gorgeous redhead. She was the one who saved us and set us free. I couldn't believe it myself."

"Susan and Bernie?!?" Tom's teeth sink into his lower lip. *What the hell are they doing down here? Susan's stubborn, but this time she's gone way too far. In her own words – she's gone "batty."*

Suddenly, another light hits Tom's face. "Get out of here now…run, run like hell!" Sal yells to James and the veterans.

The crowd funnels down the passageway, crouching, while enemy bullets ricochet off the tunnel walls and ceiling. Tom stoops behind a boulder. Sal jumps down next to him. They take cover next to an opening in the tunnel wall. Sal reaches into his utility belt. Tom's eyes enlarge, heart pacing, as Sal pulls out a grenade.

"What the hell are you doing?"

"It's for the uninvited guests," Sal says. "It'll block any last-minute run at the vets or at the very least delay them from recapturing 'em."

"What about my wife and Bernie? We can't leave them there."

With a blast of enemy fire, the sheltering rock behind them breaks off in sections. Tom and Sal stagger back. Sal fires off a burst of rounds, then tosses the activated grenade at their assailants. He pushes Tom away.

"Don't worry, we'll find 'em. Move it! Go now!"

In a powerful spew of shrapnel and debris, the grenade explodes behind Sal's back and they run wildly into another passageway.

Chapter Thirty

"Ho Dam's Questioning"

As Susan wakes up, she registers an unpleasant spell. It's partially her own sweat, plus Bernie's sweat, blood, and stinky feet. The dankness of the cave is reminiscent of a moldy gym locker. Then she registers a sharp nerve pain in her arms and shoulders.

She glances up to see that her hands are tied above her head and Bernie sways next to her, his face bruised and cut. Their feet barely touch the ground as they stand on their toes, hanging like slabs of dead meat, ripe for affliction and possible death. The crazed butcher walks in front of them, grinning.

"It truly is amazing to have you, Dr. Susan, Tom Andrews' wife, here to save the day! What a stroke of luck, indeed." He taps the sword fastened on his left hip. He pulls it out and waves it, drawing Ls in the air. "Now, your job is to tell me the exact location in the River Mountain cave where you found the vitrellium, then I'll let you and your young fat friend go back to your happy little lives."

Susan frowns and shakes her head. "You think I trust you? You already tracked us there and stole our files, data, and equipment. What else do you need?"

"That's true, but we didn't get all that we need."

"Obviously you found out about the Kilauea fault zones and fracture lines. *We* don't even know the exact location of the vitrellium deposits in Southeast Asia since your stupid cronies cut my line before we could record it. You're just sick," she says. The hoarseness in her voice undermines her bravado. *I won't tell him a thing.* She steadies herself, even while the pain intensifies and zips down from her wrists to her lower back.

"I'm sick?" Ho Dam says with chuckle. "You are working for the imperialist warmongers. Funny how people can just disconnect from their realities..." He waltzes over to Bernie and pokes the boy's exposed belly with a finger. He draws the sword closer. "Then tell me about it, chubbo. You must have some info."

"He's a nobody really, just a college student," Susan says. "He doesn't know anything."

"Your full name!" Ho Dam screams in Bernie's face. The blade wavers above his head and lowers down below his chin.

"Ber-Bernard Wilkes," he manages to say while a stream of urine trickles down his legs and puddles near Ho Dam's feet.

Disgusted, Ho Dam takes a step back. "What the hell are you doing here?"

"It's total coincidence, sir, I swear. Like she said, I'm a college student. I'm the Andrews' intern," he says, gulping. For a moment, he's relieved, too tired to be embarrassed about the pee puddle. "And if it counts for anything, Mr. Ho Dam, I'm also a serious, devoted student and fan of your country's Tae Kwon Do."

"So that's what you were doing? I was most impressed with your demonstration."

"You were? Really? Thanks."

"No, you imbecile! You don't impress me. It was terrible. Extremely amateurish and offensive, too. But, what amazes me is why would the world's most powerful military send a nobody like you?"

"They didn't. I came on my own to help Dr. Sue. She tried to stop me, but I had to come, because I know what setting off more explosives will do…"

"A suicide mission?" Ho Dam says.

"Don't say anything more," Susan interjects.

Ho Dam smiles. "Interesting. So…tell me, Bernard… what will happen?"

"Could you get me a stool to set my feet on for a sec'?"

"Yes, we can find something…" Ho Dam alerts an assistant to bring a backpack over to Bernie. His dangling feet settle on top of the pack.

"For starters," Bernie says, "an explosive would magnify a disruption in the fault zones near the Kilauea caldera, possibly loosening the volcano's shield. And it would cause major earthquakes and eruptions and perhaps even rip this entire island apart. It would also collapse the Big Island's southern cliffs, which run for miles, causing a mega tsunami that would destroy the coastal areas in Hawaii, and maybe even the entire Pacific Rim!"

Susan glares at Bernie.

Ho Dam plays along and straightens his posture, eyebrows twitching.

"That's precisely what I'm planning to do," he says. "But thank you for confirming our theories. You're a good student after all. Just one last thing, then I'll let you go."

"Yes, of course, anything. I swear I'll tell you, just name it," Bernie begs.

"You don't have that information," Ho Dam barks back. He whips his sword around to Susan. "How is the U.S. military planning to stop us?"

"I have no idea," she says.

"All right, hmmm. But you do know where the vitrellium deposits are?"

"I can't tell you that either. And you've already asked that!"

"Or you *won't* tell me? So then, I wonder, how does a house divided against itself stand?" he muses, circling the area. He picks up another sword, admiring its sharp edge. Then he whisks back around with both swords pointing at them.

"I know from my own recent experience - it cannot stand!" he shouts, advancing toward them, swinging both swords and slicing the air.

"No, don't. Please, don't!" Susan squeals.

Ho Dam winds up and the swords zig-zag in a blur of high-speed *whish-whooshes*. Bernie unleashes a scream. Susan squeezes her eyes shut. The sword blades whip and slice, closer and closer to the petrified Bernie. She can almost taste the scent of blood in the air, but when she opens her eyes she sees that Bernie is still alive.

His clothes have been shredded into pieces and his shirt hangs in tatters. He looks like a shipwrecked sailor with his waistline slashed and pants falling to the floor. Urine drenched boxer shorts cling to his nearly naked, bleeding body.

Ho Dam assesses the damage. He examines the blood oozing from shallow, multiple cuts on Bernie's torso. "Now, Dr. Susan, you must say goodbye to your young friend," Ho Dam spits out. He winds up again, swinging the weapons toward Bernie.

"No! Stop it! I'll tell you everything I know." Susan's voice cracks. "I can't let you hurt him."

Ho Dam ignores Susan, continuing to swing with violent intent.

"I'll tell you, I swear," she pleads.

With the last swerve, both blades stop abruptly at Bernie's neck. The boy's eyes close. His whole body trembles. His torso looks like an over-ripe melon with leaf-shaped gashes.

Susan whines. The ropes tear at the flesh on her wrists, but Bernie is in much worse shape, traumatized and shaking, his mouth agape as though he's been electrified, his face ashen white.

"I'll tell you what you need to know," she says.

With measured grace, Ho Dam swoops back to face her. "So now, you're ready to negotiate?" He watches her head nod. She frowns with reluctance and then he smiles. "Now, that's a good girl."

Chapter Thirty-One

"Divide and Conquer"

Tom signals Sal to follow him into a new area of the tunnel. They sprint ahead, thinking the terrorists will catch up to them soon. They have to pause when they see the tunnel splitting in two.

"Which way now?" asks Sal.

"Hard to gauge. We could go either way. If I remember from the map, the tunnels both lead to the terrorists' cavern."

Sal clears his throat. "You can be sure that those Koreans will be following us, so I suggest we go separate ways. We can't have two men down." He unstraps his .40 Beretta sidearm and passes it to Tom. "The safety's off and the clip's full. Here's an extra round, too. Hope you're a good shot. Bear in mind, bullets will bounce off inside here."

"Wait a minute," Tom says, nervously. "I've never fired one of these before."

"It's easy. Point and shoot. You're in close range. Hey, any jerk-off can do it. Go as far as you can. Our reinforcements should be here soon."

"Have you made contact with them?"

"Nah. I'm just estimating the time frame and hoping for the best." Sal turns and jogs away, disappearing into the pitch black.

Tom scowls. Even with his wild brother and wilder Dad, he's never actually fired a real handgun. BB and pellet guns, but this is different.

"Better get moving," Sal's voice faintly echoes.

"Alright. Have pistol, will travel." Tom preps himself into a firing stance and practices aiming the pistol. It feels awkward at first. He can't say he's a gun guy. Despite studying the ferocious activity of volcanoes ,and all the dangerous escapades, he considers himself to be a peacemaker, a sensible gun control advocate, and an Earth lover.

But there's the weight of the pistol and a power contained within it. He'll trick his mind into acting brave. He'll practice a John Wayne stare or

Clint Eastwood grimace. Whatever it takes. He shakes his head and runs down the eroded right side tunnel.

Meanwhile, under a low ceiling, Sal slides a bayonet onto his rifle. The tunnel is dark, secretive, disorienting. The environment unnerves him, but it will provide concealment. He scurries to a corner, hides behind a ledge, and flicks the headlamp off. While he catches his breath, he realizes there's an unbearable heat that overwhelms the space.

He hears boots shuffle on the ground. Gravel crunches. The soldiers are walking toward him. They are about to pass by him when he bounds out in front of them and opens a round of fire. Shocked, they have no time to respond and they immediately collapse to their deaths.

Sal stands on guard. Two more soldiers rush at him. He plunges a bayonet into the first one. The soldier coughs and gags. Sal pins him to the tunnel wall, as a torrent of blood guzzles out from the soldier's abdomen. Sal spins past the helpless man and throws a kick at the other soldier, knocking him unconscious. He pulls the bayonet out of the first soldier.

Close range combat in relative darkness. It's terrifying.

Then two more soldiers appear and fire at him. One bullet hits. He groans, suppressing a deeper cry, before he places a hand on his left thigh. It's a superficial wound, but hurts like all hell. The blood is warm and sticky as tar pitch when he tweezes his fingers and reaches under the skin. He examines the hole. The bullet went completely through his outer thigh. The shot wasn't enough to send him into oblivion, but enough to slow him down for a bit.

But I can't stop! Time to ramp up and fight back.

Falling to his knees, he returns fire and hits the last two soldiers. Then a rifle barrel jams into the back of his head.

"Drop it," the soldier's voice commands. Sal drops his own weapon and stands, raising his hands above his head. He steps forward. The burning pain in his wounded leg intensifies. He's been shot a dozen times before, but *damn, it always hurts. You forget the pain and then it happens again.*

The soldier prods Sal along. Sal sidesteps and halts. Quickly, he pivots around, bringing his right hand down onto the rifle barrel. The soldier fires bullets that ping off the tunnel walls, while Sal pulls the weapon down toward the ground. It continues to fire around their feet. A bullet lodges in the soldier's ankle. He screams in agony. The clip is empty now.

Sal wrestles away, pawing at the gravel. The wounded and agitated soldier shouts while he finds his footing. He retaliates with a firm thrust to Sal's thigh. Sal moans, but rises back up. The soldier pounces on him and swings with the rifle once more. As the rifle hammers into the ground, triggering a thunderous crack, Sal manages to scurry away.

In mere seconds, he discovers the cause of the intense heat. Sal and the soldier both drop onto a thick, porous slab with lava flowing underneath them. Rocks and debris rain down. Sal crouches. The soldier hunches over him. A large rock falls and strikes the molten liquid with such force that the liquid splashes up, hitting the soldier in the face with a bubbling hiss. The man lets out an agonizing screech that sounds like it comes from the depths of Hades. He reaches up to wipe his face and struggles to free himself from the flesh melting globs. He loses his balance and topples off the floating slab, landing backside into the molten river.

What a way to go, Sal thinks. It's terrible, but it's way too late to offer a truce. He shields his eyes from the heat. He's seen some gruesome deaths in his tenure, but this one's got to top the list. He knows what memories they can imprint, so he's not about to watch the lava swallow up the soldier in its fiery embrace.

The lava river gains momentum. Sal clings to his life-raft-rock-slab as it flows downstream. He centers himself in a balanced contraposto stance, raising his arms in opposite directions for balance. He shuts his eyes from the blinding heat. The tunnel narrows and the lava gathers speed. A low rumble amplifies to a roar. Swiveling his head around, he's shocked to see a lava wave rising up to a vertical wall, several feet behind him. It crests, reaching out above him, forming a cylinder.

"God help me…" he whispers. He lowers himself into a squat stance, covering his head with one hand and holding onto the slab with the other. Then the liquid wave pitches out over him. He shifts his weight to the inside edge of the slab. The lava flow speeds up. He's slab surfing in the hollow lava tube as it curls over his head. Disappearing behind a curtain of hot liquid, he yells out –

"WHOOOOA-A-A-H-H-H! …."

On the other side, Tom clambers down the pebbly right-side tunnel, stumbling every few seconds. *I sure hope Rosetti has fared better than I have.*

Broken-down rocks litter the tunnel floor. He makes a slight turn where the tunnel narrows to five feet across. He stops at a chest high tube opening in the wall and pulls out his flashlight to examine the tube. It emits a low, grumbling noise that becomes progressively louder.

He drops to the ground and covers his head. A hot white vapor blasts out of the tube like a dragon's fetid breath. The blast subsides. He stands up again and shakes it off. He's only read about horizontal vapor plumes, but never actually experienced them.

Then a sound echoes down the tunnel – footfalls and the unmistakable voices of men in pursuit. Seconds later, three Korean soldiers stand in a line twenty yards away. Lights flash and they point their rifles at Tom. He raises his hands. One soldier approaches, with another one right behind him, shouting orders at him in Korean. They probably know who he is and want to take him as a hostage.

"I'm sorry, I don't understand you," Tom says, stepping to his left.

One of the soldiers keeps his rifle trained on Tom and the other soldier sticks his head and flashlight into the glowing plume opening. With a whoosh, the lava tube explodes in another vicious blast of hot white gas.

The air consumes both the soldiers, boiling one man's head and pinning the other one's body against the wall, scalding him to death until he collapses in a fried heap. Tom backs away, pulls his pistol from behind, and fires, hitting a third soldier. In shock, Tom whirls around and ducks, running as fast as he can.

He pants and slows down when he enters into a dense, warm fog. He wonders if this could be where the remnants of the vapor blast condensed. He switches his headlamp off. The fog swaddles around him like wet cloth. He reaches out and his hands hit a wall. It's a dead end.

The light from the two remaining soldiers infiltrates the fog. No doubt they watched Tom disappear into the milky soup. Tom crouches down and holds his breath while a soldier ambles toward him, arms outstretched. Shifting his leg, Tom dislodges a pebble by accident. They'll find him for sure. Just as he's about to curse out loud, the soldiers shoot, but the bullets ping off walls and bounce back at the soldiers in an auto-fire melee. It's chaos. Tom wants to cry out. And then, the tunnel goes silent.

"Hello?" Tom whispers. A queasy sensation tingles throughout his body and he feels an odd sense of victory that he isn't sure he deserves. He rises up and looks around. He flicks on his light, but there is no movement from the dead men. As he walks over, he tries not to look at the bloody mess, half-expecting a hand to grab his calf or a groan to issue forth from a body, like a scene from a zombie horror flick. But nothing happens.

He jogs back to where the tunnel split. He passes the vaporized bodies and walks for a few more minutes. There's an increase in temperature and then he sees a hole in the tunnel floor. He looks down into it, shielding his face with his hands. Heat pulsates out of it. Several feet below, molten lava flows in undulating waves.

His eyes cannot adjust to the lava's brightness, so he turns away. And there, right next to the hole, is a M-16 gun, property of Colonel Sal Rosetti.

"Oh no…"

He squats and glances down at the lava again. With an achy numbness, he envisions the Commander falling into the abyss. As much as Tom feared the possibility of horrendous death for himself, he doesn't wish to be the survivor, the lone wolf. And how strange to meet a man, not like him, then subsequently have to say "goodbye" without warning. The disappointment weighs down on Tom. Disillusionment too. Underneath that, there is the sadness.

We never really know people, do we?

With a long exhale, he reaches for the pouch in his backpack. He opens the pouch and pours the ohelo berries into his hand. He's heard they are edible, a delicacy for the nene geese, and he drops one in his mouth. It's chewy and tart, not quite ripe and not exactly delicious. Keoki referred to them as sacred. He questions that, but then again, he's desperate.

He lets the rest of the berries roll out of his palm and drop down into the lava beyond his vision. He closes his eyes and breathes as deeply as he can. *God, if you do exist, and you're out there, please look after Sal Rosetti…* His lips move in quiet prayer. Then he hears the thump of approaching feet. He whips around to meet the sight of twenty armed soldiers.

So much for answered prayers, but I can't keep running.

The men approach and he recognizes the heat-resistant Hazmat suits. With night-vision goggles, gas masks, and Kevlar body armor under their suits, they look like strange astronauts. They bark muffled orders in English. Tom relaxes. He steps back until a soldier reaches out and grabs him.

"Wa-sh ou' there buddeee…" the Hazmat alien mumbles as he pulls Tom away from the lava. Then he tears off his gas mask, goggles, and headgear, revealing a handsomely rugged face.

"You must be Dr. Andrews," he says.

"Yes?"

"I'm Lieutenant Jarvis, commander of this Spec Op team."

The Lieutenant's face is lean, weathered by years of service in the Armed Forces, but it doesn't look like he's willing to quit any time soon. He clenches his teeth before he whispers in a reedy voice, "You all alone here? Where's Commander Rosetti?"

Tom wags his head and mirrors the Lieutenant's own anxiety as he points to the hole.

"No way. That would be an awful end for him. We'll just have to hope for the best and prepare for the worst," Jarvis states with a trace of remorse. "Great soldier. A solid commander, too." The soldiers standing next to Jarvis gesture in agreement.

"He was," Tom says. "We probably shouldn't have split up, but it made sense to him at the time. Our underground monitor readings stopped functioning. Didn't expect to be this deep into the tunnel. I do have… a map."

"Where?"

"In my mind."

"Interesting," Jarvis says. "That's the first I've heard of a mental map of this place. But at least the veterans are all safe. Are the Koreans anywhere nearby?"

"It appears Sal and I eliminated all the ones they sent after the hostages."

"Good," Jarvis affirms, "then let's keep moving and try to find their command center."

He nods to his team to follow Tom and together they walk in silence, with only the sounds of their boots shuffling against the rocky floor and the Hazmat suits crinkling with moisture. The tunnel narrows. They lower their heads and bend their elbows to avoid brushing against the jagged walls.

Tom stops and turns to them, imagining the lines of the map. "I think we're getting close."

Chapter Thirty-Two

"The Underground Fire Fight"

With two military escorts from Jarvis' Special Ops team, the fleeing veterans walk back through the tunnel. Despite their thirst and hunger, the trek seems shorter than before. Soon they see light from the cleared rubble of the tunnel cave-in and then – *Hallelujah!* – the entrance. Military personnel greet and help them, carrying the weak civilians up to the base camp where three Blackhawk helicopters await the arrival.

Still feeling protective, James inspects the faces of the weary crowd. Their clothes are filthy and tattered. Some of them are covered with blood. For poor Irene, the pain of losing Howard may never fully dissipate. Everyone is in shock, but the relief overwhelms them.

An officer welcomes James into the clearing and informs him, "We got a call from your wife. Helicopters are here to transport you folks. And you got the last flight outta' here."

James grins, anticipating the embrace of his daughter and the honeysuckle voice of his wife. "It's a miracle."

The officer smiles. "Sure is, brother, sure is."

Tom and the military team reach the end of the tunnel and the entrance of the Koreans' hideout. Crawling up, they peer down to see fifteen Korean soldiers in various states of repose. The soldiers on guard-duty lean against a wall and talk in hushed tones to one another. Others sit and recline, smoking cigarettes.

"Amazing," Jarvis whispers to Tom. "I would have expected to see more soldiers on alert. They must be thinking that they've won already."

Jarvis points to two of his men and whispers. "Load the RPGs." The soldiers prepare the rocket propelled grenade launcher attachments for their rifles.

"No." Tom grabs Jarvis' shoulder. "It's not a good idea to fire those things."

"We've been ordered to blow 'em out of there."

"But you can't…"

"Why? The hostages have all been released."

"I'm pretty sure my wife is in there. That's what one of the hostages told me."

"Your wife? Why didn't you say something earlier?"

"And our apprentice. I thought you knew. You didn't?"

"Nope," Jarvis says.

"That's crazy. They must have gone through a more direct tunnel entrance at their own risk. Unbelievable."

Jarvis addresses two of his men. "We still have civilians inside. So, here's the approach. We have to be as covert as possible. Put these on." He pulls out camo caps and jackets that look like the KUF uniform.

"Are you serious?" Tom asks. "I didn't think this happened in real life."

"We got them off of the dead ones we found in the tunnel. This will give us an advantage for a few seconds and I do mean a few seconds."

He passes caps to two of his men. The soldiers change quickly. They look to Jarvis with their thumbs up and he nods at them to start their mission. Pulling their hats down low, holding AK-47s that they also took from the dead Korean soldiers, they proceed into the cavern. The rest of the squad stays concealed behind a ledge, watching closely, their weapons drawn.

One of the Koreans stands and shouts at them to come over. "Eri-wa!"

Jarvis' men don't reply. Instead they keep their heads down while they approach two unsuspecting Korean soldiers. Jarvis motions to his team and leads them in a sudden charge.

The disguised soldiers lash out with knives, jabbing into the guard soldiers with speed and fatal accuracy. The two men collapse as Jarvis' men hold them up, effectively using their bodies as human shields against the other Korean soldiers that are firing at them.

Loud weapons fire. Battle cries in Korean and English issue forth, blending into a linguistic Babel, intensified by the cave's echoes. The entire SO team rushes into the cavern entrance.

Tom sits alone, hiding and listening to the war cries. The operation is not so quiet and covert anymore. He worries about Susan and Bernie, but he's also deeply remorseful about Sal. Their personalities clashed and Tom didn't appreciate the taunting, but he wouldn't wish any suffering upon the poor guy. It's disheartening to think there was no recovery of the body, as though Sal evaporated like a volcanic mist, entombed in a river of lava. He was too tough to go out without a fight.

No, that cranky old bastard deserved to live!

The sounds of artillery boom in Tom's ears. He imagines an oasis pool, somewhere to wash off the grim and sweat that have collected on his face and body. With the heat and humidity, his fingers have swelled to a puffy sausage consistency. To relieve the pressure, he takes off his wedding ring for a moment. He studies the band – *Gold, Au, atomic no. 79, diamagnetic, solid, malleable transitional metal, tensile strength 120 MPa.* Inscribed on the inside of the band, in small block letters – Token of Love.

Then he snaps out of his reprieve and realizes he can't just sit here. He has to rescue Susan. He puts the ring back on his finger and pulls out his pistol muttering to himself. "Time to join the insanity…"

The Koreans take on heavy casualties as the SO team advances. Tom scurries up next to Lieutenant Jarvis. Rounds clink off the walls.

"They're retreating farther into another tunnel," Jarvis says.

"I don't think they can go much further," Tom says.

Jarvis rises up and fires at the enemy, signaling his men to continue their advance. "We'll soon find out."

Tom flicks off his pistol safety and looks to one of the soldiers next to him. "Okay, cover me, I'm going in."

"You know I can't let you do that."

"Hell, you can't. My wife's in there. They could kill her!"

Tom leaps up, bolts, then dives behind a low rock pile before an onslaught of bullets narrowly miss him. He exhales, then darts behind a few of the U.S. troops. While the battle ensues, he spots something moving in his peripheral vision. One of the Koreans turns and flees down a passageway. Tom jumps up and bounds after him, striding down the tunnel. In a few minutes, the man leads Tom to the command center.

Hiding against a wall by the center's cavern entrance, Tom peeks around the edge to see Ho Dam circling Susan like a hungry shark. He waves a long, thin sword at her, his expression fixed in murderous resolve.

Tom bites his lip to swallow a yell. He sees Susan's hands tied above her head, wrists bleeding. Blood saturates her face and hair. Bernie hangs nearby, naked except for his tattered t-shirt and underwear. Ho Dam's sword cuts the air. Then Tom sees him raise his left hand and slap Susan. Hard.

"Ah, no," Tom whispers, soft enough for no one to hear. But anger seethes in him. He flinches, breathing with a quickened pace. His heartbeat accelerates and he grips the pistol handle as though he was wringing Ho Dam's neck.

"I gave you the exact coordinates of the vitrellium deposits," Susan says. "I swear that's all I know. Please. You now have all the intel you need, so let us go!"

"We'll see about that," Ho Dam says. He tramps behind Susan and Bernie to a partitioned off area. Through the underground radio transmission, he talks with Commander Lee.

"Most Supreme Commander, we have lost the veteran hostages, but you will be happy to know that I captured a worthier ransom. Dr. Susan Andrews. She was one of the scientists at the cave discovery and she is Dr. Tom Andrews' wife. And, she gave me the exact locations of the vitrellium deposits."

"That is worth it," Lee answers.

"She is not disclosing any more information besides the coordinates."

"It is enough. We will dispense our agents immediately to the province and secure the location. You have done a great service for us today."

"Now the Americans are attacking," Ho Dam says.

"Then you know what to do. We thank you for your service. And your life."

Ho Dam turns the radio off. One of his soldiers enters the partitioned area, a worried look on his face. "Captain, we cannot hold them much longer."

"Bring me the detonator."

Still hiding against a wall, Tom peeks around the edge to see Ho Dam continue to circle Susan and wave the sword at her. A Korean soldier walks to a console while Ho Dam turns his back to the newly acquired hostages. Suddenly, he looks back at Susan. He slides up to her and slaps her across the face again. She cries out.

Watching, Tom winces with phantom pain and real outrage. It's just a game to this psychopath Ho Dam. Tom exhales his last breath of self-control. Then he leaps from his hiding place, dashing to beat the soldier for the detonator.

Ho Dam screeches. The soldier grabs the detonator and raises his AK-47, but Tom fires a shot at him before ducking behind the console. A direct, lucky hit. The soldier keels over on the console and drops the detonator.

Tom rushes in and grabs it

"It's over now," Tom says.

"Not quite," Ho Dam answers. He slips behind Susan, the edge of his blade to her neck. He brings the shiny blade close to her jugular vein. Susan's eyes bulge as she quivers.

Tom hesitates and steps forward keeping his pistol directed straight at Ho Dam's head, the detonator in his other hand. Sweat trickles down Tom's forehead, but he looks into Susan's eyes as if to reassure her – *I won't let him harm you*. His heart flutters, his insides twist with a pang of fear, thundering like a washing machine. But he refuses to let the anxiety show on his face.

"Drop the gun and bring me the device," Ho Dam says.

"No, let her go first."

"Just do as I say Dr. Andrews. We'll both move at the same time. You hand me the detonator and I'll let her go. First, you must drop the gun. Do it now or she dies." He retracts the sword out from under her neck, making a small, clean cut under her chin. Bright blood spurts out. Her eyes squeeze shut.

"Let me die, Tom," she moans. "You know what's right."

"No." He bends forward and sets the pistol on the ground. Then he walks toward them. "I'm unarmed, now let her go."

"Set the detonator down and move back."

"Just let her go…"

"Set it down!" Ho Dam pulls the blade back to her throat, pressing it into her skin.

Reluctantly, Tom puts the detonator down and takes a step back. "Now, as I said. Release her as you promised."

Ho Dam scoops up the detonator. "Good boy, Professor. A-plus." He laughs. "How many times have we seen *that* old trick before?" He swings the sword's blade to cut the rope around her wrists. "But, see, I'm an honest man."

With shaky knees, Susan staggers to Tom, until suddenly Ho Dam reaches out and grabs her by the hair, almost jerking her off her feet.

"Let her go!" Tom shouts. "What the hell is your problem?"

"As you wish." With quick force, Ho Dam shoves her violently at Tom and she falls into his arms. They take a moment to regain their balance, holding onto one another in a moment of liberated reunion.

Ho Dam turns and bolts in the direction of the surface tunnel exit, with his sword in one hand and the detonator in the other. Bernie attempts to lash out and kick him as he passes by, but misses, causing him to swing by his tied hands.

"I'll never lose you again," Tom says, embracing his wife. With a small towel from his backpack, he gently presses her chin. The blood soaks through the towel. Her lips tremble and she sniffles, quivering.

Bernie rustles. "Uh, excuse me, guys? Don't forget about me. I'm still hung up here. Hello?"

Distracted and lovelorn, Tom and Susan stare into each other's eyes. Indigo blue meets green-gold, locked in silent communication. "I'll never go it alone again," he says.

"You better not. 'Cause if they don't kill you, I will," she says. "Ah, hell. Laughter is the only reliable shock absorber. I'm so exhausted. Delirious." She tosses her head.

Tom smiles, pulls her close again, and strokes the top of her hair. He holds her hands to his chest. "From now on, we're an inseparable team, Suzie Q. I swear, it will be every job together."

Bernie clears his throat. "Hey, I really hate to interrupt your second honeymoon, but my hands are going pins and needles and there's a sociopath on the loose who's about to blow apart this volcano."

"He's right," Susan says. She searches the cavern surroundings and grabs one of Ho Dam's swords. "Here take this. All right, I guess this is another solo assignment," she says, snickering, handing the sword to Tom.

He slices Bernie's rope, freeing him. Bernie rubs his hands and sighs in relief, pulling up his shredded pants.

"I promise I'll stop this guy," Tom says. "You two follow me up, okay?"

"We'll be right behind you," Susan says, handing him his pistol.

He turns and slashes the sword in the air, with all the bravado of a musketeer, dashing through the tunnel toward the entrance.

Chapter Thirty-Three

"The Eruption"

The crazy terrorist with the detonator - I have to stop him.

Tom dashes up and out of the hidden lava tube, a quick exit after the meandering entrance. It's two a.m. He switches on his headlamp to illuminate the gray patina of the volcanic mounds, a smoothness only interrupted by sprigs of trees and grassy shrubs. He peers down the crater's cliff, detecting movement.

Ho Dam scampers down a trail, the same pathway his men took to surprise the U.S. incursion team a few days earlier. Tom aims his pistol at him and fires, but misses.

Tom sprints along to the trail's slope and then slows down. Clouds shift, obscuring Ho Dam's path. Suddenly, Ho Dam jumps out and starts swinging his sword at Tom's head. Tom moves away and drops the pistol as he falls down. The sword blade misses him and chips a small rock outcropping. Sparks fly. Ho Dam scowls. They both scramble for the gun and Tom comes up with it.

"It's over now." He points the weapon at Ho Dam's head. "No more games. Hand over the detonator."

Ho Dam holds it up. It's innocuous looking, like a garage door opener, and yet it has the ability to activate the volcano and destroy all surrounding life forms.

"Too bad you'll have to say goodbye to your wife and your friend." Cackling like a mad animal, Ho Dam presses the switch. "Death. Destruction."

"No!" Tom shouts as he pulls the gun's trigger. He clicks several times. The gun is out of ammo. He tosses it aside and stands, lifting his sword to attack Ho Dam.

But at that moment the earth ripples with a violent quake. They both stagger to stay on their feet. Ash spews into the atmosphere. Tom charges

Ho Dam and just before they are about to make contact, another powerful explosion surges, which sends them both sprawling to the ground, scraping their bodies on sharp rocks. When the quakes subside, they look around to see a transformed landscape.

Curtains of fiery red and orange lava fire soar hundreds of feet above them. Steam vents, resembling white cloud funnels, open up and release gas, while large, molten, incandescent lava rock bombs eject from the surface with sonic booms. When the rocks hit the ground, they explode loudly, forming instant craters upon impact. It's Hell on Earth.

Far to the southeast, the Big Island's coastal cliffs buckle and crack. The remaining miles of the non-fenced coastal section crumble into the sea with a deafening roar.

Immediately, the impact causes large waves to roll and surge up against the Navy ships anchored off shore, swamping and sinking some of the smaller vessels. A set of fifty-foot tsunami waves rise in height, fanning out along the coast, before they wrap around the Big Island and approach landfall. Moments later the waves slam into the shoreline, inundating the entire coastal sea level areas.

Beyond that, in the evacuated city of Honolulu, the ocean begins to roar and recede to the horizon line, exposing a vast, dry seabed of reef, rock, and sand. Then the massive tsunami waves build and race toward the deserted city. The first waves hit, exploding into the harbor and coastline, decimating everything in the way. Boats, docks, buildings, cars, trucks, and debris sweep up, plunging inland in a massive torrent.

Waves rush up the streets and alleyways. Some skyscrapers collapse. Others crumble, gutted in a matter of seconds by the waves and the mounting sea of debris. Smaller buildings dismantle, wobble, and fall into the rushing currents, or they topple over each other, domino style, imploding with loud crashes.

Several more waves follow, decimating every tangible thing, until the waves finally slosh up against the foothills of the Ko'olau mountain range. Then, as swiftly as they ascended, the waters ebb, sucking back and speeding away, taking anything loose along with them back to the shoreline and out to sea. Only a few minutes have passed and the once spectacular, tropical island city surrenders to a state of ruin.

On the flanks of Kilauea, Tom sits up and holds his hand against a nasty gash from a flying projectile that winged his head. He takes a minute to recover from the ear-splitting blasts. Dazed, he looks around, awed by what he sees. It's a mega July Fourth, minus the fun, as the landscape erupts with an incredible display of volcanic power. Momentarily, he observes the scene, fascinated by Mother Nature's might.

Then, from a short distance behind him, he hears the sound of maniacal laughter. Ho Dam perches above him, brandishing his sword. Tom turns around to face him. Ho Dam blends with the rocks, like a demonic image silhouetted against fiery fountains and colorful, cruel mayhem.

Ho Dam yells above the explosions. "Just you and me! No survivors!" He waves the sword at the sky.

Tom grasps his own sword and charges, leaping up to meet Ho Dam, but the wild man scurries up and out of range.

Tom follows. "I'll kill you! Son of a bitch."

They face off and circle each other.

"Don't talk about my mother!" shouts Ho Dam. "She was a victim of your country's brutality. Don't like losing your family? Well, neither did I!"

"Maybe Susan is still alive," Tom says.

"Doubt it," Ho Dam answers. He advances, wielding the sword with precision and power.

Tom steps back to deflect the blows, realizing he is up against a trained swordsman. Tom can only do what he can. He shudders and tries to avoid contact, when suddenly his opponent's weapon swipes his left shoulder. He grimaces, looking down at the bleeding wound.

No quarter. The terrorist releases a frenetic onslaught. Blades clash. Weakened, Tom's sword flies out of his hand.

"Time to meet *your* ancestors," Ho Dam says.

Tom backs away, raising his hands and closing his eyes in fitful anticipation, when the ground shakes and erupts again, sending them both to their knees. A fissure opens up between them.

This volcano is on my side, Tom thinks.

From the fissure, a thin curtain of highly pressurized molten lava shoots up, over twenty feet into the air. They both back away from the hot splattering of liquid fire. Then they turn and run in opposite directions. Tom stops to apply pressure to the shoulder wound. When he looks up, he sees Ho Dam making his way around the vent, charging toward him.

"You're crazy!" Tom shouts. He bolts, but Ho Dam catches up to him. He evades several sword blows from the madman. But Ho Dam is fast, moving like a young, lithe rabbit. He corners Tom against a rock formation.

"You'll die for sure now," Ho Dam says. He clutches the sword, teeth clenched in potent anger. When Ho Dam swivels toward him, Tom lifts a football sized, lava rock above his head and deflects the blow. The sword slams into the rock, breaking it in half. Tom tosses the broken pieces at Ho Dam to injure or distract him. It doesn't work. He's dodging every pebble.

Tom scrambles away, but he's fatigued. Still backed into the corner, he raises his hands in surrender or as a natural response to shield himself. Ho Dam steadies the sword with both hands and rears back. He hesitates for a moment as his eyes meet Tom's.

It's then that Tom sees sparkling gold rings around Ho Dam's irises. The color of wealth. The rings are beautiful. *Meeting eyes with your enemy and it's almost poignant.*

Ho Dam grins as he brings his sword down for the final death blow. Just before it hits Tom's skull, Tom swings his arms and turns aside. The sword blade misses him and instead it clinks down into the rock, a fraction of an inch from Tom's right ear. Splinters of lava rock strike the back of his head. And yet, to his surprise, he hears Ho Dam screeching.

The sword is lodged in solidified lava rock. Tom rolls away and looks back at how close the blade came to splitting his skull in half.

Ho Dam bends down and with all his strength tries to pull the sword out. A small glowing crack forms around the blade. Again he attempts to wrestle the blade free. A thin faucet of hot, pressurized lava erupts from around the blade. It shoots up, spraying onto his face and upper body. He releases his hold on the embedded sword and steps aside, letting out a deafening scream."Ahhhhhh!"

Crouched, Tom watches him. He hopes it's all over, but he sees Ho Dam shaking lava off his burned face, which now resembles the rough-hewn texture of sizzling bacon. His frantic anger short-circuits the pain and he careens in Tom's direction. He pulls out a large, deadly-looking combat knife from his belt. He leans forward above Tom and raises it. In self-defense, Tom coils up and kicks with the last burst of vigor, his shoes thudding against Ho Dam's abdomen.

Stunned, Ho Dam stumbles toward an edge above a drop-off. He teeters there, trying to gain stability. He wipes his face in an obsessive manner and yells as the embers scorch his face and hands. Then he loses his balance and free falls backwards off the small cliff.

He lands in a crevice, fifteen feet below the edge. He screams, his upper-right thigh impaled by a three-foot tall, sharp, basalt pinnacle. Lying on his back, pinned there, he struggles to free himself, but he's helpless. His left leg is broken, bent unnaturally, like a strange jigsaw puzzle piece. He moans and cries out. He curses loudly in Korean.

Tom looks down at the suffering man, aghast at the sight. *Is he getting his just rewards? After all, he almost killed Susan a few times. He destroyed the islands.* But then there's a pang in Tom's heart. *Is it pity? Should I spare his life so he can have a fair trial?*

Tom looks for a way to scale down the vertical ledge. There's no option within the vicinity. Too many steep, jagged rocks. If he jumped into the crevice, he would break his own bones or maybe worse. Meanwhile, the crack around Ho Dam's sword has expanded into a foot-wide, pulsing, lava stream. Tom sees it flowing downhill to the cliff edge, directly above the paralyzed man.

"Lava's heading your way," he calls down to his rival. "I'll try to dam it up." Then he turns and hastily gathers several rocks and sets them in the flow's path, trying to redirect it. But the flow switches, pulled by gravity, right toward Ho Dam.

Tom bolts back to the cliff edge, screaming. "Hey, get out of there now, the flow's heading right for you. I can't stop it!"

The impaled Ho Dam struggles to get up and away, but he's immobilized in his condition and can only fall back, shrieking in pain. He lies there, in shock, about to pass out. The lava flows into a shallow crevice and inches its way over the ledge right above him.

Tom waves and motions him to get out of there. "Move! Get outta' there now!"

Then a few deadly trickles of lava drop onto the ground in front of Ho Dam, splashing his legs and stirring him out of his stupor. He looks up and panics. He pulls his legs up and struggles to move, but he's paralyzed. The flow picks up momentum and volume, beginning to drip down on him. He's stuck under the flow and he cries out again – a high-pitched, primordial scream – "Eeeeeeehh-aaaahh!"

Now, with full force, a molten rod of liquid fire descends down onto his mid-section. As it bares down, it moves slowly up his body, ripping into his mid-section in a hideous fashion – melting, burning, and dividing his flesh.

With nature's indifference, the lava slowly and tortuously inches its way up to his chest and face. He twitches, trembles, screeching out in delirium.

Tom has never heard such an agonized cry before – it's part human, part animal, part monster, like a sound from the depths of the earth's core. Hot, tortured, hellish. *"Whoa,"* he says. *The lava is literally sawing him in half.*

He looks away from the gruesome sight and drops to his knees, his body spent, his mind overwhelmed. He feels sadness, yes, but moreover he wants to spare himself this horror. He won't ever forget the image and the sounds of Ho Dam's death.

Chapter Thirty-Four

"Survivors"

It's surreal. The earth's violent tremors and explosions, his fight with Ho Dam and the poor man's tortured death...these memories will linger for years to come. But now, there is survival to consider, and Susan.

Dirty, bruised, and bloodied, Tom drags himself up the cinder cone hillside to the lava tube entrance. Halfway there, he's overjoyed to see two survivors pulling themselves out of a fissure. Covered in layers of soot, the first figure is not quite distinguishable, until Tom's headlamp light shines on her.

"Susan!" he shouts in disbelief.

She peers down the embankment, waves, and runs to Tom's embrace.

"It's finally over," she says as they cling to each other. Her tears wet his face while their collective dirt and blood mingle. "It was awful. We almost didn't make it out. The entire cavern collapsed behind us. No one could've survived." They kiss and pull back from the hug.

"The entire platoon?" he asks.

She frowns, nodding her head.

"Whoa. It's a miracle you made it out," Tom says.

Bernie stumbles next to them, rubbing ash off his body. He sits down and looks to the horizon line, too tired to speak.

"Where's Ho Dam?" Susan asks.

"Dead," answers Tom. "It was unbelievable. He fell and a lava flow..." he begins to explain when the thunderous clanks of helicopter rotor blades drown out his voice. An Army Blackhawk comes into view. It circles, hovering overhead.

Bernie jumps up. "Here we are, down here!" He pulls off his shredded t-shirt and waves it like a flag.

They all watch the helicopter descend. It loiters thirty feet above the top of the hillside, trying to find some even ground. Suddenly, a lava bomb erupts from the surface. Like an incandescent rocket, the bomb speeds skyward, glowing as it lands in on the helicopter. Before the pilot can react, the bomb arches into the cockpit, smashing the underbelly of the cockpit's nose cone. The pilot and co-pilot die in an instant.

Losing control, the helicopter spins and careens downward. It veers to its side as the main rotor blades plow into the ground at the base of the cinder cone hillside. It tumbles over, exploding in a massive fireball.

Tom, Susan, and Bernie look on, bracing themselves and shielding their faces from the explosive shock-wave that sends bits of metal streaking past them. They wait a few seconds. From a short, but protected distance away, they watch as the helicopter wreck burns and smolders into a heap.

Susan cries out in frustration.

"How are we ever going to get out of here?" Bernie whines.

Tom turns and surveys the landscape. It's a war with the elements – lava flows, lava rivers, and now, the explosive rock bombs. "Well, that was probably our only hope for a rescue. Looks like we're just gonna' have to…walk out of here."

"What? Through all of that? No way," Bernie says.

Bands of lava run downhill while crimson fire sprays into the pre-dawn sky. Searching for a route, Susan looks back up the hill to a tunnel entrance. "Hey, look up there!"

At the top of the cinder cone, a stocky figure emerges from the tube carrying a limp body. As the man approaches, they see he resembles a human sized Hulk, with ripped clothes and bulging muscles. In lieu of the green skin, his skin is reddish brown in some areas as if he's been deep fried. He's burnt and blistery, the singed hair on his head sticking straight up in thin patches. He ambles down the hill, stops in front of them, and sets a body at their feet. He straightens up and raises his head, blinking his lashless eyes.

"He's not one of ours, but he's still alive," he says to them.

As he bends down again and wipes the dying man's forehead, they recognize the standing man, eyebrows still intact.

"Rosetti? What the hell? How on earth?" Tom says.

The three of them stare and Sal continues. "More like, I was in hell *under* the earth. You wouldn't believe it. Glad I had some surfing lessons in San Diego when I was a cadet. They sure came in handy for this mission. I rode a wave of lava on a frickin' slab, until it spit me out onto this bank."

He pauses to inhale. "I made it out somehow and then found this guy. He was the only survivor. He's shot up pretty bad though. Do you have any water on you? He needs it more than I do this point."

Susan unclasps a water bottle from her belt. She bends down and holds the man's head, helping him drink. "If you can hear me," she asks, "Please tell us who you are."

With charred lips and labored breath, he struggles to speak up. When he does, it is in a heavy accent. "My name is Kim Sung."

Tom kneels next to him.

"The Korean Commander," Sal says. "He was the original leader of this operation."

Kim Sung closes his eyes. "I tried to stop him."

"He won't be setting off any more explosives," Tom says.

Kim Sung bobs his head and attempts a weak grin. He leans forward and grasps Tom's hand. His hoarse voice whispers, "But there's one more."

"What?" Tom asks.

"One last bomb," he says fighting for a breath. "Au-to-matic, detonation, one hour after…"

"What?"

"Must deactivate. Inside the large fis-sure -- another tunnel to the cal-dee-aa…that way."

Kim Sung struggles to sit up and points north. Then he leans back.

"You can end this war…begin again." His eyes open wide, directed to the sky as a bombastic array of orange and violet lights reflects back in them. He smiles in relief, sighs deeply, and dies in peace.

Tom lowers his ear to the man's chest. "He's gone." Tom lays Kim Sung back to the ground.

"Did he say another bomb is planted?" Bernie asks.

"I'm afraid so," says Sal. "He held on this long. Seems like he was telling the truth and genuinely wanted to help us."

"We gotta' find that bomb," Tom says. He grabs Susan's hand and they strike off in the direction that Kim Sung pointed. Sal and Bernie follow.

With the sun slowly rising, the sky turns rosy-pink. The foursome cautiously walk across the rugged landscape, until Tom sees the large fissure crack. It's ten feet deep, twenty feet across, with a lava tube opening at the far end.

"All right, this has got to be it," he says. He climbs down into the fissure and turns around to help Susan. Sal follows suit, but Bernie waits behind him, vacillating.

"You just spent a night underground in the dark. You can handle this," Susan says. She speaks with a soft, reassuring voice. "I really think you can do this."

"I know, but we had flashlights and I was on a comic book adrenalin rush. It may be best if I just stay up here. You might need someone here in case help arrives."

"Good idea," Tom says. "You know what, Suze? I think you should stay here with him."

"So much for being together I guess. Sheesh. Alright. But Tom, please make sure you two both get out of there before it detonates. Okay?"

"Don't worry, we'll make it back."

She clasps at Tom. "I love you, darling," she says. Tom hugs her back and then helps her climb out of the fissure. He turns to Sal's direction.

The Colonel is waiting for him at the tube's entrance. He leads the way, grunting when they leave the fissure and approach the tunnel.

"Feeling a little déjà vu here, eh?" Sal muses.

"Yeah, I don't think it's as far to go this time, thank God."

"Hope so," Sal says as they scramble further down the tunnel. Then Sal spots an orange glow in the distance. "There's something up ahead."

They hustle down to the end of the tube, which opens onto the edge of the caldera. Inside it, at the bottom, a massive cauldron churns and boils.

Twenty feet out into the heated lake is a pinnacle shaped island, with lava bubbling up the sides. On the flattened area of the island, a camouflage canopy drapes down and under it is an object about the size of a small car.

"The military didn't detect this?" Tom says.

"Ho Dam's minions must have set it up last night under the cover of darkness. The last call to total destruction. The heat may have distorted the satellite images and most of our forces were out at sea with the tsunami prevention. Well, if that *is* the bomb, I'd say this might be the most unpredictable mission I've ever been on...and you?"

"Definitely. And the most dangerous, too."

Tom looks around and spies a twenty-foot long metal plank. "That must be how they got to the middle of the lake. I guess they didn't think we'd be alive or scouting out bombs. We can use it."

"They assembled the device on the island," Sal says. "Clever bastards."

Tom grabs hold of one end of the plank and Sal picks up the other side. They lift it toward the lava, tilting it down. Then they drop it over the edge. The end of the plank reaches across the expanse to the island. They struggle to steady it, their arms shaking from the weight and the heat emanating from below it. The plank barely touches the island and it's only a foot and a half above the lava.

"Hope it holds," Sal says. "We should cross it one at a time. I'll go first." Arms outstretched for balance, he leads the way over the wobbly plank.

Tom holds his end steady and waits, observing Sal hustle to the other side. "I don't know if I can do this, Rossetti."

"You can, just like you did before. Only now it's not as claustrophobic, but damn, it's hotter than hell."

Tom stares straight ahead. He calculates the walk to be twelve long paces. He looks down at the cauldron as it roils and bubbles, the heat irritating his eyes and infiltrating his pores.

"C'mon Doc. I need your help," Sal says, with his feet on the island end to steady the plank.

Tom steps ahead and moves slowly. The plank flexes from his weight. He quickens his pace and darts for the last few feet. The Colonel moves out of the way and congratulates him with a quick pat on the shoulder. They both scale up the island's flank to the bomb.

"Here goes round two," Tom says.

"We gotta' find the timer and the activation device," Sal answers. He hunches over to inspect the apparatus. "Let's have a look at this baby."

Together they pull off the camouflage tarp covering it. Sal looks down at it in amazement. "Now, that's one helluva' bomb."

The bomb sits on a wooden platform. It consists of a dozen large, metal, fifty-five gallon drum barrels ("drums") filled with ammonium nitrate and wired together with metal straps. Individual blasting caps top each drum. Sal zeroes in on the central drum where the timing device is attached. The digital clock on it reads 10 MINUTES, 7 SECONDS and counting.

"Dang," Tom says. "It's the Holy Grail of Bombs. Do you really think you can deactivate it?"

"We have ten minutes to find out." Sal stares down at the activator. "It's ammonium nitrate and can't detonate from heat alone. It needs an explosive ignition. I have to separate the blasting wires. You got a knife?"

Tom pulls out a small Swiss Army pocket knife and hands it to the Colonel. Sal opens the knife and looks at the pinky size blade in confusion. "Really?"

"Sorry, it's all I got," Tom says, "but it's sharp."

"We got what we got, all right." Sal shakes his head and points to the small boxes attached to each drum. "Okay, so on top of each of these are blasting caps. If I cut the right wires, it'll disconnect them from the main drum with the activator, but..."

Tom looks across the expanse to the tunnel and then down at the lava. It's creeping up closer to the bottom of the plank. "If you cut the wrong ones?"

"I'd rather not think about that." Taking a seat on an adjacent crate, Sal eyes the wires. "If I can detach them, without blowing us to smithereens, we'll still have to get the main drum outta' here and try to deactivate it away from the others. The risk of it exploding here would set the rest off."

"Let's worry about that later." Tom glances around the area. "I'll see if there's something around here we can use to pry the drums apart."

As Sal examines the wires and various connections, Tom walks around to the other side of the bomb until he happens upon a long handle pickaxe. "Looky, here." He smiles, mumbling to himself. He grabs the tool and strides over to Sal. "Try to separate them with this. Just please, be really careful."

With Tom's knife in his hand and tension etched across his face, Sal cuts the last electric connecting wire. Wiping the sweat from his brow, he lets out a deep exhale, and reaches for the pickaxe. Tom watches him as he steadies the tool in his hands, rises and takes aim, knowing he has to make every move count.

The axe comes down with force on the metal straps. Sparks fly, but the axe springs off the strap without breaking it. He lifts it again, rears back, and swings mightily. The strap breaks and frees one of the barrels.

Tom looks back to the tunnel. "Good job! I'll try to secure our exit," he says to Sal, but the Colonel is hyper focused and not listening.

Tom eases down the side of the island to the plank. He notices the lava is now less than foot below and the plank is smoldering. He rears back and leaps across it, his feet burning with every step until he jumps off to the other side to the tunnel entrance. He douses his feet with some loose dirt.

Then he turns and rifles through a discarded pile of construction debris and finds a long, thick wire cable.

"Thanks for leaving your KUF stuff," he snickers. He untangles the cable and drags it to the edge of the lake. Sal is taking another swing at a barrel strap. He braces himself for an expected explosion, but only sparks emit when another barrel breaks free.

"Good work," Tom calls over.

Looking overhead, he spies a rock ledge protruding out from the tunnel ceiling, fifteen feet above him. He ties a weighty piece of scrap metal to the cable's end. Then leaning out, he hurls the cable to the ledge. After a couple of attempts, the cable catches. He pulls on it, testing its strength, satisfied that it should hold the weight.

Sal looks at the last barrel and shouts back to Tom. "Can't cut this last barrel. It's attached directly to the detonator."

"How much time we got?"

"Five minutes, twenty seconds."

"We gotta' get it over here and you back here, too." Tom attaches another piece of metal onto the cable. "We'll try to get it as far up the tunnel as we can and deactivate it there. Sal, are you listening?"

"I hear you, but I got more wires to cut."

"We have to move it. If it explodes over there it could rip the entire rift zone open."

"Look, I'm not so sure I can do it," Sal protests. "You better leave now."

Tom looks down at the plank, glowing orange as the lava inches up. "I'm not leaving. Here catch this!" Tom shifts back and heaves the cable end toward Sal.

Sal scampers down and catches it. He takes the cable back up to the platform and secures it to the barrel, then pushes the barrel off the platform toward Tom. The barrel sways halfway across the expanse. But before Tom can reach it, it swings, pendulum-like, back to the island.

Sal backs up with the attached barrel, runs, then pitches it, shoving it out again with more force. As he lets go, he loses balance and falls forward. Clutching onto the top of the barrel, he's hurled out and over the lava.

"Gotcha'!" Tom bellows as he catches the barrel. Above, the rock ledge crumbles under the weight, scattering pebbles down onto Tom's shoulder. The momentum and weight are too much for him to hold and he loses his footing too.

He falls forward, joining Sal on the swinging barrel ride. Holding on for dear life, they sway back over the lava toward the island. Pushing off the island, they lob back to the tunnel again. The ledge above them gives way and disintegrates.

They yell, screaming in unison as the cable releases, and they fly into the tunnel. They land and push off from the barrel, tumbling away from it. The barrel comes to a thudding halt. They scuttle back to it, viewing the timer – 3 MINUTES, 33 SECONDS.

"We've still got a little more time. Let's try to move it," Tom forcefully shouts.

Sal pulls and Tom pushes, but the tunnel's uphill grade is another unpredictable challenge and they are only able to roll it a couple yards. Then they stop and catch their breath.

"You better go now. I can handle it from here," Sal commands.

"No, let's move it up a little further."

"I don't think so. I'm gonna' try to de-activate it here, so get up to the surface now. And that *is* an order."

"What if you need me?"

Sal raises his arms. "I can do it alone. I don't need you." He shoves Tom away. "Get the hell outta' here. You've got a beautiful wife. Don't be an asshole. Take some time off with her, have some fun, and make a bambino!"

"Now, wait a second."

"Go on, or I'll kick your ass all the way up to surface. Move it, now!"

Shocked, Tom backs away, then turns, and bolts. He races up and out of the tube. The light blinds him for a second as he escapes through the fissure. Then he looks up and sees Susan and Bernie perched, sitting on the fissure's rim, waiting.

"Did you find the bomb?" Bernie asks.

"Where's Sal?" Susan cuts in.

"Yeah, we found it and he's deactivating it right now!" Tom says urgently with a pained look spread across his face. "We gotta' get outta' here!"

He climbs up and takes Susan's hand. In turn, she grabs Bernie's hand and together they sprint away from the fissure, running in a mad dash.

Back in the tunnel, Sal glances down at the timer clock. 23 SECONDS. He holds the open pocket knife in his mouth and separates a red wire. Sweat gushes from his face and body like a waterfall. Anxiously, he cuts the wire. Then he eyes the timer. Relief spreads across his face. But then... no. The timer starts up again, ticking. 12-11-10...

"Ah, dammit!"

He spins around and bolts up the tunnel, his short legs carrying him at the highest revolution per minute imaginable. Just as he spies the exit up ahead, and lowers his head to pass through, the bomb ignites behind him.

A concussive blast fires. The bomb's powerful shock wave slams into him and flings him out of the fissure and into mid-air, head-over-heels, shot out like a cannonball. Surrounded by rocks and debris, he soars up, arms flailing, before he plummets downward. He lands, trundling on the rocky surface, with his hands covering his face and arms around his head protecting himself. His ribs and femur smack the ground with a resounding force.

Chapter Thirty-Five

"The Last Resort"

Tom, Susan, and Bernie race side by side as the earth shakes and convulses.

They scramble for cover and dive into a shallow trench. Hiding, they cover their ears to protect themselves from the ejected projectiles and the blast's deafening vibration. The ground quakes again before it subsides to a low rumble. Plumes of ash rise high. They gaze up over the rim to see a huge lava bomb strike with enough power to leave a crater right outside the trench, right where they just were. They duck their heads to avoid the inevitable rain of rubble.

Suddenly, in a flash of bloody limbs and dusty clothes, Sal appears for the second time. He dives into the trench next to Susan.

She stares on, her mouth open in shock.

"It was close and I'm pretty sure I saw the legendary Pele, but I think we stopped the bomb from igniting another volcanic explosion," Sal says.

Bernie muses and shakes his head in disbelief. "This is way crazier than any comic book adventure I've ever read."

Susan closes her eyes and rests on Tom's shoulder. She sighs. Then she opens her eyes and gazes behind them across the trench. "No," she says, clinging tighter to Tom.

"What, what's wrong?" Tom says as he holds her back, looking in her eyes.

Then they all turn to where she is looking and see a widening river of molten lava, slowly snaking down the trench.

"Can't we rest for just a minute?" Bernie says, exasperated.

They hop to their feet. Lava gushes from the blown out fissure and spreads across the territory that surrounds them. Tom scans the landscape for an escape route. "This way, follow me."

One by one, they step up and out of the trench. Tom leads them through a narrow channel between the flows.

"Where the hell are you going?" Sal demands.

Tom points to a small cinder hill with a tall, white, bark-less tree on the top of it. "If we can make it to that knoll, we may be able to wait there until the flow subsides."

Nervously, they all follow him. At several points, they must leap on the protruding rocks above the flow. After a hundred yards, they reach the isolated hill. They rest on its flanks, a safe distance above the flow, catching their breath.

Susan sips from her bottle of water and then passes it along to the others.

"Sure doesn't look like the flow's slowing down," Bernie says in a squeaky voice.

"If it keeps on rising, we may have to climb that tree. I'll go check it out," Tom says. He strides toward it. At the top of the knoll, he rests a hand on the tree and then slaps it. A dead branch breaks off, almost striking him down as he jumps back.

"I better check it out, too," Sal says with a grunt. He trudges up to Tom.

"Let's just hope that's not going to be our last resort," Susan says. She snaps the nearly empty water bottle to her belt.

"I feel like I'm in hell," Bernie says.

Susan reassures him. "You're not. This is only temporary. We'll get out of here somehow. We made it this far and we're a team now. Like a family, okay?"

She puts her arm around his shoulder and they both walk up together. Below, the lava continues to chug out of the fissure and rise up the flanks of the hill. She thinks about her crazy dream. Bernie in his cape. Bernie, the super hero. She's not so sure about her recent optimistic speech, but the image of a rescue persists. *We will get out of here alive, we have to...*

The four of them sit at the base of the tree, resting and watching the lava rise closer and closer.

Finally, Sal stands and announces, "It might be a good time to check out our last resort." He grabs onto a branch and signals Tom to push Bernie and Susan up into the branches. Tom and Sal follow. Together, they cling onto the tree, like heavy-weight monkeys. In mere minutes, they watch the lava rise toward the trunk. Then the lava begins wrapping around the tree's root system.

"Keep holding on," Tom cries.

Flames lick and flicker around the shallow roots.

"Oh-my-gosh, it's catching on fire!" Bernie shouts.

Tom grasps the trunk with one arm and wraps his other arm around Susan's waist. "I want you to know," he says, "How sorry I am for the way I've treated you. I don't know what to say with death staring us down again, but can you please forgive me?"

"You have been a real jerk at times."

"I know. But I'll change. Just let me try. Suzie Q, I love you more than anyone."

"More than your Mother?"

"She doesn't even compare! I know it seems like I haven't valued you as much as I should, but I really do and if we get out of here alive, I'm going to prove that to you." He leans over to her and they kiss deeply, lingering in a pause of desire before they break.

"I love you too," Susan says. "And, I forgive you."

He sighs. "You know, honey, this would be an amazing story to tell our children."

"We don't have kids."

"Well, you never know…" he says with a grin. "I've been thinking about it. Sal said some things to me and I also realized, I *have* been too focused on my career. There are other important things in life."

"Guys, guys. I hate to interrupt the gazillioneth honeymoon moment, but this really doesn't look good!" Bernie groans as fire ignites the tree's base. The tree starts to wobble and tilt downwards.

"Stop moving!" Sal yells.

Bernie complies. As the tree's motion comes to a sudden stop, he slips off the branch. Now he's hanging from a limb and struggling to hold on with his left hand.

"Help me! I don't want to die!" he wails, dangling in the air. Sal leans down and grabs Bernie's foot and props him back up onto the branch, where he clings on in desperation. The tree now rests horizontally, with the flow rupturing only two feet beneath it.

"Nobody else move!" Sal barks. He searches the sky for any sign of rescue.

"The tree's starting to ignite," Susan calls out. The tree buckles and sinks closer to the lava. Susan looks back to Tom with tears in her eyes. "I love you, Tommy. Sorry about my anger and impatience. You can go on the assignments you want, I think I'll stay home…"

The tree descends further into the fire.

"Oh God, please, please help us," Bernie cries out.

They cling for their lives as the lava flames threaten to consume them, closer to imminent death…

Then suddenly, in the distance, they hear a thrashing, resounding sound grow louder and louder. They look up. An Army Pave Hawk helicopter circles, then hovers above them. A two-person rescue basket dangles from a cable below it.

"*Deus ex machina*. It's our rescue!" Bernie screams in delight. Despite his near death weariness, Sal smiles. Tom and Susan cheer with relief.

"I'm going to kiss every one of those rescuers," Susan says. "On their lips."

Tom laughs. "Yeah, me too."

As the cable lowers to them, Sal reaches up for the basket and motions for Bernie and Susan to enter it. Sal and Tom grab hold of the rim of the basket and it lifts off. The foursome ascend as the tree burns. The fire rises up and whisks Sal's boot and pant leg.

"Your leg's on fire!" Tom shouts.

"Man, at this point, I can't feel a thing." He shakes his leg and rubs it against the other leg to douse the flames. The tree sinks into the lava. Sal and Tom face each other and hang onto the basket rim, observing the flowing lava and explosions around them, both terrified and fascinated by the spectacle.

Onboard the helicopter, an Army Medevac team treats their injuries.

"Shattered knee, bruised ribs, and a concussion for the Colonel, but not bad considering everything he's been through." The medic turns to Susan and Bernie. "You've all fared amazingly well."

The survivors chug bottled water and munch on granola bars.

"Incredible," Tom murmurs, looking down to the coastline and the lava flowing into the ocean. "The flow seems to have altered. A new magma chamber opened up." He points to an area south of the helicopter. "The flow's paralleling the coast. That should reduce the risk of further coastline build-up."

"Long-term coastline stabilization?" Susan asks.

"Sure hope so. It's been a rough time for us, but the flow averted

Chapter Thirty-Six

"Time for a Little R&R"

One Week Later, Portland, Maine

In Bernie's bedroom, it's quiet. He lies in bed, under a comfy quilt his Grandmother made for him, reading a new issue of a Superman comic book.

"Ber-nard," his mother calls from the other room.

"Yeah, Mom?"

She pops her head into the bedroom. A smile sweeps across her plump face, her graying hair pulled back in a librarian bun. "Do you want me to leave the hall light on for you?"

"No, Mom, it's okay."

"Really? Are you sure, sweet pea?"

"You can turn it off. I'm over that now."

"Okay, if you say so. You're such a brave boy."

He nods and turns to the end table lamp next to his bed. He switches the light off, slants back, and closes his eyes. Peacefully, he drifts off to sleep.

The Grand Hyatt Resort, Kauai, Hawaii

Watching the sun set over the Pacific Ocean from their third-floor balcony, Tom and Susan recline in lounge chairs. Susan glances down to her bronzed shoulder. *Not so ghastly pale anymore.* Holding hands with Tom, she observes his tranquility as he stares off into the distance, sipping an ice-cold Hawaiian brewed beer from a frosted bottle. The color of the ocean complements his blue eyes.

"Good to know that Mahoe made it safely to the mainland," she says.

"For sure."

"Oh, and I talked to Bernie today."

"What did he want?"

"Well, he told me that he really admires you for declining the Congressional Gold Medal of Honor Award until the U.S. acknowledges the No Gun Ri Bridge incident."

"Really? That's nice of him. You know, I'm starting to like that kid. He's not such a bad nerd after all."

"There's a change of heart."

"Perhaps," Tom nods.

She grins and reaches for her glass of chilled Chardonnay. She takes a sip, stands, and then stretches. Leaning over the balcony railing, she looks out to ocean as the sun sinks into the shimmering tide. She circles back to Tom. He's now wearing his reading glasses and perusing the latest issue of Geoscience Journal. She turns back to the railing, leans on it, and sighs deeply.

"What was that?" Tom asks.

"Oh, nothing."

He sets down his glasses and magazine, then walks toward her. "No. That definitely sounded like some kind of serious sigh." He envelops his arms around her waist and snuggles against her neck.

"I was just thinking," she says.

"That's not surprising. What about?"

"Oh, about Bernie again."

"Isn't he supposed to be back home in Maine?" Tom releases her. He eases back down into the lounge chair and picks up his magazine.

"Yes, but he made me connect the dots, so to speak. Do you remember what Colonel Rosetti said to you when you were in that last lava tube together?"

"Uh, not exactly."

She steps toward him, pushing the magazine away. Her soft lips brush against his ear. She whispers with tenderness. "Wasn't it something about having a family some day? Might be nice to try…and have some fun in the process?" she giggles as he catches the twinkle in her eye.

"Beauty, warmth, loving desire. How can I resist?" He moves toward her, reaching up to kiss her lips, which part in wet expectation.

Bing-bing. Tom's cell phone cheeps next to him. He reaches for it and glances down at the screen. "It's you know who," he announces.

"Her again?"

"And there's something I've been needing to do about her for a long time. It's bye-bye apron strings."

He turns and tosses the phone, backhand, through the open slider door and into the living room. It hits the couch and bounces off, onto the carpeted floor, landing face up on speaker mode.

Susan laughs. "Thank you. Thank you."

Tom scoots over and makes room on his lounge chair. "Sorry about that. Time is of the essence, right?" he says with a wink. Before she can answer, he leans into her with a deep, passionate kiss.

Behind them, on the living room floor, a shrill voice buzzes. "Thomas? Darling, are you there? Hello? I'm so glad you're back safe and taking some time off. But please promise, you'll never go on such risky assignments again. You had me worried to death. And I just have to say…" Her words drone on and on and on….

Susan can still hear the sound of her mother-in-law's grating voice, but she doesn't care anymore. Nothing can disturb this perfect moment.

She falls into Tom's arms, the sun bathing them with golden light as it dips into the sea, a bright, red orb swallowed up by layers of aqua blue. She feels the pulse of Tom's heart, beating steady and strong, rhythmic like the sound of the breaking ocean waves.

He swings his feet out, and stands, lifting her up and out of the chair. He carries her through the slider door opening, into the living room, past the buzzing voice, past his wet towels and his clothes strewn over the chairs, and past his research papers cluttering the table. He walks, holding her, into the comfort of the darkened, luxurious bedroom.

Susan smiles, fulfilled and accepted in the arms of the man she has always loved.

Yes, right now, this is all I ever wanted.

Epilogue

The Big Island of Hawaii is home to Kilauea, the world's most active volcano. This volcanically active island is no stranger to tsunamis. The Big Island's university town of Hilo has sustained numerous long range tsunamis, yet oddly enough only two tsunamis, in 1868 and 1975, were generated by the Big Island's active volcanoes.

On April 2, 1868, an earthquake with a magnitude estimated between 7.25 and 7.9 (on the Richter scale), rocked the southeast coast of Hawaii. This was the most destructive, volcanically generated earthquake in the recorded history of Hawaii. It triggered a landslide on Mauna Loa, five miles north of Pahala, killing 31 people. The resulting tsunami claimed 46 lives and damaged several villages on the southern coast. The tsunami rolled over the tops of the coconut trees up to 60 feet high, and it reached inland, up to a quarter of a mile in some coastal regions.

In the 1920s, Thomas Jaggar, the volcanologist and founder of Kilauea's Jaggar Observatory, was the first to predict a locally generated tsunami. His prediction was not taken seriously. That event was not as a destructive event, that only killed one Hawaiian fisherman.

The city of Hilo, located near the slopes of the Kilauea Volcano, has sustained the worst damage in Hawaii from long-range, generated tsunamis. The most destructive tsunamis to hit Hawaii came from thousands of miles away, traveling over vast, deep stretches of the Pacific.

The first was in 1946, which struck without warning. It was generated from an earthquake in the Aleutian Islands. Hilo's north facing bay and offshore underwater canyons channeled the waves' intensity and focused them into town. Estimated to be over fifty feet, the tsunami waves took the lives of 159 people, including twenty-five students and staff at a sea-level school north of Hilo on the Hamakua Coast. Calculated in today's dollars, the tsunami destruction caused $300,000,000 in damages.

Fourteen years later, after Hilo was rebuilt, another tsunami struck. This one was generated by an earthquake in Chile. Even though the residents were forewarned, some refused to leave. There had been prior warnings (in 1952 and 1957) that produced small tsunamis with little damage and some people were not concerned.

The first small waves struck and reached only three feet high. So residents that had evacuated earlier came back to the tsunami zone. But then, subsequent waves exceeding 35 feet hit the town and 65 people perished in the disaster. In today's dollars, the property destruction totaled $125,000,000. That same tsunami continued on to Japan, where it hit with such force that over 200 people died. Since then, a large portion of the Hilo Bayfront land has been designated to grassy parks and is a no build zone.

On November 29, 1975, a 37-mile-wide section of the Hilina Slump (a chunk of the south slope of the Kilauea Volcano that is slipping away), dropped twelve feet and slid toward the ocean. This movement caused a 7.2 magnitude earthquake and a resulting 48-foot-high tsunami. Once again on the southern coast, the tsunami destroyed oceanfront property, washing homes off their foundations. Two deaths were reported and 19 people were injured form the tsunami and debris.

Presently across the State of Hawaii, there are advanced warnings for tsunamis. Tsunami evacuation signs are placed along most Hawaiian coastal routes, advising the public how to get to higher ground. On the first workday of every month, the Pacific Tsunami Warning Center (PTWC) tests its loud sounding warning sirens. PTWC is an early warning system that was first established in 1949, after the '46 tsunami devastated Hilo without any warning.

With an area of 4,028 square miles and a population of 185,000, the Big Island of Hawaii has 63% of the Hawaiian archipelago's combined landmass. All three other main Hawaiian Islands could fit inside of the Big Island. It is the third largest island in Polynesia, just behind the two islands of New Zealand.

Scientists monitor the possibility of large, locally generated earthquakes on the Big Island's southeast coast resulting from volcanic disturbance or eruption. If this happens, a sizable tsunami could occur, flaring out and wrapping around the Hawaiian Islands with little or no warning time. The resulting infraction, or wrapping tsunami waves, could reach Hilo and Kona within 5-10 minutes, Maui in about 20 minutes, Oahu in 30 minutes, and Kauai within an hour.

The Big Island is so massive and volcanically active, that it could break apart into several smaller islands, causing a major catastrophic event. The story you have just read is fictional, but could happen.

Acknowledgments: To the Korean Survivors of No Gun Ri Massacre and U.S. Korean War Veterans - may you live on in the memories of your loved ones. Thank you to William Britt for your creative cover design and help with publishing. Thank you, C.J. Kale, for the cover photos and images from Lava Light Galleries. Chuck Blay, Hawaii geologist, we appreciate your knowledge of Hawaii's geology and topography and we thank you for understanding our creative liberties. U.S. Army ex-Special Forces, Tony Colgrove, thank you for being an adviser on military matters.

Thanks to Wikipedia for general information on the Big Island and volcanoes, to Barbara Demick's non-fiction book Nothing to Envy:Ordinary Lives in North Korea, and Jayne Anne Phillips' fiction novel Lark and Termite. Kudos to Katherine Von Pelt for structural editing, and gratitude to our copy-editors/proofreaders - Matthew Toffolo, Dan Patching, Shane Roberts, and Julie Foss - who helped us edit the manuscript.

Reviews

It's not hard to see that the Millers are a talented and dynamic duo after reading their action adventure novel, Fault Line, which takes place at Hawaii Volcanoes National Park on the Big Island circa 2005.

Fault Line is chock full of intrigue and witty dialogue. The main characters are as daring, fit, and romantic as they are intelligent, which are things one might expect from a novel of this genre, and yet the novel delves deeper still. There are strong, relatable themes portrayed through the complex relationships between the characters. Fault Line is sure to captivate readers.

-Monique Rowan, writer, Garden Island Newspaper, article "Adventure, Romance in Locally Authored Book"

FAULT LINE

Michael Miller is the owner and publisher of Big Island and Kauai Adventure and Romance Magazines, established in 2004. He has been writing magazine articles and working in promotions and marketing for 35 years. Michael's visitor publications and web sites can be viewed at: www.kauairomance.com

Alison Miller, a National Scholastic Writing Award winner for poetry and prose in 1994 and 1995, graduated from Brown University in 2003 with a degree in Comparative Literature. For fifteen years, Alison has worked in education on Kauai. She is the editor of her husband Michael's magazines.

Made in the USA
Columbia, SC
28 May 2025